This book should be returned to any Lancashire
County Council Library on or before the date shown

1 9 JUL 2019

Lancashire County Council Library Service,
County Hall Complex,
2nd floor Christ Church Precinct,
Preston, PR1 0LD

Lancashire
County
Council

www.lancashire.gov.uk/libraries

Also by Eleanor Webster

No Conventional Miss
Married for His Convenience
Her Convenient Husband's Return

Discover more at millsandboon.co.uk.

A DEBUTANTE
IN DISGUISE

Eleanor Webster

MILLS & BOON

First Published in Great Britain 2019
by Mills & Boon, an imprint of HarperCollins*Publishers*
1 London Bridge Street, London, SE1 9GF

© 2019 Eleanor Webster

ISBN: 978-0-263-26914-7

MIX
Paper from
responsible sources
FSC® C007454

This book is produced from independently certified FSC™ paper
to ensure responsible forest management.
For more information visit www.harpercollins.co.uk/green.

Printed and bound in Spain
by CPI, Barcelona

To my family, who has always supported my dreams
and encouraged my persistence.

To my daughters, who demonstrate their own steadfast
persistence as they find and follow their own dreams.

Prologue

1812

It was one thing to be named after a leafy green vegetable, but quite another to resemble one.

Letty stared morosely at her reflection. Her mother had read somewhere that green flattered auburn hair and green eyes. In her opinion, this in no way compensated for the gown's vibrant colour nor its plenitude of ruffles. Moreover, her eyes were largely obscured by the wire spectacles she wore.

She sighed, tugging at the stray curl her mother's maid had forced into her stick-straight hair. If only her father was still alive. Of course, he would not have directly opposed the enterprise. He had never directly opposed her mother in anything. But they would have laughed. Together they would have poked fun at the marriage mart, the ludicrously complex dances, the trite conversations and endless rules of etiquette.

And the thought of standing surrounded by pretty girls in their pretty gowns making their pretty speeches would not have seemed so daunting.

Of course, if she were six inches shorter, with natural waves and pleasantly brown hair, pretty girls, gowns and speeches would have been considerably less daunting.

'Gracious, Letty, must you frown so?' Her mother bustled into the bedchamber, making a *tsk*ing sound to signal her disapproval. 'You will turn the milk sour and I am certain neither Lord Randolph nor Sir Edwin wish to sit across the breakfast table with someone having a disagreeable disposition.'

'Any more than I wish to breakfast with anyone having Sir Edwin's Adam's apple or Lord Randolph's whiskers.'

'Sir Edwin can hardly help his Adam's apple.'

'It bobs. And Lord Randolph could certainly do something about his whiskers,' Letty retorted.

'You could part him from his whiskers were you to marry him.'

'Except I do not plan to marry him, not even to save the world from his whiskers.'

Letty kept her voice light, but her stomach plunged somewhere near her feet at the very mention of marriage. It wasn't even that they needed the money. Her father had made a gadget, which had greatly expedited the manufacture of cloth, leaving them financially secure.

Unfortunately, it had in no way guaranteed their social status and her mother hoped that an advantageous match would serve where her father's ingenuity had not.

Besides, in her mother's mind, marriage was a woman's only choice.

Mrs Barton made a second *tsk*ing sound. 'Lettuce, stop frowning. You are old enough to be realistic. What other option do you have unless you wish to be the unwanted spinster in your brother's home? Not an enviable position, I assure you. Your father too greatly indulged you, allowing you too much time on science which has a most deleterious effect on the female mind.'

Letty did not bother to reply. She did not even hope to explain how articles about science and medicine had opened up her world, transporting her from this sleepy village to ancient ruins, battlefields and the cosmos beyond.

Her mother could not understand. It wasn't that Mrs Barton did not wish to, rather that she could not. Her world revolved around her husband, family and society. The concept that such a life might not be enough was foreign to her.

'And do leave your spectacles here. You look so much better without them,' Mrs Barton added briskly.

Letty groaned. 'Except everything becomes annoyingly blurry.'

'Then you will not be bothered by either Lord Randolph's whiskers or Sir Edwin's Adam's apple, will you?'

With this statement, Mrs Barton firmly removed the offending spectacles, closed her lips with a final *tsk* and marched from the room.

Two hours later, Letty leaned against the wall at Lady Entwhistle's ballroom. The heat had made her carefully placed curls frizz except for those now plastered to her forehead and dangling into her eyes.

Thankfully, she'd not had to dance, except one time with Lady Entwhistle's eldest son. His toes had remained unscathed, but Letty was quite certain she'd miscounted her steps and sadly lost the rhythm.

It would be bad enough to lack co-ordination if one were petite with tiny dainty feet. It was worse when one was tall with feet which could never be called dainty.

He had not asked again.

Still, even blurry, the scene was pleasant to observe. Dancing had a science to it, she decided. Some individuals moved with fluidity, as though innately able, while others stepped with measured care, each movement requiring concentration. Sometimes, she wondered if the ability to move rhythmically was but another skill just like her brother could write while she retained everything she read so easily.

Which reminded her... Letty straightened with sudden determination. Lord Entwhistle had the most delightful, wonderful of things: a fully stocked library. Since her father's death, her mother had cancelled the subscriptions to all scientific journals and Letty almost salivated with her eagerness.

With a furtive glance, Letty sidled along the wall. Her mother appeared to be conversing with a lady some distance away. Given the frequency of her nods and the way she leaned into the speaker, Mrs Barton's attention seemed unlikely to waver.

With another furtive glance, Letty slipped from the bustle of the ballroom and into the corridor's cooler air. She inhaled, thankful to escape from the noise and warmth of the dance. Now, she need only walk the few steps to the library and hope that it was not otherwise occupied.

It wasn't. The large dim room was wonderfully empty. Its curtains were not yet drawn and pale moonlit shone through the windows. Wall sconces bathed the room in a golden light so that the embossed titles glinted with magical promise.

She loved libraries. She liked the excitement of seeing those bound volumes, each promising information, knowledge and unknown worlds. She liked the smell of them, that dusty, leathery scent, as though the air itself was steeped in history.

Anticipation mixed with the nostalgia of childhood memories pulsed through her as she stepped forward, running her fingers across the smooth leather spines. She knew exactly which title she needed. Ah, there it was. Grabbing the *Edinburgh Medical and Surgical Journal*, she pulled it off the shelf and clutched it to her chest. There was a fascinating article that she'd been wanting to read for ever. Well, since her brother had written to her about it. Ramsey was a wonderful brother, so like her father it hurt. It was quite possible that life as his spinster sister would be better than that of some bewhiskered worthy's wife.

Except she didn't want to be wife or spinster. She wanted the impossible.

Still, she refused to descend into the doldrums, particularly when she'd just found her favourite scientific journal. Sinking into the cushiony depths of the armchair, she pulled out her spectacles, thankful she had thought to secrete them in her reticule.

Positioning herself under the wall sconce, she glanced furtively to the door. Likely her mother would look for her soon, but she was a fast reader and able to skim through the words, retaining almost every word for review later.

Running her fingers gently over the leather bindings, she opened the tome. Very carefully, she found the article and with a sigh of deep content started to read.

Tony strode into the library. He felt like a fugitive. Indeed, if he had to talk to one more vapid school miss... What did those mealy-mouthed governesses teach anyway? Certainly not the art of interesting conversation—he did not know which was worse: the tongue-tied, big-eyed silence or the foolish chatter about ribbons, bonnets and the like.

A noise startled him. He scanned the room, irritated that even here he had failed to find solitude. To his surprise, he saw a female figure curled within the library chair and apparently perusing a large volume. She wore a dreadful, ruffled gown of vibrant green. Her hair was an equally vibrant red and she was so absorbed in her reading that she had not looked up. He cleared his throat.

She glanced in his direction. Her brows, surprisingly dark, drew together over gold-rimmed spectacles as she eyed him with an intense gaze. 'I thought I was alone.'

Her tone and expression indicated that solitude would be preferable. Indeed, her rather stern aspect did not contain any of the giddy girlishness he had come to expect.

'My apologies for disturbing you,' he said.

She nodded, offering none of the usual polite platitudes and turned back to the book, an obvious dismissal which would irritate if it were not so damned amusing. For a moment, he watched her, fascinated by the apparent intensity of her concentration as well as the strong lines of her face, chin and high forehead.

Again momentarily aware of his presence, she glanced up, removing her spectacles. 'Please sit, if you would like.'

She fixed him with her direct gaze. Her eyes were very green, a true green, not that wishy-washy mix of brown or grey which people called hazel. He sat, momentarily discomforted by the intensity of her gaze.

'You also find dances overwhelming?' she asked.

'Pardon?'

'You looked pale. You sat with an abrupt motion as though off balance. However, you appear too young and healthy to suffer from any malaise. And you do not seem intoxicated. Not that I have a great deal of experience with intoxication, but I saw my brother the worse for drink on one occasion and his speech was slurred and voluble while you have said little but with clear enunciation. Anyway, I wondered if you also found the noise and movement of the dance floor exhausting?'

'Um...not usually,' he said after this monologue. Indeed, this was a tame event, too full of debutantes, anxious mothers and warm lemonade to encourage inebriation. He would not have attended except for his sister. 'I take it you are not enjoying the festivities?'

She pulled a face, but then smiled. He found the change from a serious demeanour to one of mischief intriguing. 'Not entirely, although having access to Lord Entwhistle's library is a solace, to be sure. You won't tell?'

'I am the soul of discretion.' Although he doubted that the kindly Lord Entwhistle would care. He glanced at the book which so obviously fascinated her, uncertain what to expect. His sister liked novels and botanical books from which she would copy flowers and ferns with scrupulous attention to detail.

More recently, she had also taken to devouring fashionable journals and often begged their mother for the latest mode.

'Goodness!' He gave a spontaneous chuckle as he read the title of the article. '"Cowpox"? You are reading about cowpox?'

'Yes, and smallpox. Neither of which is a subject for amusement,' she said reprovingly.

He straightened his countenance. 'No... um... I should not have laughed.' This rather odd female seemed to have made him abandon a decade of niceties. And he was not exactly inexperienced. He had travelled the Continent and attended any number of balls and dances in London without feeling in any way socially inadequate.

'You likely found the peculiarity of the subject amusing. My mother says that discussions about such topics will make me an oddity.'

'She may be correct,' he said, his lips twitching again.

'She usually is. Or if not, her conviction of her own infallibility makes everyone believe it must be so.'

'She sounds rather like my father,' he said.

He was still angry about a lecture his father had given him on a large sum of money he had lost in a bet. It had started with a card game and ended with a fast gallop across Rotten Row. Fun, but not good for the pocket.

'Did your father tell you to come here, then?' she asked.

'No, that was Mother, actually. She is quite positive that my presence will greatly enhance my sister's marital chances.'

'And will it?'

'Possibly. I decided that if I had to suffer, I would ensure that my friends were similarly afflicted.'

'Misery loves company.'

'Indeed.' Although his best friend, George, did not seem particularly miserable.

Infatuated, more like. What did one feel when one's best friend suddenly falls head over heels with one's sister? And George had always been such a sensible fellow. And he'd known Elsie for ever, except now he looked at her as though she was some miraculous creature—as if gowns and ribbons had the power to transform.

'So, what is the fascination with cowpox?' he asked, searching for a more pleasant topic.

She did not answer for a moment, again fixing him with her disconcertingly direct gaze. 'Did you want to know? Or do you merely aim to be polite?'

'Actually, I find I want to know,' he said, rather to his own surprise.

'Very well.' She spoke with the tone of a schoolmaster. 'The concept of introducing a pathogen to develop a strength is so interesting. And then there is the controversy. You see, Dr Jenner is thought to have first identified that a person may be less likely to contract smallpox if they have been previously infected with cowpox. But Jesty the farmer may have had the idea first.'

'Controversial cowpox—even more entertaining.'

She frowned, fixing him with a dubious gaze. 'Not the adjective I would use, but I surmise you are an individual frequently in search of entertainment.'

She spoke with surprising perspicacity for one so interested in cowpox.

'Perhaps,' he said. 'My brother is the responsible one. Do you not find that life can become remarkably dull, remarkably quickly?'

'At times,' she agreed, nodding her head for emphasis. 'But you have no excuse for boredom. You can read whatever you want and likely no one cancels your scientific journals.'

'Er...no,' he said.

He had never subscribed to a scientific journal in his life. He nodded towards the open book on her lap. 'I take it yours were? Hence your interest in Lord Entwhistle's library?'

'Yes—you see, I would like—' She stopped abruptly.

'What would you like?'

'I believe my aspirations might be considered odd. You will not laugh?'

'I have managed thus far in our conversation.'

'To provide medical care.'

The remark was so unexpected and unusual that he could not contain his reaction, which was a mix of both shock and amusement.

'You mean like a—a—' He had been about to say midwife, but realised this was hardly appropriate. 'Like someone who gives out herbs and… and poultices,' he concluded lamely.

'Or a doctor, surgeon or even an apothecary.'

'Good gracious, why on earth would you want to do so?'

She shrugged, the dreadful green ruffles rustling. 'I've always wanted to do so. I cannot explain it. It is somewhat like questioning why one would want to walk or do any number of things which are instinctual to us.'

He was about to say that walking did not involve the removal of body parts with a handsaw, but there was again something in the green intensity of her eyes that made him stop. It was ludicrous, of course, for a lady to wish to be a doctor. It was ludicrous for a gentleman to do so, too, for that matter.

'I imagine your mother doesn't endorse that ambition?'

'My mother's sole desire is for me to marry someone of a higher social status. She keeps introducing me to titled gentlemen. Anyway, it is not possible. I mean for me to become a doctor. A female cannot enrol in medical college or even apothecary school.'

He laughed at her disgruntled expression. 'I am certain you will find something more pleasurable to do.'

'And is that our purpose? To find pleasure?'

'Generally. At least it is the principle I adhere to—except on those occasions when I must march around a square.'

'You are in the military?' she questioned.

'The lot of the younger son. Although my brother also joined in an excess of patriotism. For me, it was either that or the clergy. I did not find myself well suited to the latter occupation. So, I take it you are currently hiding from your mother?'

'And the latest gentleman she has procured for me.'

'She might have found someone young and pleasant.'

The young woman glanced down so that her long lashes lay like fans against her cheeks. Her skin was pale, but touched with just the hint of pink along her cheekbones. 'Except I will not marry. I am quite decided on it.'

He was struck by the room's silence. For a

moment, time and space seemed distorted, stilling and narrowing so that everything seemed focused on this one moment in this one room.

'That almost seems a shame,' he said.

Then she shifted again, her smile widening and transforming her serious demeanour into one of wry humour. Her amusement was contagious and her smile engaging, the more so because it seemed a rare thing. 'Not at all. Indeed, I believe it would be a goal quite destined for disappointment, given that I resemble a cabbage.'

He looked at her and, while she was quite strikingly different from other young ladies, he would not put her in the category of leafy vegetables. Indeed, she was almost beautiful in a strange, unconventional way. Her eyes widened as hot colour flushed into her cheeks at his scrutiny. He saw her inhalation. Her lips parted.

'I apologise.' He stood abruptly. 'I was rude again. I seem to be making a habit of it. And really, I should return to the dance and doubtless your mother is looking for you.'

'Indeed. Her brows drew together as she looked to the mantel clock. 'And I am not even done the article.'

With renewed urgency, her gaze returned to her book, and he had the odd and unusual feeling that he had been dismissed in favour of the more fascinating topic of cowpox.

He strode to the door, but paused, his hand on the handle. 'What is your name?'

'Lettuce Barton,' she said.

Chapter One

August 2nd, 1815

His head hurt. The pain thudded, pounding and stabbing into his temples with every beat of his heart. Tony pulled himself to an upright position, squinting at the obnoxiously bright daylight flickering through the narrow gap of the drawn curtains.

'Good day, my lord,' Mason said, crossing the floor and pulling open the curtains with a raucous rattle. Bright sunlight spilled through the glass, filling the bedchamber.

'Must you make it so infernally bright this early in the morning?'

'It is past noon, my lord.'

'Fantastic, time for another drink,' he muttered. 'Why are you here anyway? Didn't ring for you. Sleeping.'

'Lady Beauchamp is downstairs, my lord.'

'Actually, not so much "downstairs" any more,' his sister announced, laughing from the doorway.

'Elsie!' he said, keeping his injured hand hidden under the bedclothes. 'You can't come barging into a gentleman's bedchamber, even if I am your brother.'

'I have visited for three days and I am tired of waiting. You are either out or sleeping or in your cups. Besides, you do not return one's calls.'

'And you insist on visiting in the middle of the night. Anyway, what is so damned urgent?' He spoke too loudly so that he winced at the noise of his own voice.

'I need to go to the country.'

'Then go. You do not need my permission.'

'I wanted to talk to you first. Provided I could catch you in a moment of sobriety.'

He glared. 'Fine. We will chat, but for goodness sake, wait outside while I make myself decent.'

'Very well, I will see you in the breakfast room, but do not think you can lope off again.'

With those words, his younger sister gave a

decisive nod and, thankfully, left the room, the door shutting firmly behind her.

He again flinched, glaring irritably at the closed door. Truthfully, he had been avoiding her. Her presence reminded him too much of the gaping holes within their family.

As well, there was this peculiar, detached feeling. He knew her to be his sister and knew that he loved her, yet could not seem to find the emotion.

He lay back on the bed, staring between half-closed eyes at a crack in the ceiling. Even the concept of rising felt exhausting.

And his bloody head hurt.

'My lord?' Mason said, clearing his throat.

Tony groaned.

'She will be back.'

He nodded, pulling himself upright. His sister had always been persistent. 'Stubborn and obstinate as a mule,' their brother had said.

While George, her husband, had called her 'steadfast' and 'resolute'.

But she was his family. Even though he couldn't find the emotion, he knew he loved her, or had loved her. He knew he had been best man at her wedding. He could see himself. He could see George. He could see Elsie.

But everything felt distant. As though recalling something he had observed—a wedding that was pretty, charming, happy, but in no way closely connected to himself.

Perhaps that was it. Everything felt distant. Both the wedding and that which had come next: the cannons, the corpses, the smell, the blood...

And Elsie and George and Edgar and his father, the happy and the sad, all seemed intertwined, so that he wanted only to shove them from his mind and lie within the dark, oblivion of this room.

Shaved and dressed, Tony exited his bedchamber. He still had a headache. As always, movement hurt. It was not excruciating any more, but rather a raw tautening, as his skin and muscles moved where the bullet had lodged within his ribcage.

He was already looking forward to his next drink.

Elsie glanced up as he entered the drawing room. As always, she wore the latest fashion. Of course, she was in deep mourning but even this suited her. George, Edgar, their father. Gone.

He hated black.

Sitting opposite, he stretched his feet towards

the hearth, wincing slightly with the movement. 'So why are you going to the country?' he asked without preamble. 'It seems a departure from your usual habits.'

Elsie had a low tolerance for boredom. In their youth, he'd tended to egg her on while Edgar, always responsible, had bailed her out of numerous scrapes until she married George, who had then assumed the role.

Until Waterloo.

'I have been feeling unwell.'

He glanced up sharply. She looked pale, he realised, although her appetite must be fine. She had gained weight. 'Too many late nights, I suppose.' While grief and injury had made him a hermit, she had become a social butterfly.

'You are one to talk—well, at least about the late nights. No, it is not that.' Elsie paused, glancing downwards, her fair ringlets falling across her forehead. She rubbed the black silk of her dress between her fingers. 'You see, I am having a child.'

He heard the words. They hung in the space between them, almost visible within the room. He felt nothing. He knew he should feel something: joy, worry, sorrow that George would never see his child…

'Right,' he said.

Elsie frowned, scrunching up her face almost as she done when younger. 'I am announcing that you may soon have a nephew, that George, who was your best friend, might have sired an heir prior to his death and all you can say is "right"?'

'I am happy for you.'

It was not entirely a lie. It was not that he was unhappy. Rather he was nothing. He felt an odd remoteness as though everything was miles from him—distant and inconsequential.

And then it happened. One moment he sat within the pleasant decor of the sunny salon opposite his sister and, within the next second, the salon had somehow turned into a mire of muck, churned and muddy from cannon balls.

He could even smell the war, a mix of blood, smoke, sweat, manure and urine.

His body felt different. His feet were heavy and his boots sank deep into the mire with a sickly sucking squelch. All around he heard the groans of dying men, their whispered prayers and anguished calls.

'Tony?'

His sister's tentative voice came as from a great distance.

'Tony, you're white as a ghost. Should I get Mason? Are you in pain?'

'No,' he ground out. His hand tightened over the chair arm, the pain intensifying about his ribs. 'Do—not—I—do—not—need help.' He pushed the words out.

And then that other landscape disappeared, as quickly as it had come, and he was back in the neatly appointed room with its pleasant floral curtaining and sunshine-yellow walls.

'Sit down, Elsie,' he said as she stood, reaching for the bell pull. 'No need to raise the alarm. I am fine.'

'You're certain? You still look pale.' She glanced at him and then away. People tended to do that as though embarrassed to see the scar snaking down his cheek to his collar.

'I am fine. Happy to hear your news and to know I will be an uncle.' He pulled out the trite words, relaxing as her worry eased and she sat back in the chair.

'Oh, Tony, I didn't even realise, at first. It was my maid who suspected. I am six months along and usually a person would know before that, but I didn't. When I felt ill, I thought it was the grief. And now I am so very happy and sad all at once. It was so—so terrible losing George, but having his child—that will make it easier. It will make life worth living again.'

'Yes,' he said, again feeling inadequate.

He should feel something. George had been his closest friend. He'd watched the man die. And held him as he did.

'And Father. This would have been his first grandchild. He would have been happy.'

'Yes,' Tony said.

He had been recovering from his own wounds in the hospital when their father died. He'd dropped dead like a stone to the floor when he'd heard about Edgar's death.

That hurt. Even through the numbness, that hurt.

'He cared a lot for George. He was happy when you married,' he said, again because he felt that he ought to do so, that something was expected.

'Anyway, I have decided to go to Beauchamp and I wanted to talk to you prior to my departure. Since Waterloo, you know, and after losing Father and George and Edgar, I stayed here to keep busy and to keep Mother company. I was afraid to be alone, afraid of my thoughts.'

He looked down. He had been so overwhelmed with his own pain, he had failed to see hers. She'd lost her husband, brother and father. Again, it seemed that he ought to feel more and that his emotional response was inadequate. Since when had feelings ceased to be spontaneous, but become 'shoulds'? Like one should wash one's hands before tea.

'Tony?'

He looked up. 'I'm sorry, I was miles away.'

'Anyway, these days I am feeling so tired. My head aches and everything is so noisy here. And even near my house, London does not smell pleasant and vehicles pass day and night. Besides, I am not so afraid of the quiet.' Her hand touched her belly. 'I think I will almost like it.'

'Is there a good doctor there?'

'I— Yes. I think so.'

'And Mother?'

'She is doing well. She socialises much as she always did. She thinks the country will be good for me and will visit after the child is born.'

'I will go with you.' He spoke suddenly and felt a jolt of surprise at his own words.

'You will? Why?'

He didn't exactly know, except that he was failing his remaining sibling and must make it right. 'I might like the quiet, too.'

Besides London was too filled with people and empty chairs.

He and Elsie had never been particularly close as children. He'd been closer to Edgar. He remembered fishing with him at Oddsmore, learning to ride that bad-tempered, stout little pony, sharing a tutor, Mr Colden—except Tony had insisted on calling him Coldfish.

He'd viewed Elsie rather as an irritant as she tried to chase after them. Indeed, it had taken a month at least to adjust to the fact that his best friend had suddenly, and without any warning, fallen in love with her.

Still, Elsie was his only living sibling and his best friend's widow. He should feel something… He frowned, trying to find evidence of sentiment mired within this odd, cold, numbness.

'You are not going to Oddsmore?' she asked.

'No.'

'It is your estate.'

'Oddsmore is fine. Mr Sykes does an admirable job and doesn't need me interfering.'

He had not been there since his father's death. George… Edgar… Father… Like dominoes.

'Very well,' Elsie said. 'I will enjoy the company and you might be able to help run the estate. I have been feeling I should do more, particularly now.' She patted her stomach again with a mixture of pride and protection.

'I would imagine you should do less, particularly now.'

'Perhaps. Anyway, Oddsmore is not far—'

'No,' he said.

'Well, at least the country will be healthier for you than drinking your days away here,' she said with some asperity.

He smiled grimly. 'I doubt the countryside will preclude me from pursuing that endeavour.'

The delivery of Mrs Jamison's third child was not as easy as Letty had hoped. She'd had to reposition the baby and the labour progressed slowly so that the night seemed long within the stuffy, airless room. She'd tried to convince the family that fresh air would not cause any harm on such a warm summer night, but country folk were not ready for revolutionary thought. The fear of bad spirits still lingered.

Letty scratched her head. The ancient, old-fashioned, powdered wig always made her scalp itch and prickle with sweat. Of course, by now she had largely got used to her 'disguise'. She quite enjoyed the freedom of men's trousers, loved the ability to wear her spectacles whenever she wanted, but still resented the wig.

At least she no longer had to wear it daily as she had during her training, or rather Dr Hatfield's training.

The fifth Jamison arrived with a lusty cry as her mother collapsed against the birthing stool, her face wet with sweat and tears. The maid wiped her mistress's face while Letty cut the cord. Taking the damp cloth, Letty wiped the blood from the red, wizened, angry little face. Then she swaddled the infant in the blanket, handing her to her mother's waiting arms.

'Thank you,' Mrs Jamison whispered. There was a sanctity in the moment, Letty thought, a joy that was also pain.

She turned away, rubbing away the sweat from her own forehead. What would it be like to bring life into the world, to be responsible for, to protect and love this fragile, new human being? She hadn't attended many births during her training at Guy's Hospital. Most people that came there were incurable, clinging to life by the merest thread. There had been more death than birth.

Helping Mrs Jamison to rise from the birthing stool, she settled her more comfortably on the accouchement bed and tidied the bloodied cloths needed for the birth.

'A girl. I'm that glad—Lil, my eldest, will be wanting to get wed herself and it will be nice to have someone to help out around the house, mind,' Mrs Jamison said, bending over the child cradled within her arms.

'Lil can't be ready to marry yet?'

'Well, no, she's only eleven, but they grow up so quickly, mind. It seemed like only yesterday she was this size.'

'A few years to wait yet, then. Anyway, perhaps your lads could help.'

Mrs Jamison chortled. 'Have you met Cedric? He's a one. Likely burn the house down as like as not.'

Letty smiled. She'd given Cedric stitches on more than one occasion. 'I have indeed. He is a repeat customer.'

For the next hour, Letty kept busy, the afterbirth was delivered and then the Jamison family trooped in solemnly to meet their new sibling. Of course, Mr Jamison offered a sup of something to wet the baby's head and, as always, Letty refused.

She never lingered. With the child born, Mrs

Jamison would be more likely to notice her doctor's feminine features, too poorly disguised. She might see the tufts of red hair peaking from under the wig, the swell of her breasts, despite the binding, or that her hands were too small and delicate for a man.

While treating any patient, Letty seldom worried that she would be discovered. It was as though her mind was too occupied with treatment, remembering the details of anatomy, relieving pain, determining the correct poultice or herb, or placing stitches into flesh. But once finished, her mind circled, worry omnipotent.

At times, she still could not believe that the crazy idea she and Ramsey had concocted four years ago on a bright, starlit winter walk was working...*had* worked.

Besides, she was too hungry and exhausted to do anything save return home with all possible dispatch.

So, after checking once more on patient and child, she packed her belongings into her doctor's bag, made sure any stray hair was tucked under the wig, adjusted her jacket, straightened her shoulders and strode out into the bright daylight with a masculine swagger. The Jamison lads had already hitched up her horse, the stalwart Archimedes, and Cedric stood on the second plank of the fence, balancing precariously, a long yellow straw clenched between his lips at a jaunty angle.

'Hello, Cedric,' she said, clambering into the trap and watching as he climbed down to open the gate. 'You happy with your new sister?'

'She's all right. A brother would have been better.' He peered up at her, wrinkling his freckled nose. 'Girls are dull. Still, at least I'm not the youngest no more.'

With that consoling thought, he swung open the gate and Letty tapped Archimedes into reluctant movement and he ambled forward, happy to find his own way down the narrow lane.

At times, she missed the lectures at Guy's Hospital, the lively discourse between students, the classes in anatomy and the excitement of the illegal autopsies and new procedures.

Today was not one of them. In London, there had also been an undercurrent of fear. She remembered hurrying through poor, narrow streets with her collar turned high and her shoulders hunched, even more determined to hide her gender than at the hospital.

Sewage from the Thames tainted the air. Garbage littered the streets and beggars and drunks would lie at the entrances of the shops, hospital and along the river bank while urchins would run up to her, grimy hands out-thrust. Sometimes prostitutes would sidle up with their toothless, painted faces, taken in by her male garb.

This was much nicer, she thought, gazing through heavy-lidded eyes at the country's clean, morning brilliance. It was nice, to relax to Archimedes's rhythmic movement, the reins limp in her hand.

Sometimes her secret felt heavy, but on this fresh, shimmering hopeful dawn it was delightful and precious.

As always, she took the back route, skirting the village centre so that she could approach the stable by the lane. Doubtless, the villagers thought the doctor an odd recluse and Miss Barton equally eccentric. Still, she could take no chances. She had worked so hard for this life and it still felt fragile—like the houses they'd constructed as children from playing cards and toothpicks.

The lane behind her house smelled of lavender. Already the day promised to be warm. It had been an unusually hot summer and the air had that heavy, lazy perfumed feel of August. Mixed with the lavender she detected manure.

Likely Arnold had been gardening, already eager to beat the day's heat.

'Ah, there you be, miss.' Arnold stepped out from the stable. She'd known him since childhood: groom, gardener and friend. He always kept an eye open for her when she was out at night and irritatingly insisted on calling her 'miss' despite trousers and wig whenever they were alone.

He was quite stooped with his years, moving with a rolling nautical gait as he stepped forward, taking hold of the reins. 'You must be that tired. You go up to the house. Sarah will have a bite ready for you, no doubt.'

'Thank you.' She gave Archimedes's wide girth a final pat before getting down from the buggy and entering the stable.

She found her clothes in the small valise under the hay and dusted away the yellow straw, before hurriedly removing her trousers and thankfully pulling off the powdered wig. She shoved this into the valise, running her fingers with relief through her straight red hair. Then she pulled on her dress and exited the stable's dustiness.

In the winter months, she'd likely abandon this practice. Even now it seemed like an excess of caution, but worry was deeply rooted and in these bright, long summer days she feared that someone might see 'Miss Barton' enter the doctor's house or vice versa.

Thanks to her inheritance from her father, she owned both the two stone houses visible at the far end of the garden. Eagerly, she hurried towards the one on the left, stepping across the paving stones of her overgrown herb garden. The leaves brushed against her skirts which would likely be yellow with pollen.

'I am that glad to see you back.' Sarah came to her the moment she'd pushed open the back door.

Sarah had first worked as a nursery maid and was also more friend than servant. 'Sit there. I have fresh bread and the kettle is hot so I can make tea.'

'Thank you. I was going to head straight to bed, but perhaps I will eat first,' Letty said.

She had not eaten for hours and the kitchen smelled delightfully of cinnamon and fresh bread. Kitchens always smelled wonderful. Even as a child, she'd loved kitchens above all other rooms, except the library. Of course, her mother had seldom entered the kitchen, or had done so only to lecture the staff. Her mother was the daughter of a housekeeper and had spent her life trying to forget this fact.

'Well, I have food enough, but you won't be having that much time to sleep if you're planning to visit your sister-in-law.'

'Good gracious, I didn't know I was!' Sarah sat rather heavily, propping her head on her elbows, too tired to stay erect.

'It is the fourteenth and your mother and Mrs Barton invited you weeks ago—most specific she was.'

Letty groaned. She loved Flo. She owed both Flo and her brother everything. She would never have been able to register at Guy's Hospital without her brother's help. Certainly, her mother would never have allowed her to live in London if Flo had not offered her accommodation. Nor would she have pulled off her peculiar double life without Flo's ingenious excuses.

However, the garden party would doubtless involve her mother.

Letty was a tremendous disappointment to Mrs Barton. Indeed, her mother would have disowned her except she feared it would cause talk. Mrs Barton hated to be the topic of 'talk'. Besides, Ramsey had convinced one of his more aristocratic friends to provide some mumbo-jumbo about the upper classes adoring eccentricity.

Living alone in her little stone house was certainly eccentric.

Not that Mrs Barton knew about the doctoring. Letty smiled grimly. That information would doubtless have sent Mrs Barton into a decline or given her fits. Indeed, the fact that Letty had wasted almost two years in London without finding a husband was sufficiently dreadful.

'I suppose I must go,' Letty said, her head sinking lower.

'A failure to show might result in a visit from the elder Mrs Barton.'

Letty groaned. 'I'd best avoid that.'

'Indeed,' Sarah agreed.

'Give me an hour to sleep,' she instructed. 'Then get me up for this flower party.'

'Garden party, I believe, miss.'

As expected, her mother's influence was clearly visible and nothing had been done by half-measures. Liveried servants lined the flagstone path leading towards the comfortable brick façade of Letty's childhood home. The box trees now resembled African animals and the ornamental fountain frothed and burbled. The flower beds were colourful perfection, the dark soil freshly turned, the weeds removed and a statue of a lion placed in the very centre of the rose garden.

A huge tent stood on the emerald lawn. Long tables covered in white linen extended from its shadows, laden with food, drink, silver cutlery and crystal stemware. Meanwhile colourful groupings of the local gentry and other notables chattered, protecting their pale complexions under ruffled sunshades in pastel hues.

Letty frowned. What was the point of a garden party if one erected a house and hid from the sun?

Just then, she saw her mother. Mrs Barton was not as tall as Letty, but was still slim. She had been talking with several ladies close to the box tree giraffe, but stepped forward on seeing her daughter.

'I am glad you are here and on time,' she said, with a bob of her white parasol as she presented her cheek for a kiss. She looked well. She had Letty's pale skin and reddish hair, but her locks had a pleasant auburn shade, threaded with a few strands of grey, as opposed to Letty's more vibrant hue.

Letty tried to think of a suitable but truthful response. She couldn't really say that she was glad to be here. In reality, there were any number of places she would have preferred to be.

'I am glad you are happy,' she said. 'Sometimes I wonder if there is not a connection between one's physical health and one's emotions.'

Her mother's forehead puckered, as though uncertain how best to take that statement. 'Well, never mind all that. And where is your sunshade? You know how dreadfully you freckle. And why must you insist on wearing such dull shades?'

'Likely a reaction to the overly bright hues of my youth,' Letty murmured.

'But grey? It is such a raincloud of a colour.'

'But serviceable.'

'Which you would not need to worry about if you had not decided to waste money buying a house. I am quite certain your father did not intend for you to fritter your inheritance.'

'The purchase of a house hardly seems frivolous.'

'It is when you could stay with me at the Dower House or with dear Flo and your brother. Well, no matter—I have a gentleman I particularly wanted to introduce—'

At that moment, Flo, or Florence, approached, her smile wide and genuine. 'But first, Lord Jephson is here and I absolutely promised him an introduction. He wanted to meet you as he has a lively interest in humours. You do not mind, do you, Mama?'

She addressed this last statement to Mrs Barton while expertly steering Letty towards the house.

'Humours! You know science has moved beyond humours. And who is Lord Jephson?' Letty asked as soon as they were out of earshot.

'A rich lord without a wife which will absolutely thrill your mother. But don't worry, I don't think he has any interest in acquiring a wife. Besides, I wouldn't do that to you. Ramsey is in his study and will be so delighted to see you. He says you are the only person outside of London able to provide intelligent discourse—'

Just at that moment, a disturbance occurred beside one of the long tables and both Letty and Flo turned abruptly.

'Good gracious.' Flo lifted her skirts so that she could move with greater efficiency. 'I think someone has collapsed or fallen.'

Letty hurried after her sister-in-law. Quite near to the tent, a cluster of women encircled a young female reclining on the grass. The woman wore black, but looked to be young with fashionable blonde curls peaking from under a dark bonnet.

'Do not crowd her,' Letty directed.

'Really, I can get up,' the young woman said, struggling to stand.

'A fallacy. You are as white as a sheet and look ready to swoon again.' Letty pushed through the bystanders, kneeling beside the young woman, instinctively reaching for her wrist to feel for a pulse. 'Give yourself a moment. You are likely still dizzy and—'

Before she could complete this sentence, a second wave of interest coursed through the group of onlookers. A tall man approached, striding from the house, his gait uneven. From her kneeling position, the newcomer's height was extenuated, his broad shoulders all but blocking the sun so that his size appeared superhuman, like Zeus or Neptune.

'Elsie? What happened?' His voice was harsh. 'Are you in pain?'

'No, I just went dizzy with the heat. Really, I am quite fine now.' The young woman again tried to rise. Two splotches of colour appeared on her otherwise pale cheeks. Her skin looked damp with perspiration. Letty saw miniature beads of moisture along her upper lip and forehead. Moreover, her face had a fullness or puffiness which Letty did not like.

'I disagree,' she said, releasing her wrist. 'Your hands and face are bloated. I cannot accurately measure your pulse in present circumstances, but it seems too fast which could indicate a more serious condition.'

'Young lady—' The man addressed Letty sharply as he knelt also beside the prone woman. 'Who are you? And why are you attempting to scare my sister witless?'

Letty glanced at him. His face was still shadowed from the sun, but there was something arresting about him and she found herself momentarily bereft of breath.

'I do not intend to alarm her,' she said, her mouth peculiarly dry. 'Merely to ensure that she seeks medical treatment.'

'She is already under medical care.'

'It doesn't seem to have been entirely effective. I would advise further consultation.'

'Thank you for that. Obviously, I will ensure her physician is called immediately.'

'Please, Tony,' the young woman said. 'Can we move from here? Everyone is looking.'

'Let them. And don't flatter yourself. They are likely more interested in me than you.'

It was true, Letty realised. The group of on-lookers had grown and stared openly with an avidity at the gentleman which seemed oddly devoid of good manners—particularly among a group who could forgive murder more readily than a lapse of etiquette.

Letty nodded. 'Indeed, I would strongly advise moving out of the heat.'

'It is still quite cool indoors,' Flo said, now also bending. 'I can help.'

'Rest assured I can support my sister,' the gentleman said, putting out one hand to help the young woman.

This single-handed gesture seemed oddly awkward, Letty thought, as she stood, also supporting the young woman.

'Perhaps— however, you appeared injured when you walked here. You are only offering one hand and, depending on the nature of your injury, the strain might do further harm.'

'You need not concern yourself. I am quite capable of managing my own physical condition,' he said tersely.

'Now, rise slowly and you will be less likely to feel vertiginous,' Letty said, ignoring the irascible gentleman as they helped his sister rise.

Together, they moved towards the familiar

stone bulk of her family's home, crossing the lawn, an odd, unwieldly threesome, while Flo walked ahead. They left the crowd behind and the quiet deepened as the chatter of voices fell away and Letty could better hear the young woman's laboured breathing.

With her arm about the woman's waist, Letty could feel the bulge of pregnancy—about five or six months along—although these new fashions made her belly less noticeable. Occasionally, she peeked at the gentleman, but he kept his face averted and largely in profile, silhouetted against the bright summer sky.

Although tall and broad, he had a thinness also, likely due to whatever hardship he had endured. There was a familiarity about him. She saw it in his profile and the timbre of his voice. She could not place him, but she had likely met him during her eighteen months in London and her peculiar double life, that odd mix of days and night within London's brightest ballroom and the morgue.

'The front Salon will be hot,' Letty said, as they stepped out of the warmth into the familiar front hall. 'We should go into the library. It will be cooler.'

'Yes, of course,' Flo agreed. 'And is there anything you need? Smelling salts? Brandy? Well, there is brandy in the library already. But if there is anything else?'

'Solitude and quiet would be nice,' the man said.

'Yes, yes, of course,' Flo replied, her hands making the fluttering motions she always made when nervous. 'I will let Letty—Miss Barton—take you to the library.'

'You didn't need to be rude,' Letty said to the rather formidable gentleman, as soon as Flo had left.

'It proves effective in clearing a room.'

'So does the discussion of pustules—that doesn't mean one has to do it.'

The man gave a sharp, spontaneous bark of laughter, which struck her as familiar. 'You speak from personal experience?'

'Yes. Well, it was actually an abscess.' It had been during her adolescence and her mother had spoken rather harshly to her on the issue of suitability. She had learned some restraint since then.

He looked her, his expression intent, and she had the feeling he had not properly noticed her previously. 'Right,' he said. 'Might we focus on my sister and not my manners? Elsie, why don't you sit here on the sofa?'

'Thank you,' the young woman agreed as they helped her sit. 'I am Lady Beauchamp, by the way, and this delightful creature is my brother, Lord Anthony. And thank you, Miss Barton. Truly I appreciate your kindness.'

'It is nothing. Hopefully, you will feel better after a rest. Oh, and I would advise keeping your feet elevated,' Letty said, placing a brocade cushion under Lady Beauchamp's feet and helping her to lift them. 'Are you in any pain?'

'No. I was just dizzy.'

Letty stepped back, trying to better study the woman's face and wishing she could wear her glasses, but she dared not. Whenever possible she only wore them as Dr Hatfield.

'Your lips are dry,' Letty said.

'Yes, my doctor advises that I do not drink too much.'

'What?' Letty straightened. 'You mean wine or spirits?'

'No, anything.'

'Then we will get you lemonade or water immediately.'

'Miss?' Lord Anthony said, his tone again sharp and any hint of humour eradicated. 'It would seem you are contravening the doctor's advice.'

'I am contravening a load of nonsense,' Letty retorted.

'You base that opinion on your extensive medical knowledge?' His tone was unpleasant and yet again oddly familiar. Letty glanced at him, but he had turned away.

'Some. I used to talk to the midwives,' she said, truthfully enough.

She narrowed her gaze, looking carefully at Lady Beauchamp. Even without glasses, Letty could see that Lady Beauchamp was definitely increasing and her face had a fullness that did not look right. There was a puffiness about the wrists. Indeed, the skin just above her gloves appeared taut as though stretched too tight.

'Lady Beauchamp, are your ankles similarly swollen?'

'What? Why, yes, my slippers no longer fit. Indeed, I had to order new ones and now they are also dreadfully uncomfortable.'

'Headaches?'

'A few.'

'Double vi—?'

Before Letty could finish the question, Lord Anthony turned, cocking his head towards the far end of the room. 'If I might speak to you for a moment, Miss Barton.'

Letty nodded and followed him. When he turned, she noted that one side of his face had been recently injured, a mark like a burn snaked down his cheek while the skin was stretched taut, an odd mix of red and white until the scar disappeared under the collar.

'I was injured at Waterloo,' he said.

'A burn, I would surmise.' She studied the tautened skin with a clinical regard. 'About third-degree, according to Heister and Richter.'

'Are you insensitive or just plain rude?'

'Interested. I have not seen that many burns and I have an interest in their care.'

For a moment, he said nothing. He fixed her with a steely grey-blue gaze, his expression unreadable.

'You are unusual. What did you say your name was?' he asked at length.

'Lettuce Barton.'

Chapter Two

The words, the voice, melodious but firm, brought everything back. Tony remembered that last Season before he went to war. He remembered the dances, music, laughter, warm, perfumed rooms glittering with mirrors and chandeliers. He remembered card games, horse races, fox hunts and his facility for wit and humour—for saying the right thing.

Now, he said nothing or said nothing right. He was in a foreign landscape, uncomfortable within his own skin. He avoided his friends, hiding within the fog of alcoholic stupor.

Whereas before he'd enjoyed friendships and a good story or joke, now he was the story, always under curious scrutiny. Or an observer and everything about him was but a play, a bad play which evoked little interest.

She'd worn a bright-green dress, he remembered. She had been reading about smallpox or cowpox and she'd had remarkable green eyes.

For a moment, the memory was so vivid, it shook him. It was as though he could almost see the girl in her bright ruffles, with those mesmerising eyes.

The clarity of this memory was oddly shocking because, since his injury, his memory had been peculiarly warped. His recollection of his life before Waterloo had felt distant, separate from him as though details from another person's experience.

But those insignificant moments with the peculiar Miss Barton seemed more real than anything else in this peculiar existence which had been so distinctly dissected; the before and after.

'Right,' Miss Barton said crisply. 'Unless you wished to talk to me further, I will provide Lady Beauchamp with some water.'

'What?' He was jerked back to reality and felt again an oddity, a stranger in a world which should be familiar. 'No, you will not. Lady Beauchamp's medic advised against water, you should not advise otherwise, certainly not based on a few conversations with a midwife.'

'Midwives,' she corrected. 'And I have never

read that a woman's fluid intake should be limited when with child and I have read extensively on the subject.'

'No doubt.' Again, the image of the odd girl in her odd dress flickered before his inner eye. 'However, I am certain our physician has also read a considerable amount. Indeed, I do not feel that we need impose upon your time any more. I am certain a servant can get anything we might need.'

'Actually, likely I *do* need to get you anything you need, because my sister-in-law has every servant out on the lawn and you scared her off by your unpleasant demeanour. Anyway, I am happy for the excuse. I am not particularly fond of chatting.'

'I remember.'

She glanced at him, a frown puckering her forehead, and he realised that she had not yet placed him. Not surprising—he had been a man of fair looks and now—

With a tiny shrug as though tracking down his reference was not worth the effort, Miss Barton walked back to Elsie. She moved briskly, her unfashionable grey skirts swishing. He wondered that neither the elder nor the younger Mrs Barton had not yet improved her style. Although the gown oddly suited her, the soft grey making her hair and green eyes the more vibrant.

'You are with child,' Miss Barton said to Elsie, in that direct way of hers, which would have been shocking in any other unmarried female, but seemed in no way unusual for this woman.

'Yes, six or seven months.'

'Your wrists are swollen. Your ankles, too. And your fingers, although that is hard to discern as you are wearing gloves. From your comment about your slippers I would surmise that your feet are also distended. In addition, your face appears unnaturally puffy.'

Elsie laughed. 'You certainly have a way with words.'

'As I recall, Miss Barton is under the misapprehension that she has medical knowledge.' Tony spoke sharply, although this was in part because he realised the woman was right. Elsie looked puffy and the bracelet she always wore was tight, as though cutting into the skin. Why hadn't he noticed?

'I am not under any misapprehension. I do not suffer from misapprehensions in general. Now I must get you water.' Miss Barton took a glass tumbler from the tray which held water and other refreshments.

Her positivity grated. She seemed so sure of herself. This irritated—perhaps because he had once been sure of himself and now was sure of nothing. He remembered his amused curiosity as he had chuckled inwardly at the quaint girl with her strange ideas. He had told Elsie about her, although she'd scarcely attended. That was also the night that she and George had fallen in love. They had known each other for ever, but on that night, friend had morphed into suitor.

And two months later, Father had walked her up the aisle. Elsie had looked happy and beautiful. Edgar had been typically pompous in his regimental uniform and George had looked as though he would burst for joy.

Then the church bells had rung jubilantly as the wedding party stepped out into a bright, cloudless day.

The splash of water into the tumbler caught his attention, piercing through the memories clogging his brain.

'Miss Barton!' He spoke hardly. 'Lady Beauchamp's doctor says she should not have water.'

'Then her doctor is a fool.'

'He is a trained physician,' he retorted.

'One does not preclude the other.'

'You are little more than a school girl and you suggest you know more than a qualified doctor?'

'Based on my experience—'

'Your experience? What experience?'

Colour flushed into her cheeks and she opened her lips before snapping them shut. 'I—'

'I don't care,' Elsie said suddenly and loudly from the couch. 'I am so thirsty. It is all I can think about. Surely a sip will not do me harm.'

'It will not. We have water here.' Miss Barton handed her the tumbler. 'And keep your feet elevated. You said you have been having headaches. What about vertigo?'

'Yes, some. I told Dr Jeffers. He did not seem much concerned. Do you—do you think the baby is fine?' Elsie asked.

Tony heard her fear and felt his worry balloon.

Miss Barton nodded, but Tony saw concern flicker across her mobile features and felt another twist of fear, cutting through his usual numbness.

'I will summon Jeffers here,' he said.

'No, no, please, do not,' Elsie begged. 'I feel so tired and I would so much prefer to go home.'

Tony paused. To his irritation, he found himself glancing towards the authoritative young woman in her unfashionable garb and ruddy hair.

She nodded. 'Likely Lady Beauchamp would feel more comfortable at home.'

'See!' Elsie said.

'The fact that a young miss approves is hardly a deciding factor.'

'But the ride is quite short—little more than an hour. Most of it is in the shade of the woods and, if we keep the windows down, there will be a breeze and I am feeling much improved.'

Elsie sipped her water, sighing, her relief so palpable that Tony wondered whether perhaps this irritating young woman was not in the right and not the self-important Dr Jeffers.

'You are looking better,' he acknowledged. 'I will summon the carriage and request that a servant be sent to Jeffers so that he can meet us at Beauchamp.' He went to ring the bell, but was stopped by Miss Barton's sudden interruption.

'I realised where we met before,' she said, her usually serious face lit with delight. 'It has been bothering me—you know, like a blister when one is walking. It was at my debut and we talked in Lord Entwhistle's library. You have changed.'

'A bullet hole and burns will do that.'

He said these things, he knew, to intimidate, to push people away.

'Yes, although the scarring is limited.' She eyed him critically.

Oddly, he felt a peculiar relief. Usually people would look his way as though oddly drawn to his wounds and then, their curiosity satisfied, glance away, their distaste and disgust evident.

Turning from her, he tugged on the bell pull, his movement awkward.

'You are still injured?' she said.

'It is nothing.'

'It impacts your movement which is not nothing.'

'Regardless, it is certainly not your concern,' he said, tightly. 'Now, if you will permit me to focus on my sister, I will transport her home where she might receive the attention of her qualified physician. Provided you approve, of course.'

'Indeed, that seems an admirable plan,' Letty said.

Letty slept well. Perhaps she was just too exhausted to do otherwise. No child arrived and she did not wake until late the next morning. Indeed, the sun was high in the sky and brightly shining through the lace curtains when Sarah roused her.

'What is it?' she asked drowsily, rubbing her head and squinting against the sun's glare.

'It is past noon and Mrs Barton, your mother, is here,' Sarah explained.

'Huh.' Letty pulled herself up to a seated position, still squinting. 'No wonder you are looking perturbed. Bring me some tea and I will get dressed. Best make it strong.'

'Be quick. She hates waiting and does not approve of sleeping in of a morning.'

'Very strong,' Letty muttered.

Some thirty minutes later, Letty entered the morning room. Her mother sat, as always, ramrod straight, having chosen the most uncomfortable chair available. In reality, her mother was not old. Letty had patients still bearing children at her age. Moreover, she didn't even look old, her hair had only a few strands of grey.

However, Mrs Barton's worried aspect always gave the impression not only of age, but of her never being young.

'Lettuce, I am glad you graced us with your presence,' Mrs Barton said, pushing her lips together with that characteristic click of the tongue.

'I aim to please.' Letty crossed the room, placing a dutiful kiss on her mother's smooth cheek, before seating herself in a more comfortable chair opposite.

'Although I do not know what time you think this is to be rising?'

'One in the afternoon,' Letty affirmed, glancing at the mantel clock.

'Are you ill?'

'I do not think so.'

'Only severe illness is sufficient reason to lie abed until this hour.'

'I will try to remedy the situation. Would a cold or chill suffice?'

A frown puckered her mother's forehead. 'Your sense of humour is too much like your father's. And you disappeared yesterday almost as soon as you had arrived.'

'Disappeared—gracious, I feel like a magician at a village fair. I went into the library and then home.'

'You were invited to a garden party, not to skulk in the library.'

'Indeed, skulking sounds positively criminal.

You always make my life feel so much more exciting than its reality.'

Her mother's forehead furrowed into a deeper crease. 'Criminal is not "exciting". And you always talk in riddles. Your father was much the same. We are lucky that your brother had the good sense to marry a young lady related to a duke.'

'I believe the relation is distant and Father's money, as opposed to Ramsey's sense, might have had more to do with it,' Letty murmured.

'Your comment is ill bred and ungrateful. Your brother's marriage to dear Florence provides you entrance into a level of society I never enjoyed. But do you not take advantage of this? No. You spent close to two years with her in London and did not acquire a single suitor. In fact, you hardly seemed to socialise at all—or only under duress. Now you live here on your own in a ludicrously eccentric manner while squandering your inheritance which is the only thing likely to entice a suitable husband.'

'My delightful personality and good looks will not?' Letty quipped. 'Anyway, my lifestyle is much too frugal for much squandering.'

'You have purchased a house and must run that establishment.'

'Two, actually. I rent one to the doctor next door.'

'Who is also odd, from what I hear. No one even sees the man. Anyway, back to the garden party. Dear Florence purposefully invited Mr Chester. Indeed, she arranged the party all specially for you, you know.'

'I didn't. It certainly looked lovely. I appreciated everything. Particularly the elephant. And the giraffe.' Letty sat in the chair opposite, lolling in excess as though to compensate for her mother's stiffness.

'Elephant? I do hope you are not losing your reason. It is not done, you know.'

'I was referring to the box tree sculpted like an elephant. In fact, the box trees all resembled wild animals. Combined with the stone lion, it felt like a veritable African adventure.'

Her mother's frown deepened. 'I am uncertain if African adventures are entirely appropriate.'

'Really, that quite ruins my plans for next week. By the way, did you want tea or any other refreshment?'

'Can Sarah make tea?'

'She can boil water.'

'Fine, but I won't be diverted. Florence wanted

you to meet Mr Chester. We both did. It was excessively irritating that you did not.'

'Chester?' Letty frowned. She remembered a middle-aged gentleman of that name.

'He has a sizeable income and is related to an earl.'

'Doesn't he also have a bald head, a bad temper—and a wife?'

'She's dead. A month since,' Mrs Barton announced with unseemly enthusiasm.

'Gracious, I can't drag the poor man down the aisle when she is hardly cold in her grave.'

'You wouldn't drag him down the aisle immediately. You would reach an understanding. The wedding would come after a seemly interlude. And really, you cannot be too picky. You are not in the first blush of youth and no great beauty.'

'Certainly, I am guaranteed not to become vain,' Letty muttered.

'Moreover, you have chosen this eccentric lifestyle,' her mother continued, ignoring the comment. 'I mean you do not have a proper cook, butler or scullery maid. And sharing Sarah with that young doctor, I don't think that's the thing at all.'

'I hardly think my virtue will be compromised because my maid also dusts for a gentleman.'

Her mother made another tutting sound. 'You can scoff all you want. But Florence and Ramsey will have their own family soon. I know your father left you comfortably placed, but your funds are not unlimited. And Ramsey cannot be expected to support you in this nonsense.'

Letty rubbed the cloth of her skirt between her fingers, then stilled her hand. She'd heard this all a thousand times and refused to believe her mother's doomsday prediction. After all, she was *almost* self-sufficient.

Although she did tend to be paid in rather a lot of root vegetables which, she supposed, might lead to a healthy lifestyle, but hardly one of affluence.

Yes, it was a tenuous, fragile success and one based on smoke and mirrors. The purchase of the two houses and the doctor's buggy had taken a considerable sum and her training in London was not without cost. Moreover, it would only take 'Dr Hatfield' to make some mistake, or some sharp-eyed individual to see beyond the wig, spectacles, her flattened chest and man's attire.

Briefly, her mother's face softened. 'Besides, this must get lonely. Your father and I weren't close exactly, but we shared a common goal to look after you and Ramsey, to secure the best for you. Surely you must want a family, children?'

For a moment, Letty remembered Mrs Jamison's expression as she held her baby. It would be something to feel such love. It would be something to create new life. Yet she remembered also the mothers she had seen in hospital whose children could not be saved. She remembered the desperation in their eyes. They had been broken by the loss.

The pain of losing a child must be more awful than anything she could imagine. She'd felt broken enough by her father's unexpected death. Even now she could see him in stark detail, his face ashen, contorted with pain as his hand flew in a futile gesture to his chest before dropping to the floor.

There was nothing she could do.

Was that when she'd decided that she must find a way, however desperate and crazy, to pursue medicine? Was that when she'd realised that she could not be satisfied with reading alone or even sneaking after the midwives?

Those visits had started a few years earlier. Whenever her mother was in London, Letty would wander to Mrs Soames's cottage, fascinated with its bundles of herbs hanging from the ceiling, air heavy with the scent of caudle. Later, she became more daring, tagging along when Mrs Soames was summoned to attend a birth. At first, Mrs Soames had shooed her away, but eventually she'd been allowed to boil water or bring in the hot caudle for the mother to drink.

Of course, she'd been motivated in part by rebellion, a need to experience something before becoming enclosed within the noose of societal expectation. But it had become much more than that.

'I don't think I have quite the same aspirations as other women.'

'Tell me something I do not know,' her mother said with a rare glint of humour, albeit grim. 'Again, I blame your father. He educated you in a way which did not prepare you to fit into society.'

'Perhaps you are right about that,' Letty said.

'And I was away too much in London. I always found the country so dull. Besides, I worried about the wrong things. One fears one's daughters will go to dances before they are officially come out or make a fool of themselves over some handsome boy, not wander about as a ministering angel.'

At that moment, the door swung open and

Sarah bustled in with the tea tray, placing it on the round table with extra care, as though well aware of Mrs Barton's critical eye.

Thankful for the interruption, Letty poured the tea and for a few seconds the room was quiet except for the trickle of liquid and Sarah's soft retreating footsteps as she exited into the corridor and towards the kitchen. Letty handed her mother the cup and Mrs Barton sipped, making no comment.

Fortunately, Mrs Barton chose to abandon the topic of Letty's adolescence. It had not been pleasant. Her mother had eventually learned of her escapades and put an abrupt stop to those excursions. Even her father had not entirely approved when he'd become fully aware of her activities. Indeed, he'd suggested that she would do better to read about modern advances than to acquire knowledge too steeped in superstitious folklore to be of use. He added also that the former would be safer and considerably less distressing for her mother.

As she drank her tea, Mrs Barton focused more intently on recounting Mr Chester's virtues and insisted that she introduce Letty to that gentleman as soon as she could determine an appropriate and timely manner to do so.

'You must realise that a widower of good character and sizeable income will not remain available for long and it is incumbent upon us to move in an expeditious manner.'

'But—'

'And if you wanted a younger man with hair, you should have acquired one while in London with Florence, which was the perfect opportunity.'

Letty opened her mouth and then snapped it shut. She had no desire for a husband, with or without hair. In fact, she knew she would be a dreadful wife, but it would be impossible to convince her mother about this.

Instead, she listened stoically, hoping that Mrs Barton would eventually run out of adjectives to describe Mr Chester. Surely, there was only so much one can say about a dead wife and a solid bank balance.

Standing at last, Mrs Barton glanced around Letty's drawing room. 'Sarah keeps it tidy enough, I'll grant you, and I am pleased you do not have too many of those books in evidence which absolutely screech "bluestocking". But living here with only a servant for company is no substitute for family.'

With those words, her mother left. Letty saw

her to the door and then flopped down with un-abashed relief, lying on the sofa with her legs inelegantly draped over its arms as the carriage wheels rattled into the distance.

Departure was always the best thing about her mother's visits.

Her poor mother—she would have been so happy with a nice girl who wanted to get married to a nice gentleman of superior social status with a moderate bank account and have nice children who also wished to marry nice individuals with superior social status and moderate bank accounts.

At times Letty wondered whether she should be grateful to her father for enabling her to escape such a dire fate, or angry that, as her mother said, he had ensured she could never fit into an appropriate role, as prescribed by society.

The door opened. Sarah entered, her face crinkled with worry.

'What is it?' Letty asked, lowering her feet and sitting upright.

'A note, miss. For the doctor.'

'Very well.' Letty took the note. It appeared to be on good-quality paper and more literate than the usual summons from a villager or farmer. Her gaze skimmed the terse lines. The writing was in bold black ink and in a masculine hand and she felt a start that was half-panic and half-excitement.

'Good gracious—Dr Hatfield is requested to provide a consultation to a Lady Elsie Beau-champ,' she said.

Tony glared out of his window. He sipped his coffee which was strong and harsh the way he liked it. He was being a damned fool, he knew. It was ludicrous to be swayed by the notions of a redheaded miss with interesting eyes, but lacking a shred of medical knowledge. Dr Jeffers had trained in Edinburgh. He plied his trade successfully, or so it would appear, given his horse, carriage and clothes.

Tony drummed his fingers against the window sill. Indeed, Jeffers had turned up promptly enough following their return from the garden party. He had immediately suggested leeches to withdraw the excess fluid in Elsie's arms and legs, which made sense, he supposed. The physic had also directed the continued limitation of Elsie's fluid intake, which also made sense.

After these pronouncements, Dr Jeffers had settled himself with Tony in the library and dedicated himself to his own fluid intake in the form of several brandies.

And Elsie had almost cried when she'd heard she should not drink water or lemonade.

Today she did not look a whit better.

She looked worse.

A lot worse.

Tony could feel the fear. It cut through his numbness. It lined his stomach. It made his mouth dry and his body hollow. Elsie was his only living sibling and the child she carried was his best friend's heir.

He rang for Mason. 'Has that new doctor come yet?' he asked as soon as his man had entered the study.

'No—sir—but the footman returned and said that he would attend her ladyship.'

Tony nodded. 'It cannot do any harm to get a second opinion. I would take her up to London, but she begged me not to do so. She said the journey would make her feel too ill, especially in this heat.'

'Yes, my lord.'

'I will not have my sister suffer because Dr Jeffers is too busy drinking brandy to properly concentrate on her.'

'No, my lord.'

'And you said he was good?'

'According to the cook's sister. She spoke quite highly of him, sir.'

'I am relying on Mrs Greene's sister?'

'Mrs Peterson, my lord. Mrs Greene is the housekeeper.'

'I am relying on the report from a random relative of one of the staff here?'

'Two, sir. The second footman's mother had a good report. She didn't like Dr Jeffers, sir, although you were kind enough to pay for the cost of his visit. Called him foolish, sir.'

Then her doctor is a fool.

He smiled, remembering Miss Barton's words. 'The second footman's mother is not alone in her opinion.'

'Er—no, sir.'

Tony had felt something yesterday as Miss Barton had brushed by him. He'd experienced a tightening within his stomach and an added level of awareness as she'd skewered him with that bright luminous gaze. It was like a shadow— a reflection of what had been. Or what he had once been capable of feeling.

Before Waterloo, he would have noted her curves, the creaminess of her skin, the elegance of her neck, that russet hair and the firm line of her lips, the bottom lip full and slightly pouted. The very dowdiness of the grey dress almost enhanced her appeal, like an intriguing package, delightfully obscured.

He swore. His hand had jerked, spilling the coffee.

'My lord?'

'Clean up this mess. I seem intent on burning my good hand, as well.'

'Yes, my lord.'

'And tell me as soon as that new doctor arrives.'

'Yes, my lord.' Mason dabbed at Tony's hand and at the liquid spilled on the sill.

Tony brushed away his efforts irritably. '"Yes" and "no"—is that the extent of your linguistic capabilities?' he muttered. 'You sound like a bloody parrot. Go. You know I hate hovering.'

'Yes, my lord. I mean, no, my lord.'

Chapter Three

Letty sat within the shaking chassis of the doctor's elderly vehicle. Arnold was driving and she began to wish she had chosen to do so herself. Arnold drove somewhat ponderously which, when combined with Archimedes's aversion to over-exertion, meant for a slow journey. Besides, if she had driven herself, she would have been outside which would have been considerably pleasanter than this sweltering heat which seemed to exaggerate every noxious scent ever contained within the vehicle.

Sweat prickled her palms and armpits while her stomach tightened so that she felt quite ill. The window did not open so there was no way to ensure a breeze and her scalp under the wig itched quite dreadfully.

Trying to distract her mind, she applied herself to the study of the passing scenery. It had been a hot, dry summer. The fields had turned yellow and the cows huddled under the shade trees. What should have been small bogs or shallow ponds were dried mud, beige patches marked with a criss-crossing pattern of cracks.

At least, as the doctor, she could see the view with clarity. As Miss Barton, she never wore her spectacles and her world was blurred.

The trap swung from the main road and into a small copse, a shady pleasant place. It reminded her of afternoon visits with her mother when they had called in on Lady Beauchamp—Elsie's mother-in-law, she presumed.

Letty pushed a finger under her wig, trying to make it more comfortable. She felt a fluttering of nerves. Sarah's fault, no doubt. She'd hovered about earlier, her face so furrowed she'd all but resembled a death mask at a feast.

So why had she taken this extra risk? Letty supposed she could rationalise it from a purely financial viewpoint. At some point, she needed to grow her practice and to be paid in money, as opposed to root vegetables.

But why start with Lady Beauchamp and Lord Anthony with his sharp, hard eyes and bitter smile?

Generally, she understood herself well enough, but today her motivation seemed more complex. She was genuinely worried about Elsie. She'd read about a condition where the expectant mother's face and extremities became puffy and swollen. She'd also spoken to local midwives and had once seen a mother, with similar symptoms, have fits.

She had died.

Letty also knew there were preventative measures, but no cure. Indeed, she might well be unable to help.

She placed her forehead against the carriage window. No, it was not only worry for Elsie, but something else. There was another element, a thrill of excitement, a feeling of daring and exhilaration. The very riskiness of the enterprise appealed.

But this was not logical and, while she had taken risks in the past, they had been calculated. By any measure, she should avoid Lord Anthony at all costs. He had seen her as a woman and a cynical intelligence glinted from those grey-blue eyes.

She'd liked his eyes.

She frowned at this errant thought, pushing her hand further under the wig. She hated it. She hated having to dress up in this stupid disguise to do the job she was meant to do.

As they passed through the woods, twigs and branches scratched against the buggy as it bumped over the uneven path before pulling on to the well-tended drive. For a moment, Letty knew a sudden longing to return to the dim, shadows of the woods.

Shafts of bright sunlight returned, spilling through the carriage windows. Trees flanked the drive so that the light flickered as they progressed towards the mammoth structure at its end. Good heavens, she had quite forgotten its size. It made Oddsmore seem but a country cottage. On either side, she could see the green expanse of the immaculate park, punctuated by bright flower beds, shimmering ponds and neatly trimmed box trees.

At least, payment would not be in root vegetables.

But the very elegant opulence of this place served to spike her worry. These people had power. Any complaint, any disclosure would be believed.

Arnold pulled the vehicle to a stop. Up close, the house seemed even more imposing; a three-storey structure with a stone façade and turrets.

Ramsey had enjoyed a brief fascination with architecture and they'd studied turrets with their tutor.

Arnold clambered down and opened the carriage door. For a moment she hesitated, then climbed out, looking up with a shiver of apprehension at the wide staircase and imposing bulk.

'Good gracious, they even have lions,' she muttered.

Indeed, two stone lions flanked the staircase as it ascended towards an impressive black-lacquered door.

This portal opened even before she'd walked up the stairs and a rather grim-faced butler stood within the doorway.

'Dr Hatfield...' the elderly butler intoned, more like a statement than question, as though announcing her entrance to a grand banquet.

'Yes,' she agreed, keeping her voice gruff, her spine straight and her shoulders square.

He had a squint. Hopefully, the squint indicated limited vision.

'Her ladyship is resting in her sitting room,' the butler continued. 'I will lead you to her. And His Lordship also requested that you visit him before you leave.'

'Naturally,' Letty said brusquely, ignoring the peculiar fluttering within her stomach.

After removing her hat and cloak, she followed the tall, somewhat stooped gentleman along a narrow passageway and into Lady Beauchamp's sitting room.

A maid opened the door and Letty stepped into a dark apartment, the curtains so tightly drawn that the only light entered through a tiny crack between the cloth.

'Good Lord, it is like a morgue in here,' Letty said impulsively.

'Not the best turn of phrase perhaps, Doctor.' The voice came from a form just visible within the gloom.

'Lady Beauchamp?'

As her eyes adjusted to the low light, Letty recognised Elsie. She lay on a daybed and gave a wan smile. 'You are Dr Hatfield?'

'Yes,' Letty said. She must keep in mind that the doctor had never met the woman.

'My brother wanted me to see you. I suppose that must mean you are the best. He always gets the best.'

'Your brother is kind,' Letty said.

'That adjective is not frequently used to describe my brother, at least within the last year. Although he was different before.'

Letty curbed a flicker of curiosity. She longed to talk about Lord Anthony. Indeed, the man at the garden party had seemed in stark contrast to the young gentleman at her debut.

But Lord Anthony was not her patient and, even in the dim light, she could see that Elsie was not improved. Her face had a roundness she didn't like and her speech lacked the brisk clarity she had recalled from their previous encounter. In fact, there was a listless apathy which seemed quite contrary to the woman she remembered.

'Is it possible to open the curtains so I might better examine you?' she asked.

'No, please. The light makes my head worse.'

'Your headaches are worse?'

'Yes. So much.'

'Very well. I will ask your maid to light a candle. Close your eyes if you must.'

She heard the striking of a match and the maid's movements as she lifted the candle to provide a small, puddle of light.

Within its amber glow, she could discern the woman. She lay on the daybed, her eyes scrunched tight shut against the limited light.

'I am glad you have your feet up. But keep

them elevated higher than your heart.' Letty took a pillow from an armchair opposite, placing it under Lady Beauchamp's feet. 'May I see your ankles?'

Lady Beauchamp acquiesced. Gently, Letty lifted her skirts. As she had surmised, her ankles had swollen. Her feet were so distended that she had discarded her slippers.

She let the skirt fall back with a soft swish. 'You have headaches, you said. Blurriness of vision?'

'Terrible headaches, but my vision is not impaired.'

'And what treatment has Dr Jeffers recommended?'

'Leeches for my headaches. Limited fluid. Rest.'

'Leeches?' Letty muttered. That treatment had gone out with the ark.

'What would you suggest?'

Letty paused. Truthfully, she knew that birth was the only 'cure' and Elsie was only in her seventh month. She also knew her condition to be serious, but feared that increased anxiety would aggravate her symptoms.

'No leeches. Plenty of water. Rest with gentle walks when you feel able. Bland food. Meat and eggs. I will also prescribe a draught from the willow tree. We will start with the water now.'

'I can have water?' Elsie asked.

'Yes.'

Elsie smiled. 'Then I do not care if you call this whole house a morgue. It is a morgue. In fact, it is a mausoleum to George, Edgar and Tony.'

'Lord Anthony? But your brother is alive?'

Elsie looked down. In the candlelight, Letty saw the shimmer of tears just visible under the lashes. 'Perhaps. But he is so changed. Sometimes I hardly recognise him.'

Again Letty had to curb that quick sharp pulse of curiosity.

'Perhaps he is still adjusting to his injuries.' She turned to the maid. 'Do you have a jug for water?'

The girl bobbed a curtsy and hurried from the room. The opening of the door brought a welcome draught of cooler air.

'Also, this chamber is too hot. At least during this warm weather. Is there a cooler room you could spend time in?' Letty asked.

Elsie shrugged. 'I suppose. The house is gargantuan.'

The maid re-entered, handing over a glass of

water. Letty gave it to Elsie, watching her relief as she took a sip.

Then she turned back to the maid. 'Make sure her ladyship spends time in a cooler area.'

'Yes, sir. The other side of the house is usually in shadow.'

'Good, make certain that she goes there and keeps her feet up. And she can drink. But not too much all at once.'

'What will happen if I drink that whole jug?' Elsie asked, with greater energy, eyeing the jug which the maid had put upon a dressing table.

'I am uncertain, but I believe in moderation.'

Elsie giggled. 'You are an unusual man.'

Letty stiffened. 'How so?'

'You said the word "uncertain". So unusual for a man and a doctor,' Elsie added with another tiny giggle.

But it should not be unusual, Letty thought. There was so much doctors did not know—the mysteries of physiology and disease. The exact method involved in the spread of disease and how one could help the human body to withstand illness.

'Doctor?' Elsie queried.

'My apologies I was thinking we have so much we need to learn and to research.'

'Tomorrow—will I also be able to drink tomorrow?' Elsie asked, focused on this more important issue.

'Yes.'

'Thank you,' Elsie said.

Letty nodded, preparing to leave.

'Dr Hatfield?' Elsie asked.

'Yes?'

'Are you the best?'

'That is a subjective question. However, I keep accurate records and, to date, more children and women have survived childbirth when I have been retained than other physicians within a twenty-mile radius.'

'This baby—I need this baby to be born healthy. My husband—he died. And his parents are already dead.' For a moment, her gaze swam with tears.

Letty bent to buckle up her doctor's bag, then straightened. 'I never make promises I cannot keep and I cannot promise you that everything will be fine. I can promise that I will do everything I can.'

'Thank you.'

'And I am the best.'

Letty exited Lady Beauchamp's bedchamber and followed the footman towards the front hall.

She felt quite certain Elsie had not suspected anything. The place had been too dimly lit for one thing and Elsie's headache likely too bad for critical thought. Moreover, while intelligent, she didn't seem to be an individual with a suspicious nature.

Moreover, Letty's natural height helped and she always bound her breasts so that the jacket showed no unnatural curves. This, combined with the wig, spectacles and a certain squareness to her jaw, made her appear quite masculine.

But what of Lord Anthony? He seemed of an entirely different and more suspicious nature. Indeed, she felt a tension, an uncharacteristic shivery feeling that was half-anticipation and half-apprehension.

In reality, she should seek some excuse to leave immediately. Perhaps she might mention another patient or some other commitment and then write her notes and recommendations.

'Dr Hatfield?'

Lord Anthony strode into the front hall.

'Yes.' She deepened her voice, hoping it did not tremble.

'Come into the library. Bring more brandy.' He slurred his words together, directing the last statement to the servant.

'Yes, sir,' Dobson said.

Letty followed, again noting his uneven gait, although whether this was from his injuries, or the alcohol he had apparently imbibed, she did not know.

He poured himself a drink from the decanter. 'Brandy?'

'No, thank you.'

He threw himself into an armchair, stretching his legs towards the hearth with a lack of grace that she would never have seen as a woman. To her relief, the lamps had not been lit and, due to the heat, the fire was neatly laid but not burning.

Still, to be safe, she chose a seat some distance from him.

'A doctor who does not drink? You are an anomaly, sir. I did not know there was such a creature.' Lord Anthony lifted the glass, swirling the amber liquid and watching as it moved within the glass with apparent fascination.

'I must still travel home.'

'Never seemed to bother your predecessor. So, what of my sister?' He tossed back the drink.

She watched him. 'Do you drink heavily because of your injuries?'

His brows pulled together. His jaw tightened. She saw a muscle twitch along his cheek as anger suffused his face. 'I drink because I enjoy drinking. I hope you are not under any misapprehension that you are here as *my* physic?'

'Not if you don't wish it. I ask because I could prescribe an ointment made of yarrow and a tincture of chamomile which might be more helpful than alcohol if you are seeking to numb the pain.'

'I find alcohol does well enough.' He paused, frowning as though his next statement required considerable concentration. 'Dr Hatfield, I have no wish to be uncivil to a man I invited to my home, so let me state here and now that I have had enough doctors poking and prodding me to last a lifetime. Your capacity here is only to consult on my sister's condition, do we understand each other?'

'Absolutely, you have answered my question with great clarity.'

His brows pulled together further, although the effect was more of confusion than anger as though trying to properly understand her words or suspecting some hidden meaning. Likely the brandy was inhibiting the clarity of his thoughts.

'Anyway,' he said, after a moment, 'may I ask your conclusions?'

'Lady Beauchamp shows signs of a condition of pregnancy where the body swells considerably with fluid. It can result in fits.'

She saw his body flinch as though her words had been a physical onslaught. His hand again tightened about the tumbler. She had spoken bluntly because that was what men did. Now she wished she'd softened her words.

'This…swelling is serious?'

'It can be.'

'Could she die?' he asked. His jaw tightened.

'Yes.'

'You do not mince words.'

'Would you want me to?'

'No.' He stood, pouring another shot of the amber liquid. The glass decanter clinked into the sudden silence. She saw that his hand shook.

'I have not been so forthright with Lady Beauchamp as I fear worry may worsen her condition.'

He walked to the window and stood facing away from her so that his large bulk was silhouetted against the glass. 'I am thankful for that. So what treatment do you prescribe?'

'Rest. Water. A bland diet with plenty of milk. A cool environment and an occasional walk when it is not so hot.'

'Milk? And rest?' he ground out. 'That is all you have? Milk and rest?'

She nodded, aware of a nervous tightening within her stomach.

He turned, stepping closer, so that she was able to see his clenched fists, his face and the steely, piercing brightness of his gaze. 'Good Lord, man. I do not pay you to come here and suggest the ingredients for a nursery tea.'

'At present you do not pay me at all. You may well want to retain Dr Jeffers, which is quite within your rights.' She stood abruptly.

'Sit down, man. Feisty as a woman. But milk? She is not a child.'

Apprehension slithered down her spine at his words. She felt her palms dampen, but she forced herself to relax, to assume that innate confidence of a male. He was angry at the world, but he would not guess her identity. Besides, at the rate of his current alcoholic consumption, he would not even remember the interview by morning.

'It is nutritious and will certainly do no harm.'

'Hardly a stirring endorsement,' he muttered. 'And if this nursery tea doesn't help?'

'I have prescribed a draught from the willow tree. I can attempt to bring about a speedier delivery within a few weeks. The only cure is for the child to be born. Treatment options are limited—'

The last words again seemed to ignite something in him. He tossed back the drink, slamming the empty glass against the table with such force she feared it would break.

'Bloody doctors—is that all you can say? "Treatment is limited". And "You should be glad to be alive". Do they give you a book of phrases when you train? Trite words you can proffer at any opportunity?' He paced, crossing in front of the window and back.

The last words were slurred so much that it took her a moment to comprehend. As though suddenly devoid of energy, he paused, sitting down again. The movement was heavy and ungainly. His body slumped. The anger seemed to dissipate, turning from molten heat and becoming but a sad smouldering thing. Letty studied him. The one side of his face was still so perfect while the other showed the harsh scars of his wounds. She noted also the slight tightening of his mouth with his movement as though still in pain. His gloved hand hung limp.

The impression of pain and anger and loss was so powerful that she felt a need to cross the space and provide some measure of comfort. Indeed, she had taken a step before she stopped, forcing herself with an almost painful energy to remain still.

She was a doctor and supposedly a male. This peculiar surge of emotion was not professional or in character.

'I presume we are talking about yourself and not your sister?' she said, making her tone calm.

'What?' He twisted towards her.

'I imagine you are quoting the words spoken to you by various medics following your injury.'

'You are now a mind reader, sir?' The muscle flickered across his cheek, the scarring fiercely red.

'No, but your recovery must have been difficult given the extent of your injuries.'

'Another one to add to that list of trite phrases— "the extent of your injuries". Let me tell you something, Doctor. Recovery is impossible, given the extent of my injuries.'

Impudent upstart—Tony glared at the odd man with thick lenses and ludicrous powdered wig. The style had gone out in the last century. He should send the fellow packing. Indeed, he would if he could summon either the energy or coherent words.

Except Elsie had already penned a quick note in favour of the peculiar gentleman.

He could, at least, send the fellow off now so that the evening was not spoiled by his nonsense. Yes, he'd do that. He'd ring for Dobson. He'd ring for Dobson and get the man to light the lamps and clear out the doctor.

And bring more brandy.

The doctor was talking again. He was nodding, the powdered wig bobbing. 'You will never be exactly the same in mind or body. There will always be scars, but I think recovery is about enduring and persisting.'

'A sound philosophy,' he muttered. 'Probably came from the same damned book.'

Although truthfully, Tony did not dislike the fellow as much as he should. Likely the soothing effects of alcohol. Or perhaps the man's blunt acknowledgement of the injury was almost a relief.

His scars were omnipresent in any relationship. He saw it in his valet's movements, in Mason's eagerness to put on his shirt to hide the damaged skin. He saw it in his infrequent conversations with his mother and the way her gaze skittered from him, addressing her comments to his hair or a lamp above his head. He saw it in Elsie's worry, the pity clouding her expression and her manner of positioning herself in any room so that she saw only the one side of his face. He saw it in the friends who had never visited.

Yes, one could almost say that the fellow's open interest was unique. Everyone else tiptoed around, mealy-mouthed and obsequious or else entirely absent.

Except for that odd woman at the garden party—Florence Barton's sister-in-law. He smiled, remembering that glint of beguiling emerald eyes.

Beguiling—good grief, he really had drunk too much. And Miss Barton was more annoying than beguiling.

The doctor cleared his throat, dragging Tony's attention back to the present.

'Right,' he said abstractedly. 'I suppose you can leave now. I will get Dobson to see you out. Bring in the lights and light the brandy.'

'I will write my conclusions and you can let me know if you wish to retain my services for Lady Beauchamp.'

'You are retained. I doubt you know much more than Jeffers, but you please Lady Beauchamp.'

'I like that you take her wishes into consideration.'

'Glad you approve. I will rest easy.' There was a pause, a momentary silence.

'Then we are agreed. I will write down my recommendations and monitor Lady Beauchamp's health.'

Tony shrugged. 'At least my store of brandy will remain intact.'

'A good thing, given your need for it.'

Tony gave a bark of laughter. 'In a previous lifetime I might have enjoyed your wit, Doctor.'

He paused. Even here in the shadows there seemed to be something familiar about this Dr Hatfield. He frowned, rubbing his forehead as though to help his sluggish thoughts. If he could only focus, if he could stop the dizzying swing of the room. 'You look familiar,' he said.

'I doubt it. I seldom socialise.' Dr Hatfield spoke jerkily, his voice oddly high before stepping so quickly to the door that he knocked over a chair. It clattered against the wall.

'Good Lord,' Tony drawled, lolling further back in his chair. 'You are a nervous fellow.'

'I must go.'

'See yourself out. When will you be back?'

'In a week, unless you call for me earlier.'

'Fine. Tell Dobson to send in more brandy.'

'I'm not certain that more alcohol is a good idea.'

'It is a damned necessity. And, Doctor?'

The man turned.

Tony's eyelids felt heavy and he felt his chin rest heavily on his chest. 'Do your best for her. She's all I have.'

Chapter Four

Elsie's note arrived two days later. The week
had been uneventful with no births, deaths or ac-
cidents. When Letty first saw the carriage with
its crest and uniformed footman rattling down
the village street, she feared instantly that Elsie
required medical attention. Indeed, she had already rung the bell to send Sarah to the doctor's
house and was pulling out the straps to bind her
chest when she heard the rapping at her own
front door.

Moments later, Sarah handed her the note.
The epistle was brief and in a female hand. Elsie
wrote that she had been ordered to rest by her
physician and was dreadfully bored. Therefore,
given that Letty was one of her few acquain-
tances in the country, she would love her to visit
and hoped that Miss Barton did not think her too

forward to invite her to tea, given their short acquaintance. Her carriage and footman was at her convenience that very afternoon.

Letty wrinkled her face. Truthfully, she wanted very much to see Elsie. She attributed this to her natural concern about her patient's health, although she felt this was not the sole reason.

Indeed, she knew that quick, almost physiological excitement, a quickening of her pulse as though she had been running. For a moment, Lord Anthony's face flickered in front of her, that odd mix of perfection and scarring.

She drummed her fingers against the table which she tended to do when thinking. Then she paused, carefully smoothing out the folds of the note, and studying it as though analysis of its form would make her decision easier.

In general, she saw little point in over-thinking one's emotion. Feelings were based on thoughts and circumstance. Therefore, it made more sense to deliberate on the logic of an action and its consequence than to perseverate on an abdominal wobble most likely due to Sarah's eggs.

She must encourage Sarah to cook the breakfast eggs more thoroughly.

Logically, she should decline Elsie's invitation. It was only sensible to keep as far removed as possible from both Lady Beauchamp and her brother. They had seen her as a man and would continue to do so, given that she was providing Lady Beauchamp with medical care. To return as a female was undoubtedly asking for trouble.

She had risked everything for this career.

Even now she felt something akin to disbelief that this façade, the masquerade, had worked—was working.

Indeed, when Letty had written to Guy's Hospital under her brother's name, it was more a last desperate act before surrender. Ramsey had opened the hospital's reply. He'd frowned and then handed it to her with a wry lift of his brow. 'I did not know I aspired to be a doctor,' he'd said. 'Life is so full of surprises.'

'Don't tell Mother.'

'I'll keep my aspirations a dark secret,' he'd said.

Later, after he'd gone out, she'd held the letter, pressing the edges between her fingertips and studying the bold words inviting 'Mr Barton' for an interview to see if he might be a suitable apprentice to become apothecary or surgeon-apothecary.

She'd stared at the words until they seemed

imprinted on her eyes, visible even when she squeezed them shut. Why had she written? As she'd stood within the breakfast room, the paper tightly pinched between her fingers, it seemed as though this was an added torture, opening her to a litany of 'what ifs'.

With a sudden impulse, she'd run up the stairs and into Ramsey's room. She'd flung open his closet, pulling out his clothes. She was a tall woman. She always hated her height, her long gangly legs which had so ludicrously lengthened during her fourteenth year. Now she felt a flash of gratitude as she pulled on a ragtag collection of trousers, shirt, cravat and jacket.

Indeed, on her brother's return, she'd had on long trousers, bagging about her hips, a pair of riding boots and a poorly fitting jacket.

'Letty? What are you doing?'

'These don't fit, but we could get some made and I could lower my voice and wear hats all the time. I—I wouldn't be Mr Barton. I mean that's you, but I could apply under a different name. I could be—I could be—' She'd gazed out of the window at the green fields behind Oddsmore and then around the room at the boots, shirts, hats and cravats tossed about so randomly. 'Mr Hatfield. I could be Mr Hatfield.'

'And now I really do think you're lost your reason,' her brother had said.

'It would work. At least for the interview.'

'And what good would an interview do? Do you know what people would say?'

'Do I care? I don't want to marry. I have never wanted to. And this way, I'd know.'

'Know what?'

'I'd know if I was good enough,' she'd said.

'I do not think you should go, miss,' Sarah said, interrupting Letty's memories with this pronouncement from the doorway 'Not if you are still planning to be her ladyship's physician. Indeed, I would urge you to reconsider.'

'What? Tea or being her doctor?'

'Both. They can certainly afford Dr Jeffers,' Sarah said.

'It would be better if they could not. The local midwife has considerably more luck in keeping patients alive.'

'It is not up to you to save everyone.'

She's all I have. His words echoed in her mind.

'They've lost so much—'

'Then if you are so determined to be the doctor, you should avoid the risk of tea.'

'I am not planning to ride Lord Anthony's bulls,' she grumbled.

'You know what I mean.'

'I know I never thought a cup of tea would be considered a daredevil activity.'

'Likely it wouldn't for them as are not living a double life of mystery and intrigue.'

Letty sighed. 'I know you're right. Every logical part of me urges me to follow your advice. But so few females have ever wanted my friendship, even when I was a small child.'

'They might have appreciated you more if you had not practised your amputation skills on their dolls.'

Letty allowed herself a brief grin. 'I didn't make a habit of it. I only did so once with that awful doll belonging to that dreadful Grismold girl. Besides she looked quite possessed. The doll, I mean, not Miss Grismold.'

'Grisgold, miss.'

'And I find myself worrying about Elsie—I mean Lady Beauchamp. She sounds lonely and I would like to see if her face and hands are less swollen.'

Sarah shook her head. 'It is not wise.'

Letty chuckled. 'Good gracious, if I wished to be wise, I would never have started this masquerade. No, I refuse to live my life in fear. Enjoying a cup of tea is hardly taking up highway robbery or treason.' Letty nodded, as if agreeing with her own words. 'Tell the footman to wait. I will come.'

'I do wish you would not be so inordinately stubborn and headstrong,' Sarah said. 'I am certain it will all go awry. And you know who will have to wipe up the tears. Muggins here.'

The maid prodded her chest to emphasise her point.

'But you do such a wonderful job,' Letty said, pressing a kiss against Sarah's cheek before getting ready for tea with uncharacteristic excitement.

The Beauchamps' coach proved considerably more comfortable than the doctor's shabby vehicle. Of course, Ramsey had offered her a more deluxe and better-sprung carriage, but she had refused. Anything too grand would have invited question. Besides, despite both her own inheritance and her brother's generosity, her funds were not infinite and she wished to be self-sufficient as soon as possible.

Still, this didn't stop her from enjoying the luxury of working springs and an interior which was not tainted with a combination of old leather, wet footwear, medicinal herbs and body odour like an aromatic history.

In contrast, this carriage was new, without any distinct or unpleasant smells, and seemed unlikely to rattle one's teeth loose from one's gums. With a sigh of content, she leaned back against the cushioning. Her body relaxed as she swayed to the carriage's rhythmic rocking. She had always found that carriage rides put her to sleep and really there was no reason to fight it. Indeed, she'd racked up enough sleepless nights to doze through a dozen carriage rides.

It was just as her lids drooped that the carriage jerked to a halt. Her eyes flew open as she half-tumbled to the floor.

'What is it?' she called out, scrambling to look out of the window. They appeared to be in the middle of the wood which surrounded the Beauchamp estate.

'Stay in there, miss. It might be a trick,' the groom shouted from the podium.

She ignored him, swinging open the carriage door and clambering out.

For a moment, she saw nothing. It was only as she stepped to the front of the vehicle that she saw the crumpled figure.

'Good God!'

A man sprawled on the ground, only five feet in front of their wheels. He lay awkwardly and appeared unconscious.

'Sir?' She stepped towards the prone figure.

The footman had now also descended from the podium.

'Miss, please go back inside. T'aint no place for a lady. Indeed, he may be a highway man—'

'Nonsense! We are miles from anywhere in the middle of a wood. An unlikely location for a highway man,' Letty said, crouching beside the man. He was breathing. She could hear his inhalations and felt it soft against her hand.

'I wouldn't say so, miss. I really think—' the footman repeated.

Letty glanced about to see if she could see any sign of a horse or vehicle but they were, as the footman had stated, quite alone.

'I think he must have knocked himself out on this rock. Get me a cloth or a shirt or something,' she directed.

'A cloth, miss?' he said as though this were a foreign object.

'Yes, his head is bleeding.'

'Miss, I am sure you should be in the carriage.'

'Where I would be no help whatsoever and you obviously require assistance unless you expect to heal him with the intensity of your stare. Now find me something that I can tie about his head.'

The firm tone did the trick and, galvanised into action, the footman grabbed a cloth from the vehicle. 'Will this do, miss?'

She took it. With efficient movements she tied the cloth tightly about the head wound, carefully moving his head to secure its position.

The gash was bleeding quite profusely, turning the white cloth quickly red.

'Bring me some water,' she directed to the groom who still stood behind her.

'I don't have none.'

'Bother. Sir? Sir?' Letty bent over him, tapping his cheek slightly, hoping to see some return to consciousness. 'Sir. This is—Miss Barton.'

The man groaned. His eyes opened.

'Right,' she said. 'Can you hear me? Tell me your name.'

The man made no response, his eyes closing.

The footman cleared his throat. 'It's Mr Cummings, miss. He's our neighbour.'

She nodded. 'Right. Well, you are going to be fine, Mr Cummings. The bleeding is slowing, which is very positive.' She turned back to the footman. 'Do you have something which might do as a stretcher?'

'Pardon?'

'To help carry him. And a sling.'

'A sling?'

'Yes, for his shoulder. I think it might be dislocated and I need to immobilise it. My shawl will do.'

'Here, miss,' he said, procuring the shawl.

'Thank you and thank goodness he is not overly portly,' she added, as they moved the man on to the board, their efforts punctuated by Mr Cummings's groans and her own gasps of exertion.

At last they had moved the unfortunate gentleman from the board and on to the cushioning within the carriage.

'Good,' she said, ensuring that the bandage had not shifted and his head rested on one of the cushions. 'Drive slowly. I will ensure he does not roll from the seat.'

'Yes, miss,' the groom responded, hurriedly ascending to the podium as if thankful to be back in this familiar role.

As the carriage lurched forward, the gentleman opened his eyes again.

'Good,' she approved, taking his hand. 'Try to stay with me, Mr Cummings, it won't be long now. Do you remember what happened?'

He blinked. His eyes were a pale blue. He was not young, appearing to be at least middle aged with a bald head, encircled by a fringe of short blond whiskers.

'Trying out a new horse. Must have got spooked. Threw me.'

'It is fortunate we came along. Not to worry. I will stitch up that wound,' she said.

'You, miss?'

'Indeed.'

It appeared tea might need to be delayed.

Tony was striding across the courtyard when he heard the carriage roll down the drive and pull to a standstill. He turned, aware of a pulse of interest and unusual eagerness.

The door flew open almost before the wheels had stopped. The woman, Miss Barton, bolted out. Again, something about her captured his attention. There was a vibrancy and energy about her which was arresting. It was the brightness of her red hair against her dark bonnet, the flush of colour staining her cheeks and her quick movements.

He felt a start of awareness, pleasure almost, and was so taken aback that it took him a moment to realise that she appeared distressed and was talking rapidly and with agitation.

He started forward. 'What happened?' he shouted. 'Miss Barton, are you all right?'

'—need help—gentleman—met with accident—' She could barely get her words out for her heavy breathing.

He saw now that she was dishevelled, her face dirty and her clothes bloodied. His pulse accelerated and he felt fear twist through him. The size of the emotion, the thud of his heart and dryness of his mouth surprised him.

'Miss Barton? Did you meet with an accident? Are you hurt?'

'No, I am absolutely fine,' she assured him and he could see that, despite the stains on her dress, she appeared as robust as usual. A mix of relief and irritation flashed through him. Tension tightened his shoulders.

Just then, the footman, Phillips, appeared from the back of the coach. His face was chalk-white and his clothes were also dirty.

'We found Mr Cummings and he has met with an accident,' the man explained, his voice shaky.

'Indeed,' Miss Barton agreed. 'But we can

catch His Lordship up on the details later. Currently, Mr Cummings is in the carriage. I need him to be moved to a clean, flat surface within the house.'

Tony stared at the preposterous woman, his irrational fear now replaced by irrational anger.

'Miss Barton, I hardly see a need for you to further involve yourself in Mr Cummings's care. I will send for a medic—Hatfield, I suppose.'

'I—' She appeared briefly uncertain. He saw her exhalation and her brows draw together over her remarkable green eyes. 'I share a stable with Dr Hatfield in the village so I know he is away. I—have—read a lot about medical issues and carry some basic supplies, so I can help. In any event, the gentleman needs to be removed from the carriage with all possible dispatch.'

She finished this statement in a brisk rush of words before turning and disappearing back into the carriage. Instinctively, Tony stepped forward. He had meant to argue—no, not to argue, but to order, to direct, to instil reason. The sensible words and phrases were already formed and waiting to be uttered.

'Miss Barton.' He leaned into the carriage. 'I—'

The words and sensible phrases died on his

lips. It was the smell. His breath left him in a sharp whistled exhalation. His stomach hurt, as though he had been punched in his gut. His good hand squeezed the doorframe so tightly that later he found a red line marking his palm.

The interior was laced with the scent of blood. And fear. And sweat.

In some part of his mind, Tony knew he needed to say something; to give direction and regain control. Again, he tried. Again the sensible, logical words formed even as his own blood thundered against his eardrums. His throat was dry, his tongue cleaving to the roof of his mouth.

His gaze was drawn almost against his will to the man reclining unconscious against the cushioning with his pallid, clammy skin and soiled makeshift bandage.

Almost blindly, Tony stepped back from the carriage. His hand dropped. His every muscle felt limp. His throat felt dry and his tongue swollen so that it was Miss Barton who spoke. He heard her words as if from a great distance or muffled by the roar of a water fall.

'Lord Anthony, you do not look entirely well. I can look after Mr Cummings. Perhaps you could go inside and explain to your sister why I might be late for tea,' she said.

Tony felt himself nod, but seemed peculiarly unable to either comply or dispute the issue. Instead, he stood, with a feeling of dislocation and odd fascination as his two footmen brought wooden boards from the stable. Under Miss Barton's direction, the footmen removed his neighbour from the coach.

He watched the limp figure lying flat against the boards.

At Waterloo, they had not even had proper porters. The entire army had moved on to continue the fight, leaving the dead and dying scattered and inconsequential. Some local peasants had come, trundling their carts through the bodies. Many had helped. He owed his own life to just such a man.

Scavengers had come also, prying out teeth to sell to the French dentists—'Waterloo teeth'. You could get them now from fashionable London dentists. He saw the advertisements in the newspapers.

'Take him to the kitchen,' Miss Barton directed.

The kitchen? Tony felt a ripple of inappropriate mirth, jarring and discordant with the earlier images as though he were on some bizarre, emotional swing. Mrs Peterson would not approve of bleeding bodies within her kitchen.

Dazedly, he followed Miss Barton and the two footmen as they carried the unconscious man on the makeshift stretcher.

'What in the name of all that is good are you doing?' Mrs Peterson thundered to the footmen.

It was exactly what he had expected her to say, he thought. He still stood in the passage, which was dark in comparison to the brightness in the kitchen, giving him the odd feeling that he was watching a theatrical production.

But then perhaps it was not so very odd. Since his return, he had often felt more observer than participant—as though he was mouthing the script of his former life.

'You cannot be putting a sick man in my kitchen. And certainly not one what is bleeding. I am making dinner,' Mrs Peterson's strident tones pierced his peculiar, inner soliloquy. 'Take him to a bedchamber, for heaven's sake.'

'No, there is no easy access to water and soap and often bedchambers are not well lit. We will use the scullery.'

Mrs Peterson reddened, placing her hands at her ample waist. 'Well, I never and who might you be when the Pope's in Rome?'

Tony knew again that odd mirth, a fleeting thing which would too soon be replaced with numbness. He must have made some sound because Mrs Peterson saw him. Her hands dropped from her waist and her mouth opened.

'Oh, my lord, I am that sorry for my tone. I did not see you there.'

She continued to look at him. Likely she was expecting intervention, a return of sanity, where bodies were not strewn about her kitchen. On another day, in another life, he would have thundered out an immediate dismissal of Miss Barton and her nonsense. On another day, in another life, he would have done the sensible thing and sent for Jeffers. On another day, in another life, he'd have done something instead of inhabiting this frozen place.

'If we could look after Mr Cummings. As I said, the scullery would be suitable.'

'Bleeding men do not belong in my kitchen and that you can tie to. Indeed, I am certain a footman can get a proper physician.'

'That would be better, I am certain,' Dobson intoned.

Dobson always spoke, Tony thought, as though making an announcement, turning every comment into an oration.

'Except Dr Jeffers is gone to London for several days,' the housekeeper said suddenly from her position behind Dobson. 'He informed Lady Beauchamp.'

Tony hadn't seen her earlier. Indeed, it was like a play in which he had front-row seats.

Miss Barton frowned. She bit her lip, appearing less confident. 'I have read extensively on head wounds. And if Dr Jeffers is away, I am able to put in some stitches. Mr Cummings will bleed considerably less and make a better recovery.'

Mrs Peterson opened her mouth and, at his continued silence, closed it. The retinue then moved through the kitchen and into the scullery. Mr Cumming was laid on the table and Miss Barton efficiently tore off his shirt with a rent of fabric.

That noise—that sound of fabric tearing—did it again. His mirth evaporated into a shivery, nauseous, thudding fear.

The kitchen become distant, a surreal, nightmarish place.

He'd pulled off his own shirt to stop the bleeding when his brother-in-law was shot. The cloth had been burned into his skin where the bullet had struck his side. He'd pulled the material away. He remembered thinking how odd it was that he felt no pain.

It hadn't mattered. It was a futile gesture. The cloth was already wet with his own blood and sodden—a useless thing.

And George had died.

After that it had felt so lonely lying on that field, oddly quiet after the thunder of the battle.

The clouds were so low he could not tell where the mist ended and mud began. The acrid scent of gunpowder coated his tongue. Gradually, the sun burned off the mist and he'd felt hot. His tongue had swollen, becoming huge and dry within his mouth, while his back was cold with the mud from yesterday's rains.

Between the bodies, a few men were still alive. Some cried out, but most groaned softly as if aware of the futility, as if knowing that no one would hear them. Or care.

He'd gone to the other wounded men. He'd tried to help. Maybe one or two had lived. Not many.

He'd felt so powerless. He'd looked over the damp, muddy, misty fields littered with bodies and felt a heavy, heartsick hopelessness, as if he was drowning in mud or quicksand.

George was dead. He could not find Edgar.

And he could do nothing to help or save those dying men.

He'd stayed beside George's body to save his teeth from the scavengers. He could see them, their dark shadowy shapes visible within the mist. Sometimes they'd loom quite close, at other times they'd slip from view, disappearing within the hollows caused by the cannon balls.

Now and again he thought he heard the click of their small efficient pliers—a click of metal on tooth, a breath of exertion and a rustle of cloth as the tooth was deposited within a sack. Click, breath, rustle…click…breath…rustle…

'Lord Anthony, if you could step aside a moment,' the clipped female voice said.

He looked around the scullery which should be as familiar as his own hand. But wasn't.

Briefly, it seemed as though the two worlds had collided; the mud and corpses oddly superimposed on Mrs Peterson's clean kitchen. His amusement came back. Some part of him almost laughed. Mrs Peterson would so disapprove of mud within her kitchen.

'Lord Anthony!' This time the words were sharper.

The mud disappeared and he was back once

again within the scullery, looking into Miss Barton's clear emerald gaze.

Their gazes met. For a moment it seemed as though she was the bridge, the connection, the lifeline between these two divergent worlds. The shadowy shapes which peopled his nightmares seemed faded. He gulped at the air, as if at some point he had forgotten to breathe.

'Sit down. Put your head between your knees. I cannot have you keeling over while I am stitching him up.' She spoke with determination but without any panic lacing her tones. Somehow, that firm clear direction was what he needed. He complied. The crazy shushing of his heart slowed and steadied so that he could hear the voices of the staff.

'I don't wonder you're not feeling the thing, my lord,' Mrs Peterson said. 'No gentleman should have his kitchen used in such a way. Not the thing at all. Most extraordinary. Should I give you smelling salts? Or camphor?'

'Good God, no,' he said, or he thought he said, although later he wondered whether he'd uttered the words only in his mind.

'I require some wine,' Miss Barton said.

'Much better,' he said or maybe said.

'I have brandy here,' the butler stated.

Yes. Ever better!

'I suppose that will do,' Miss Barton said. 'Pour him a small measure and I will add a few drops to it.'

Tony watched as his butler poured the amber liquid. Then Dobson gave it to Miss Barton who gave it to the man on the table.

Tony laughed. This time they must have heard him because everyone looked.

'Perhaps His Lordship could go to the library or his study,' Miss Barton suggested.

And he went. He followed Dobson like an overwrought bloody child. And it seemed that he felt every emotion: pain, anger, fear, guilt—

Indeed, he felt so much that he felt nothing.

Letty exited the kitchen and approached the library a half-hour later. The wound had only required a couple of stitches and she felt certain it would heal well. Satisfaction surged through her. She straightened, adding swing to her step as she strode down the hall. Logically, she knew she should never have shown her medical ability— at least not as Miss Barton. Not in this house, to these people.

Yet, despite the risk, she felt a thrill, a vindication.

She had seen their doubt. She'd heard Mrs Peterson's loud whisper to the housekeeper, 'Are you certain we should be allowing this? Just because His Lordship isn't feeling quite the thing doesn't mean we should allow torture in my kitchen.'

But she'd persisted and, just for once, she had not had to hide under the white powered wig.

Her jubilation was curtailed as she approached the library, pausing with her hand on the knob. While Mr Cummings's issues had been straightforward, Lord Anthony's were not. His Lordship had not been himself. She frowned. In fact, he had not been anyone. It had felt as though he was oddly absent.

Letty had an excellent memory and could often see and reread the words, long after she had put away the article. She recalled now that she'd read about soldiers who sometimes seemed less able to cope once they returned from the battle. Indeed, she could almost see the printed words, although the title and volume escaped her.

She would not chase the thought. She found that she would sometimes remember that which had been eluding her if she let her mind think about other things. Besides, it was entirely possible that the man had been demonstrating yet another form of inebriation. Or apoplexy.

Hopefully not the latter, as it was a serious complaint and, on occasion, fatal.

She twisted the knob with urgency, stepping forward, aware of a sudden fear almost bigger than that which she had experienced when they had located Mr Cummings.

Which was not logical.

The library at Beauchamp was large, long, with high ceilings and wood-panelled walls interrupted only by stacked shelves and paintings. She saw Lord Anthony almost immediately. He was not prone, thank goodness. So likely it was not apoplexy.

He sat very still with a rigidity which was not natural. The curtains were drawn, but even in the low light she saw that his colour had not yet returned, making his face white except for the crimson mark of his scar.

'Lord Anthony,' she said softly.

He made no sound and did not acknowledge her presence. Indeed, he still sat as though closed from the world. His eyes were open, but she had the strange sense that he did not see her or even the room or empty hearth.

If this was the effect of drink, it was one that

her father, brother or the villagers had never demonstrated.

Swallowing nervously, she rubbed her hands against her skirt. The rustle of cloth was loud in the still room.

'Lord Anthony?' she said, stepping forward.

He still made no response.

She looked about, taking in the shelves, books, the comfortable chairs and the paintings of dead Beauchamp ancestors as though for inspiration.

'I like this room,' she said softly. 'I like the huge fireplace. It must be so very cosy in winter.'

Nervously, she bit her lip. 'Of course, it is summer now so there is no fire. And outside, there are green shrubs and flowers. I—I love the colours and smells of summer...'

She paused again, looking around rather desperately. She had a foggy notion that if she could make him aware of the sounds, the smells, the textures of this place, this present, it might help. She had to do something. The contrast of the man she recalled so vividly in Lord Entwhistle's library and this person who seemed so greatly removed, hurt on a physical level. It was as though his grief or loss or pain was so huge that it had engulfed him so that the man was lost.

Again she rubbed her hands. The need to help or to comfort seemed so much larger than was usual for her. She always cared for her patients, but this was different. Or maybe it was simply that this distress was less rooted in the physical and therefore she felt less competent.

Yes, that must be it. The tightness within her chest and the clogged feeling within her throat must be due to this feeling of uncertainty.

With a desperate impulsivity, she reached for a bunch of lilies within a cut-crystal vase. She pulled them out. The cold water dripped against her skirt in huge dark splotches.

She leaned forward, thrusting the blooms under his nose so that the water splashed on to his trousers.

'What the...?' he muttered, with a jerk of his head.

The relief was huge. Her eyes smarted as though she might cry. Her hand shook, further scattering water droplets.

'Why do—I have lilies—stuck under my nose?' He blinked somewhat dazedly and spoke unnaturally with a staccato rhythm.

'I didn't have smelling salts,' she said shakily.

'Thank heaven for small mercies.'

This wobbly mix of relief and a sentiment akin to joy was uncharacteristic as she knew herself to be prosaic in nature.

'And—and because the lilies seemed much more beautiful than whatever you were seeing.'

Irritation, pain, fear, rage and a myriad of other expressions flickered across his features before hardening to a cold anger. He straightened his spine.

'Miss Barton, I am fully recovered and I do not require your ministrations. Indeed, I was merely experiencing pain from my wound.'

She shook her head. 'I do not think so. I am certain you still have residual constant pain, but I do not think it was the cause of—of—'

'Yes?' he bit out.

She replaced the lilies, shifting away from him, needing to distance herself from the bristling anger. The clock ticked, loud within the uncomfortable silence of the room.

She licked her lips nervously. 'When I was little I fell off my horse. It was in a meadow. I remember very little about the incident except for the smell, a mix of skunk cabbage and moss. Anyway, whenever I smelled anything remotely resembling skunk cabbage, I am transported back to that place and time.'

She glanced at him.

'Is there a point to this sad tale about your poor equestrian skills?' he drawled in cold aristocratic tones, with a rise of one eyebrow. 'I can suggest to my groom that he provide you with some lessons, if you would like.'

'No, I ride quite adequate to my needs. My point was that memories can be very powerful.'

His lips twisted into a smile that was not a smile. 'Tell me something of which I am not aware.'

'I hoped to counter whatever you were remembering with the scent of the lilies. I thought it might bring back more pleasant memories.'

He smiled. This time a faint glint of humour almost reached his eyes and that flicker of humour seemed to do something to her insides. 'Indeed, I am reminded of dreadful debutante balls.'

'Yes,' she said. 'Awkwardly dancing and forever hiding from my mother.'

'In the library, as I recall.' His smile grew and it almost seemed as though she saw a flicker of that man she had met—indeed—the man she had thought about at odd moments and that brief meeting that was so oddly sharp within her mind.

The warmth within seemed to grow, heating her cheeks. 'It always seemed the safer option. I had a habit of treading on people's toes or accosting them with odd topics of conversation.'

'Yes, although I actually found your discourse more interesting than many. I once had a young lady discuss her spaniel's medical problems. Did you know that spaniels suffer from ear wax?'

'I did not.'

'And flatulence.'

'That would have been Miss Grisgold. She was always giving the poor animal sweetmeats—it became portly.'

'You see, cowpox is a much more pleasant topic.'

Her mouth felt oddly dry and her pulse peculiarly quickened. The fact that he had recalled the nature of their conversation from three years ago somehow jumbled her thoughts and made her gasp as though she had just ascended the stairs extremely rapidly, which she had not. In fact, she had been sitting quite still.

Now, the room which had felt pleasantly cool was suddenly unconscionably hot. The slight warmth in her cheeks was now a raging fire and she seemed oddly immobile, incredibly aware of his proximity.

Indeed they sat directly opposite each other. His knee was approximately nine inches from her own. His hand rested on his leg, the long fingers outlined against the worsted cloth. He was a large man, in a tall, spare, big-boned way. She looked up. His gaze was a deep, dark grey-blue. His brows were straight, dark and formidable, so that he almost appeared to be glowering except when he smiled. And that contrast between angry pain and wry amusement seemed even more intriguing.

He shifted forward. She heard the rustle of cloth. Very slowly, he raised his hand and trailed one finger along the delicate line of her chin. His touch was so light, yet she felt it everywhere— it sent a strange tingling into her extremities.

Nervously, she bit her lip and felt his dark gaze move to her mouth. Again she heard the rustle of his movement. Very gently, he touched her chin once more. Everything, her entire consciousness, was focused on the feel of his thumb as very slowly, with infinite care, he ran it along the line of her chin.

He moved forward, shifting, leaning—

Her own hand lifted. She touched his jawline.

He was still thin from his injury, but that seemed to give him a hard leanness.

He jolted at her touch.

His hand dropped. It smacked against his leg, the noise surprisingly loud. He stood, almost bolting upright, so quickly that she heard him wince.

Her own hand dropped back to the cloth of her skirt.

'Right,' he said briskly. 'I am quite fine now. If I seemed...unwell earlier it was likely the heat. Terribly hot summer, this year.'

She shot back in the seat, pressing her spine against the cushioning, as though hoping to mould herself to the frame. 'Yes. Hot. Very. Extremely. Unusual—for England which is usually rainy. And damp. Very. Anyway, I—um—must go. See your sister.'

She sprang, as though catapulted, and was already halfway across the floor when the butler entered. 'Lady Beauchamp is awake and asking for Miss Barton,' he said.

'Thank you. I will go immediately.'

Dobson cleared his throat. 'Might I suggest, miss, that you freshen up? The maid says she has located some clothing which might prove adequate. She is in one of the guest rooms and will help you change. If you would like to do so, I can take you.'

'Yes, I suppose so,' Letty said, glancing at her dress which had definitely seen better days. 'Thank you.'

'And her ladyship suggests that, given the late hour, Miss Barton stay for dinner and the night.'

'No—I—don't want to inconvenience any-one,' Letty said, her refusal swift and too em-phatic for courtesy.

'Her ladyship said to say that the road is hard to navigate in the dark.'

Letty glanced towards Lord Anthony, hop-ing for assistance in avoiding the invitation that must be uncomfortable for both. Tony merely shrugged as though such domestic arrangements were not his concern. 'Discuss it with my sister. I am going out for some air.'

With these words, he strode from the room. The door swung shut. She exhaled, conscious that she had been holding her breath. She felt a confused mix of relief and anti-climax as though she had been robbed of something vital with his departure.

'I suppose I'd best get changed so I do not look as though I have slaughtered a chicken or something,' she said somewhat lamely to the butler who still stood at the door.

'Indeed, miss.'

She heard his condemnation in his tone. Of course, stitching up injured gentlemen was likely much worse than slaughtering a dozen chickens. And oddly, the incident with Mr Cummings, the kitchen surgery, those waves of disapproval and even her own sense of vindication all seemed oddly distant, as though it had occurred to her in the distant past—or as though she had been somehow immutably changed since it occurred.

Chapter Five

Elsie lay on the daybed with her legs raised upon a pillow. She looked better, Letty noted with some relief. Her face appeared less puffy, her smile genuine and her expression no longer listless.

'I am so glad you've come,' she said. 'I heard you looked after Mr Cummings which sounds wonderfully brave and gallant of you. It is so fortunate you found him. Heaven knows what would have happened.'

'His servants would have looked for him when his horse returned,' Letty said somewhat drily. 'And given that he was on the main path within a rather small wood, they would likely have found him.'

'By which point he might have expired. Or perhaps been trampled by a rider or carriage less alert than our own dear Phillips. Anyway, the good thing is that now it is so late that you absolutely must remain for dinner and stay the night.'

'I don't know...' Letty hesitated. 'I think I could make it back.'

'But it would be dark. Indeed, you must stay. I am so bored here and apparently poor Phillips is quite shaken by the episode. I am certain he will be startled by every shadow. So it would be so much kinder to let him rest. Normally, of course, McGee could take you, but his sister is getting married and we gave him the day off. Besides, now we can choose you a wonderful dress for dinner. I haven't been able to fit into anything for ages. Plus, I've had to wear black, but it will be so much fun to dress you. Indeed, I have been wanting to do so for ever.'

'You have?' Letty said with some confusion. 'We only met a month ago.'

'Actually, I saw you at my come out. Later, I heard you were staying in London and thought I would like to meet you. But George and I spent most of our time here. I mean before he—left.'

Letty could see her pain. For a split second that mask of smiles and humour left and Letty saw her naked vulnerability.

'I am glad to meet you now. And glad you are here.'

'Yes, it is both sad and restful which must sound odd, I know.' She paused before adding in brighter tones, 'Anyway, we never seemed to be in the same place, but I always thought you would be vastly entertaining if ever your mother let you talk.'

Letty laughed, touched and surprised that Elsie had even noticed her. 'My mother never enjoyed my topics of conversation.'

'Likely because they veered from the dreadfully dull.'

'I did not discuss my spaniel's ear wax, at least. Although now I come to think if it, that might be because I did not have a spaniel. I do rather like medical topics and ear wax might be under that category.'

Elsie laughed. 'You must be talking about Miss Grisgold. You absolutely must stay. Then I can choose you a dress. I would love to do so.'

'A dress? No—I mean—you are certain this is not adequate?' Letty glanced down at the afternoon gown which the maid had provided. It seemed fancy enough in comparison to her usual garb. Besides, the aristocracy's delight in changing clothes umpteen times within a single day seemed a dreadful waste of energy. Her mother had made her do so and she had resented it terribly.

'Adequate, but not splendiferous. And it would be so sad to see my lovely dresses go to waste and I am certain they will be dreadfully out of fashion by the time I fit into them again. If I ever can.' She pausing, sighing dramatically. 'I have one that would be perfect on you. It is cream, but with threads of gold.'

'It sounds rather fancy,' Letty said dubiously.

'But you will try it on. Or there is always blue or green. I am certain green would suit you.'

Letty pulled a face. 'So my mother said. Consequently I have resembled a cabbage or a bean pole or some form of vegetable most of my life.'

'Only because she loved ruffles of such size that they masqueraded as leaves. Besides she always chose the wrong shade. Now for your hair, I think we could put loose waves in it. Maria,' she called to the maid. 'Do you think loose waves would suit?'

Letty reached up to touch her hair. It was unfashionably short and she always kept it tied back and twisted into a small, neat bun. 'I don't know. It doesn't sound very tidy.'

Elsie laughed. 'Gracious, since when did any female aspire to tidy hair?'

'I do. And mine doesn't like to curl. My mother's maid would try and it would frizz.'

'Maria is ever so clever with the tongs. Please, let us dress you up. I love clothes. I am not clever at other things like Tony. You see, that was my thing. There were three of us. Edgar was the eldest. He was dreadfully responsible and just the teeniest, tiniest bit dull. Tony was funny and clever and witty. I am neither responsible nor witty, but I know clothes. I absolutely always know what will suit people.'

'Funny'—the adjective didn't exactly suit the man she had recently seen in the library. Nor the shell of the man in the kitchen.

But the boy she had met at her debut. Briefly, she saw him, tall, broad, with that careless, effortless good humour and style that seemed a part of aristocratic life.

I avoid ambition on principle. Sounds too much like hard work. She remembered the words.

'He seems to have changed, your brother?'

Sorrow and worry flickered across Elsie's features. 'Waterloo impacted his sense of humour quite dreadfully.'

Letty noted Elsie's turn of phrase. She remembered her mother's strictures. A proper lady does not display any excess of emotion—or any emotion at all for that matter.

'I'm sorry,' she said.

Tears shimmered in the other woman's eyes. Perhaps Elsie had not heard Mrs Barton's rules. Impulsively, she reached forward to touch her hand. 'It might help to talk.'

'Good gracious.' Elsie gave a laugh which was close to a sob. 'Wherever did you hear that? That is not good etiquette at all. One's aim is always to look pleasant, say the proper thing and never, ever let people know that—that one's heart is breaking.'

Letty said, still holding Elsie's hand, 'Likely why I will never make a proper lady.'

Elsie's grip tightened. 'Indeed, you are quite different than most people. In a good way. And Tony is better here than in London, at least.'

'And you?'

'Better and worse. In London, I kept so busy, I didn't have time to think and here I have nothing to do but think.' Elsie's face fell into wistful lines, but then brightened. 'Which is why it would be so wonderful to choose you a dress. It would remind me of playing with friends when I was a girl and everything seemed much less complicated.'

Letty hesitated. Firstly, her childhood had never included dressing up with friends. Secondly, her mother had always made her feel like a doll of inferior quality. Indeed, she could still hear the long litany of her faults: her hair was too contrary, her skin too pale, her figure too tall and her freckles...well, freckles should not even exist.

Yet Elsie showed an excited enthusiasm which was contagious.

'Very well,' Letty said. 'But I don't want to look like...like a lettuce or a doll.'

'Of course you don't. As though I would do that to you. Indeed, you will look like Athena or Diana or some absolutely wonderful, statuesque Roman goddess. Or Greek. I was never very good at mythology.'

'Very well. Although I've never heard of a redheaded goddess.'

'What about a Nordic goddess? Weren't they redheaded?'

'Blonde, I think.'

'Then you will be the first goddess with red hair. Quite fitting because you are definitely original.'

Letty smiled. 'I'm not exactly certain that is a positive attribute.'

* * *

An hour, Letty peered curiously into the looking glass. She didn't exactly resemble the promised deity. Her red hair and tall slender figure made that rather difficult. However, deity or not, she looked...attractive. Her eyes appeared huge and very green. Her skin was creamy and her cheeks pleasantly flushed. Even her hair, despite its hue, was almost co-operating. The maid had not tried the tight ringlets her mother favoured, but had curled it into loose waves which she'd pulled into a low twist at the nape of her neck. As always due to its shorter length, tendrils escaped, but they had been curled artfully so that they appeared part of the design, as opposed to merely untidy. Moreover, they framed her face, softening her usually severe aspect.

And the dress... Letty felt an unfamiliar thrill of girlish excitement. Elsie had chosen a gown made in the new Empire style and thus loose, flowing and somewhat diaphanous. Indeed, the light cloth made her feel naked or as if she were in her peignoir. Certainly, there was a freedom to it which was a pleasant change from the dresses of her debut, but it also incited a nervousness, reminiscent of those dreams in which one had forgotten to dress.

'Is this quite decent?' Her hand touched her throat. 'The neckline seems quite low.'

'Good gracious, of course it is. Do you not go out at all? The style is everywhere in London.'

'I go out as infrequently as possible,' Letty said, wryly. While not exactly shy, she knew herself to be awkward and both bored by subjects which interested other women and unable to feign that interest. Indeed, it was one of the many reasons she knew she could never marry. Likely she'd doom both her spouse and any offspring to being social outcasts.

Sometimes, she wondered if, despite life's hardships, belonging was not easier in the lower classes. Would one be valued more for one's practical abilities and less for one's looks and wit?

'But you must go to London on occasion. I am certain Florence would take you. And didn't you spend several months there after your come out?'

'Indeed, but I rather prefer a quiet life.'

'But whatever do you do? You must be as bored as I?'

Letty chewed her lip. She could hardly admit to the hours spent in the small cottages helping children survive whooping cough or other childhood diseases. Nor her hours of fascinating research into childbed fever.

And certainly not that she had spent more time in London wrapping wounds than listening to the opera.

'I read,' she said.

'I do, too, on occasion. *La Belle Assemblée* and *Ackermann's Repository*. Indeed, I do not know how anyone could keep up with the latest fashion without them. Have you finished the latest issues?'

'Not yet,' Letty said, thinking of her huge stack of medical journals she must peruse.

'Well, you must. I will lend it to you. Oh, I am so glad you are here. It is almost dinner. And even though I can't come down it is lovely to have had your company.'

'You can't come down?' Letty stiffened. She felt a nervous tightness within her stomach and an unusual squeak in her voice.

'No, my new doctor insists that I have rest, eat bland food and keep my feet elevated.'

Curse Dr Hatfield!

'Right.' Letty rubbed her fingers nervously across the fine silk. 'Of course, you must take care of yourself.'

'But don't worry. You won't eat alone. My brother will be there. He has been drinking much less since we came and was well known for his wit previously. Hopefully, you will enjoy his company.'

Letty nodded, although she was not certain that 'enjoy' was quite the right adjective for the peculiar mix of feelings Lord Anthony engendered.

'Maria will lead you to the dining room, as this place can be a veritable rabbit warren.'

'Um—thank you. I hope you rest and enjoy a good supper.'

Elsie sighed with dramatic effect. 'It is likely I will be fed something bland like rice pudding. It is most trying.'

Letty smiled. She wished for a moment she could share her identity. How could she ever develop friendships if she must always hide behind Dr Hatfield's persona?

The maid led Letty through long corridors and she was glad of this. As Elsie had stated, Beauchamp was vast and complex. It must have been built in Tudor times or before. The hallways were narrow, the doorways quite small and made of stone. Moreover, it seemed to consist of a network of corridors which converged at a tall staircase which led down into a vast hall.

Aware of an unusual fluttering of nerves, she descended the stairs, pausing on the threshold of the dining room. Like the hall, it, too, was huge with a vaulted ceiling of grey stone, more reminiscent of a cathedral than a dining room. At its far end, the hearth appeared as an immense dark orifice, taking at least half of the wall and topped by a heavy wood mantel. Tapestries hung on either side, patterned with hunting scenes and wild boars.

The daylight was fading so the huge candelabras had been lit and hung low over the table. They were of Gothic design, constructed of a heavy dark metal and lit with a myriad of flickering candles, their golden light reflected many times within the huge, gilt-framed mirrors hanging on the other walls.

Lord Anthony stood at the hearth. The room's size, the vast darkness of the unlit hearth and mantel, should have diminished his appearance. It didn't. Instead, it enhanced his height, the Gothic medieval tone making him look less civilised, the strong cheekbones and square jaw hard and uncompromising.

Even the scar, snaking down his cheek, seemed to only serve to make him appear dangerous. Indeed, the pain from his injuries was still visible in the leanness of his face and frame. His physique and the grim lines of his face had none of the softness of good living visible in so many of Britain's gentry.

He glanced up at her arrival. His brows contracted sharply so that he seemed to glower with greater intensity than was usual.

'Good evening, Miss Barton,' he said, although not in a tone that would suggest there was anything good about it.

His reaction surprised her. She had thought she looked…if not attractive…adequate. His expression, however, was not approving. If he had not wanted her to stay, he should have been more forthright.

'Lord Anthony,' she said, titling her chin. 'Do you look so disagreeable to all of your guests or have I displeased you in some way?'

'I—am not displeased. My face is not as flexible these days.'

She raised a brow. 'You have been caught out scowling. Do not aim to throw me off by fiddle-faddle suggesting that your injuries are to blame. The movement in your hand might be impacted, but the wound on your face is largely superficial. It might cause a slight tightening of the skin, but in no way impacts the muscles.'

His expression became darker or, at least, more unreadable.

* * *

The woman's blunt words were downright rude and the opposite to that demonstrated by any usual female.

Indeed, Tony had not wanted to have dinner with this odd woman and now wished he had not acquiesced to Elsie's notion. Phillips would have been totally capable of seeing the woman home.

Miss Barton had seen him at his weakest. She had seen him in whatever stupor or madness had struck him this afternoon. Moreover, he had subsequently behaved in a ludicrously juvenile manner. Instead of promptly and politely dispatching her for tea with Elsie, he'd almost kissed her.

He'd wanted to kiss her.

And he hadn't kissed or wanted to kiss anyone for a long time.

Besides, the woman was entirely unpredictable. Who comes to tea and stitches up the neighbour? Who wears grey or brown morning, noon and night like a governess on much reduced wages and then transforms into a flame...a burnished statue or however her current look might be described?

No, not a statue. She was too human, the silk draped too gently over her skin with none of the harshness of stone or marble.

Her usual attire had made her seem tall, accentuating her natural slim physique. In contrast, the low neckline and the soft cloth made him aware not only of her vibrant energy, but also of her curves and femininity.

'Lord Anthony, do I have a smudge on my nose or some other problem with my appearance?' she asked in that direct way of hers.

'No,' he said, dragging back his attention.

'Then may I ask why you are staring? Your sister assured me that this gown was quite the rage in London.'

'No doubt. It is just somewhat unlike your usual appearance.' And too bloody distracting.

Miss Barton gave a wonderful chuckle, low and rich. 'I have never worn anything like it before in my entire life. But Lady Beauchamp greatly enjoyed orchestrating the transformation.'

That, too, was what was so unusual—this ability to laugh at herself. Women tended to take everything so seriously, but Miss Barton's humour disarmed, all the more so because her demeanour was often solemn.

He felt his brow furrow further. Women belonged in categories. Some were like his mother and sister: kind, pleasant, amusing and appropriate.

Then there were those that one never introduced to one's mother or sister: actresses and courtesans. One took them to dances, balls, masquerades. They entertained.

Young men usually enjoyed the latter and eventually matured and found suitable wives from among the former.

Miss Barton was neither.

'Perhaps you are hungry?' she suggested. 'I always find I get into a dreadful mood when I am hungry.'

That irked him also. She appeared so calm, so entirely self-possessed and in no way threatened by his distemper. Good Lord, even Elsie tiptoed around him or had in the months since his injury. And any mention of his injury was a conversation stopper. He need only bring up the topic and people skirted away or spoke of the weather. They certainly did not give him some nonsense about muscles and study him as if he were an experiment or frog ready for dissection.

Just then Dobson entered, announcing the first course.

'Right,' Tony said, both thankful for the interruption and somewhat belatedly grasping hold of his manners. 'Shall we?' He nodded towards the dining table.

'Of course,' Letty said, walking briskly.

Despite his distemper, he had to smile at her movements. Elsie might have made over her apparel, but his sister had forgotten to inform Miss Barton that ladies do not march or stride towards the dinner table as though unfed for a month of Sundays.

Or maybe Elsie had mentioned that fact and Miss Barton just hadn't given a damn.

They sat at the vast table. Since Elsie's prescribed bedrest he had taken to eating in the library. He did not like the study, which still reminded him too much of George, and preferred the library to the solitary formality of this room.

Today, it felt more formal than ever. Good heavens, Elsie must have instructed the servants to use every crystal or silver widget available. The whole table sparkled. The huge candelabras had been lit as were the wall sconces so that the whole room seemed aglow.

Moreover, Miss Barton's gown caught the light, giving her an almost luminescent quality which was magnified and multiplied many times within the room's mirrors. The effect was captivating. Breathtaking.

And Lord Anthony was not of the disposition, either before or after his accident, to feel such a compelling reaction to any woman's looks or gown.

This in itself irritated. It was irrational. Even her proximity unsettled. Granted, he was glad that they did not have to use a foghorn to communicate, but her location so close to him gave the evening an intimacy he had not intended.

It was strange. After months of feeling nothing, now the merest sensation caused discomfort.

Perhaps it was similar to the pain of returning indoors after a snowball fight with Edgar when they were children. Their hands and faces would get so cold that homecoming and the hot nursery fire caused considerable discomfort.

He became aware of Miss Barton's scrutiny as she sat to his left, leaning forward slightly.

'Your expression is quite interesting,' she said. 'I cannot decide if you are happy or sad.'

Neither could he. A mix of everything with every feeling intensified.

'I was thinking of snowballs.'

'Snowballs? Really, I used to play with my brother. And Father, occasionally.' Her face softened with reminiscence. 'Ramsey always won, which was disheartening.'

'You are competitive.'

'No, but Father and I always based our strategy on science. Indeed, we would plot force and momentum. I am always sad when science is outdone by brawn.'

He laughed. He couldn't help it. She looked so disheartened. 'I have never heard of anyone making a snowball fight into a scientific experiment. You do know there are some things which cannot be plotted and dissected into scientific strategies?'

'I am not convinced. And to date I haven't encountered anything else which is reassuring.'

'There are other things.'

'Really? Like what?' She leaned forward, so that her gown gaped just slightly.

Lovemaking, he thought. He would like to see to see her lose that restraint and become aroused, not by logic and reason, but by passion. There was something intriguing about this love of logic, this adherence to sense superseding emotion which both intrigued and challenged him.

What would she be like without this tight control? If constraint were lost—

Damn—he put down his wine glass so suddenly that it almost slipped from his grasp.

Dobson and the footmen entered, carrying trays of soup.

'Ah, good soup!' he announced unnecessarily with the boring banality and bluster of some of the men he used to see in his club before the war.

He frowned, studying the servants' movement with apparent intent, ensuring that his gaze kept away from Miss Barton.

This afternoon he had experienced a stirring of interest. It had been like the echo of something he had felt before his accident when such feelings were appropriate. Now, that stirring was huge, like a hurricane or cyclone.

The soup was delivered and Dobson and the two footmen left. The door closed behind them with a click. A candle in one of the huge chandeliers flickered and fizzled out with the breeze.

He tasted the soup, as did Miss Barton. There was the click of spoon on porcelain.

'It is good,' he said.

'Indeed,' she agreed. 'Tomato with a hint of basil.'

'Yes.'

Now he was ludicrously tongue-tied as though the blasted bullet had lodged in his mouth and not his ribcage.

'I apologise. I am not good company,' he said, laying down his spoon and picking up his glass.

'Do not worry. I think we are feeling awkward because we almost kissed,' Miss Barton said as though discussing the bloody weather.

Again he almost dropped his wine glass, putting it down so abruptly that the liquid spilled, running down the cut crystal and forming a tiny puddle on the white linen at its base.

'I did as well,' Miss Barton continued amiably. 'But then I realised that men have these… inclinations or urges and decided not to take the matter personally. Indeed, it likely occurred because, as you said, you have not been socialising since your injury.'

He gaped. He wondered that she had even managed a single Season, never mind any time in London. 'I said nothing about my injury. I do not talk about my injuries or—or anything else.'

Certainly not his bloody urges!

'Then your mealtimes must be rather quiet.'

'I eat alone and prefer it that way.'

'Yes,' Miss Barton agreed. 'I don't mind my own company either. And it is much more time efficient to eat without having to chat. Plus, better for the digestion. However, I think Lady Elsie feels we are both lonely and has decided that we should socialise. I am certain you are only here because she entreated you and I know I only agreed to this dress for the same reason.'

'My God, you are blunt.' He laughed. He couldn't help it. She was disconcerting in the extreme, but also refreshingly forthright.

'I find it saves time.'

'Then you must be extraordinarily efficient. Although I still wonder how you survived the Season. Never mind your time in London.'

'Generally in silence or under my mother's strict supervision,' she said.

He thought he saw an expression of wistful sadness flicker across her features.

'And what would you discuss if it were not for your good manners?'

'Oh, I do not suffer from them,' she said.

He gave another chuckle. 'You mentioned that in our first meeting. It would appear you have not changed so very much and, given this after-noon's events, that you still have an interest in medicine.'

Her fork clattered to her plate. He heard her slight gasp as she leaned back in her chair in an almost physical withdrawal. He felt again a confusing mix of emotion; there was a certain satisfaction at her discomfort, although he was surprised by it—for someone so able to talk of urges.

But also regret that this tentative connection with another human might be jeopardised.

'A childish dream which I gave up soon enough.' She spoke in a staccato rush of words, her tone sharp.

He watched the nervous movements of her fingers rubbing against the grain of the fine linen cloth. 'I'm sorry,' he said.

She shrugged. 'Don't be. As I said, it was a youthful and foolish notion.'

'And you just accepted that.'

'Pardon?'

'You just accepted a reality you hated.'

'Yes. I help the villagers on occasion. That is why I had the supplies with me in my reticule. Many cannot afford any other help. That must suffice.'

'How?' he asked the question without fore-thought. 'How does one accept something one does not want to accept, that feels wrong and at odds with one's entire being?'

He watched the confused mix of emotion flicker across her face and a flush of pink stain her cheeks. 'Perhaps I am not the person to ask.'

He wondered why he had even posed the question. He hardly knew the woman. Or maybe that was the reason—sometimes it was easier to talk to a stranger. Besides she seemed different, less bound by the norms and dictates of an unyielding society. Her conversation, while odd, was not hidden behind platitudes.

Other people did not understand. They could not fathom why he had yet to go to Oddsmore since his return. And really, what was there to understand? His father and brother were dead. He was a lord, a peer, and Oddsmore was his birthright. It was his duty to go, yet he could not.

He—could—not.

'I had another brother. Edgar. He was always serious and responsible,' he said.

'Elsie said that. She said you were the fun one.'

'Edgar's role was always a given. He would be lord of the estate. I remember Father riding with us and telling him what he should do. They spoke about the crops and the animals and the tenants. I remember thinking how dull it all sounded.'

He remembered also a niggling feeling of exclusion—that father and elder son shared a bond he had no part of.

'So you decided to be the opposite,' Letty said.

'I suppose. We had horse races. I loved going

fast and jumping. There were other things. Climbing trees. Swimming. There was a pond with a huge tree. We would swing from it and jump into the icy water.'

Of course, that had stopped when the bough had broken, hitting Elsie, who wasn't supposed to have come along anyway. It was a glancing blow, but Father had given him a lecture.

About responsibility.

Miss Barton smiled, her serious features wonderfully transformed. 'Ramsey and I occasionally had fun.'

'Really?'

Miss Barton nodded. 'You sound surprised.'

'Only because by your own account you managed to turn a snowball fight into a science experiment.'

Just then Dobson brought in the next course. It was lamb and Tony again felt surprisingly hungry.

'This is very good,' Miss Barton announced, after her first bite. She nodded as if agreeing with her own statement, licking her lips.

'Mrs Peterson will be pleased with your compliment.'

'I am not certain Mrs Peterson likes me too much,' she said.

'Appreciation of her cooking will serve as a peace offering.'

She took another bite and he watched as she chewed carefully, her eyes slightly closed. 'My maid, Sarah, is absolutely wonderful and so loyal. She is used to a much bigger house, but came with me and does everything. However, her culinary skills are limited. Mother always had a good cook. I hadn't realised how much I missed good food.'

There was an almost sensual quality to her enjoyment. He dropped his gaze, focusing on his own plate, feeling the need to shift the conversation or to interrupt this moment which felt oddly personal.

'So, other than reading, and an occasional snowball fight, what else did you do during your childhood?'

She sighed. 'A series of tortuous activities. Mother tried to teach me to play piano and to sing. I can't do either. Fortunately, Father made her stop both activities.'

'He did?'

'Father said it was a waste of time when I was so obviously tone deaf and merely torturing our domestics. Mother said that I would never find a husband with a title if I did not know how to play the piano and sing. Father said in that case I'd best content myself to a solitary life unless I could find a deaf suitor.'

'You were close to your father?'

'Yes,' she said. 'He loved the scientific. He believed in thinking and learning and discovery. He said just because something was a certain way did not mean that it must always be that way.'

'So, what did you do for fun exactly?'

'Fun?'

'Yes, frivolous pursuits which did not involve the scientific? Did you go to the theatre when in London? Do you draw or dance? Ride or hunt?'

'Neither. I am hopeless at dancing and drawing as well as singing and piano.'

He laughed, a little shortly. 'Which of us is sadder—one who never learned to enjoy life or one who has lost that ability?'

Letty frowned. There was a familiarity to his words; a judgemental condescension. She recalled the foolish tea parties, the gossip and nonsense about fashion and that uncomfortable feeling that she did not belong.

Her mother would twist her hair into painful curls and dress her in frills and ruffles. And she'd sit mute. At first, she would give voice to her ideas, but the girls would alternately stare or giggle, so silence proved the better option.

Even in London, she'd felt like a misfit at soirées and social engagements. As Dr Hatfield, she'd been able to read whole articles and recall every detail, visualising the words in her mind as clearly as in the original text. She'd dressed wounds, attended anatomy labs and argued points of medical research.

But every aspect of society seemed both a waste of time and oddly designed to demonstrate her peculiarities. She stepped on her partner's toes with alarming regularity. She could think of nothing to say or said too much about the wrong things. She did not enjoy opera. And she wanted only to shop at bookstores, unless coerced by her mother or Florence into going elsewhere.

She knew herself to be intelligent, but always felt stupid.

Anger fired through her. 'Just because I do not sing or chase a fox on a horse does not mean that I am unable to enjoy life. Maybe it is that I do not need to fill my life with meaningless activities merely to pass time.'

'Apparently I hit a nerve,' he drawled in an infuriating tone, raising dark, ironic brows.

'I do not want to be a sheep, following a herd of sheep, with no self-direction or self-determination—the same as every other sheep. Why must we all be the same? Why do people dislike anyone who seems different?'

He flexed his injured hand. 'Perhaps you should not lecture about being different while you are whole and without injury.'

She felt the fire in her cheeks. 'And perhaps you should recognise that differences are not always physical.'

For a moment, she thought he would make a biting retort, but instead looked at her with sudden intensity. 'Yes,' he said, his expression turning bleak. *'Touché.'*

The moment stretched between them. She was unsure of his meaning. The footmen entered, clearing the plates. They moved carefully and only the rustle of their clothes and the occasional ting of cutlery against crockery broke the quiet.

Letty stared at the candle's flickering flame. She felt acute discomfort. She had been rude. She had lacked self-control and, worse than that, she had lacked caution.

She felt exposed.

Having collected the plates, Dobson and the

footmen left. A slight breeze whistled through the room as the door shut.

Tony turned to her. 'I apologise. You are right. I should not judge how another person spends their time. I am still readjusting to society. I will attempt to be polite for the remainder of the evening,' he said, with a lopsided smile which did odd things to her heart.

'I apologise also. I did not wish to make light of your injury.'

'At least you are willing to talk about it. I find that better than those who look at me as though I had grown two heads, but converse about the weather in an awkward pretence that I am unchanged. But we are too serious and Elsie will read me the riot act if I am not pleasant company. Let me prove that I am not totally devoid of social graces. Perhaps we might play cards later? If you know how to play?'

'I—' Letty glanced at him uncertainly. She should think of a reason to bring the evening to a prompt conclusion. He made her feel confused, jumbled and unsure.

'I won't make you dance and I promise not to sing,' he said, again with that slightly lopsided grin.

'I used to play a few card games with my father and brother,' she said. 'Mother didn't always approve.'

'I rather feel that would only enhance your enjoyment.'

She laughed, her amusement genuine. Perhaps it was the wine, but she found it peculiarly easy to talk to him. Moreover, though this seesawing of her emotions was both uncharacteristic and discomposing, there was an excitement also, as though she were more fully alive.

Any such feeling, she reminded herself, was without logic. One was alive or dead.

One could not be more or less alive. Currently she was alive and the fact that her cheeks were hot and her pulse fast did not in any way mean that she was 'more alive'.

It did mean, however, that she agreed to adjourn to the library.

As always, libraries brought Letty a sense of ease and this one was particularly pleasant. It was small in comparison to the vast medieval aspect of the dining room, but had high ceilings and a stateliness.

She sank into the chair closest to the hearth. The good weather had broken, necessitating a small fire. This burned with a friendly crackle, casting a warm flickering light about the room.

She had enjoyed the dinner more than anticipated. Mrs Peterson was an exceptional cook, despite any limits to her personality. Indeed, the dinner was a pleasant change from her usual fare. Sarah did her best, but Letty kept odd hours and most often requested egg on toast, severely limiting any culinary creativity.

And how long had it been since she'd conversed with someone other than Sarah, Arnold or a patient?

She leaned back into the soft cushioning that bespoke well-used furniture.

For once, she'd almost felt comfortable. She had the right height. As Dr Hatfield, she always felt too slight and as Miss Barton too tall, all gangling legs and awkward elbows. But in this dress, she felt different and pleasantly aware that the fire's glow made the threads in her dress gleam.

Tony sat in the armchair opposite. He leaned back, pulling out a deck of cards. The long leanness of his frame was emphasised as he thrust his long legs towards the fire. 'Piquet?'

He ran the cards expertly through the fingers of his good hand. She glanced at his other hand, still gloved, but for once said nothing. It might be pleasant, on this one occasion, not to think in terms of joints and ligaments but the breadth of his shoulders, the fascinating shadows cast by the flickering flames, the hard planes of his cheek and the bold, jutting shape of his jaw.

She listened seriously as he reviewed the rules and then carefully inspected her twelve cards.

She lost the first hand and studied her hand with greater attention on the second. She lost the second hand as well.

Tony laughed, giving her a brief glimpse of the young man she recalled from their first meeting.

'Is it not poor manners to be quite so smug in your success?' she asked.

'I believe we are agreed that good manners spoil many activities,' he said, with a tiny, unsporting twinkle in his eye.

She won the third hand. 'You were getting much too vain with your success and now I can boast.'

He laughed. 'A lucky hand, nothing more.'

He won the next hand, but then her luck turned quite remarkably. Carefully, hiding her expertise while shuffling, she handed them out ensuring that her movements were pedestrian.

She then went on to trounce him quite thoroughly in three consecutive hands.

'Apparently, you are more skilled in this than I have given you credit for,' he said.

'I played sometimes with my father and my brother.'

'Despite your mother's disapproval.'

She dealt again, smiling as she felt his close scrutiny. Again she won.

'You know,' he said as she rounded up the cards once more, 'I usually prefer my hand dealt from the top of the deck and not the bottom.'

She gave a happy chortle, shuffling with the expert movement of the hands that her father had taught her. 'You caught me. When we played we used to see if we could gull the other. It was half the fun.'

He laughed. 'Now that is something I didn't expect. Your father certainly sounds unusual.'

'Yes,' she said softly, her expression gentling. 'Wonderfully so. I was lucky. My father spent a lot of time with us.'

'Yes,' he said. 'My father and my brother were very close.'

She glanced at him, shuffling the cards again. She wondering if he had had a similar intimacy, but something in his hard expression made her hold her tongue.

'Anyway, Ramsey was quite dreadful at cards. I think that was why Father made him play. He said that he would be rich one day and, therefore, he needed to know every card trick in the book in order to ensure he was not fodder for a trickster.'

Tony pulled a face. 'I might have benefitted from such instruction. I am afraid I had to learn the hard way.'

'You lost money?'

'Some. Edgar would bail me out, which saved me from a good many lectures.'

'My mother was the lecturer.'

They played a few more hands, but Letty soon found herself almost nodding off. It was likely the good food and wine.

'I am afraid I will have to say goodnight. I am somewhat sleepy,' she said, standing.

'Roadside rescues are apt to prove tiring.'

He rang for Dobson and for a moment they both stood by the fire. There was a stillness, a magic to the moment. She glanced up, again acutely aware of the breadth of his shoulders and the strong firm line of cheek and jaw.

She had the odd feeling that she would remember this moment: the soft firelight, the shelves filled with their books, the man.

He must have been watching her gaze as she looked towards the books. He again gave that slightly lopsided smile. 'If you would like to borrow a book for the night, please help yourself?'

'Really?'

'Indeed, I even have the *Edinburgh Medical and Surgical Journal,* if you are interested.'

She had it at home, but had not yet had time to read the most recent copy and positively itched to do so. 'Yes, absolutely.' Again, she felt touched that he had remembered the peculiarities of her taste in reading. Most others would have scoffed or have forgotten.

He went to the shelf, pulling forward the volume. He handed it to her. Their hands touched and she felt that peculiar sensation of energy and awareness. The moment again stilled, broken only by the fire's crackle and the rhythmic tick of the clock.

For a moment, she wondered what it would be like to be honest—to tell him about the powdered wig, Guy's anatomy lab, the illegal dissections—

Just then Dobson opened the door. Letty jumped back. Heat washed into her face. She pressed her lips together as though the words might yet tumble out. It was illogical. She could not breathe a word of any of that to Lord Anthony or anyone—

'If you could show Miss Barton to her room and ensure that a maid is sent up, as well,' Tony said in his clear, crisp authoritarian tones.

'Yes, sir.'

She went to the door.

'And make sure that Miss Barton has adequate light,' Lord Anthony said. 'I know she likes to read.'

Chapter Six

The cannons thundered. He heard the whistle, that eerie sound, like wind blowing about the eaves, but higher and more shrill. The mud sucked at his feet, so heavy he could not move as the slick clay both anchored his limbs and paralysed his body.

Why was it so dark? It must still be daylight. The battle had started at dawn. How much time had passed? Hours? Minutes? Infinity? Everything was black and wet. He heard the shouts of men. He heard their screams as he stumbled to the ground, groping with his hands, wiping the sweat or mud or blood from his eyes.

'George! Edgar!'

He had to find them. Or George, at least. Edgar was fighting on the left flank. He'd promised Elsie he would look after George. He'd promised Elsie he'd bring him home. Except he couldn't move. He couldn't see.

'George!'

Something…someone gripped him. He felt fingers tight about his arms. He struggled, pushing against the restraints. George! He had to find—

'Lord Anthony! Tony, wake up. Stop! You're having a nightmare.'

The voice was female and came as though from a great distance, echoing down a long tunnel. His eyes were closed. He wanted to open them. He wanted to break free of the dream, but he could not. His lids felt huge and weighted.

'Tony, you are just having a dream. You are safe.'

At last, he jolted awake. Shudders still ran through his body. Goosebumps prickled his arms even as he felt the clamminess of his sweat-soaked linen. The feeling was familiar. The nightmare was familiar—his nightly reality.

Except tonight, something was different. He stared. For a moment, he could make little sense of the shadowed shapes of his room or the figure leaning so close to him. His hands rose, instinctively wanting to fend off attack, and then dropped. It was a woman. She held a candle. The flickering flame lit up her face. Huge eyes stared down at him, dark brows furrowed in concern. She smelled of flowers. Wisps of hair sprang loose, falling forward.

Reality thudded back. 'Miss Barton? What are you doing in my bedchamber?'

'Determining if you required assistance or medical intervention,' she said.

'You usually go into the bedchambers of men?'

'Only when they are screeching the house down and might require assistance.'

'I was not—I was merely having a bad dream,' he said.

She placed the candle down on the side table and poured something into a glass. 'Drink this.'

'What is it?' he asked suspiciously.

'Hemlock! Water, of course.'

He sipped. The cool fluid anchored him into the present, pushing away the shadows. He exhaled, silently readjusting to the calmness of his room, the silver slip of the moon just visible through a crack in the curtaining, the peaceful, melodious ticking of the mantel clock.

'You should leave. You will ruin your reputation,' he said.

'Fiddlesticks. I have independent means and no desire to marry.'

She stood, and went to the towel stand. She

wore a gown of fine linen. It was quite simple, but hung attractively, draping her bosom. She poured water into the bowl, placing the cloth into it. Then she wrung out the cloth with a musical trickle of water droplets. The sounds of the water and the rustle of her movements soothed. Her movements were not graceful, but capable and oddly calming.

Gradually, his panic eased, his breath becoming more even as his muscles relaxed, the throbbing in his head lessening.

'Here.' She sat on the chair close to the bed, and touched his brow with the cool, damp cloth. It felt good. That sense of peace grew.

Gently, she wiped away his sweat.

They were silent for several moments. 'Thank you,' he said at last. 'But really you should leave.'

She returned to the bowl, rinsing out the cloth and replacing it on the towel stand. The gown must be borrowed. It was a little short and fit loosely so that he could see her ankles and the curve of her calf.

'Do you have bad dreams often?' she asked.

'No more than anyone,' he lied.

'I have never before been awoken by my host or hostess making noise in their beds.'

'Then your life has been most sheltered.'

She bit her lip, obviously understanding his meaning as colour flickered into her cheeks.

She sat back on the chair beside the bed. She pressed her lips together, looking at him in that quizzical way, her composure again regained. 'I find your humour reassuring, but also intended to divert.'

'Indeed.' He sat up in the bed. His chest was quite bare as he did not sleep in a nightshirt. The cloth irritated his scar.

He'd thought either his naked chest or injuries would frighten her away. They did not. Her gaze flickered across his torso and then away.

'Has the frequency or intensity increased since you returned from the war?' she asked.

'No.'

He wished she would go. He was too aware of their isolation, too aware of their proximity and the way her borrowed nightgown gaped, the quickness of her breath and the sheen of moisture on her lips.

'Do you ever hear a whistling sound?'

He startled. She was psychic now? 'What? Why?'

'I read of something called *vent du boulet*. I believe it was identified during the French Revolution. Sometimes soldiers are impacted by the sound even when physically unscathed. I think Goethe also wrote about it.'

Good gracious, the woman was a walking medical text book. He frowned with rising irritation. He was thinking about her lips while she studied him like a bloody specimen.

'Of course you have,' he muttered.

'Did you know that the philosopher Pascal almost drowned in the Seine.'

'Must we play Twenty Questions in the middle of the night?'

'This is only one question, easily answered,' she said.

'No. Might I benefit from his acquaintance?'

'I do not think that is possible as he is dead.'

'My condolences to his family.

'There is anecdotal information that people who have been at war or suffered some other catastrophe have more nightmares and feel more apprehensive than is typical. That is what happened to Pascal, you see, and his personality was quite changed.

Apprehensive?

Is that what this woman thought he felt? He did not feel apprehensive. This was not apprehension, but fear, panic, anger, despair, hopelessness. His good hand balled the sheet so tightly that his fingers hurt, his muscles cramping.

And now he wanted only solitude. He did not want her analysis. He did not want her scientific theories. He was a man, not a specimen—certainly not *her* specimen.

'Fascinating,' he drawled. 'However, might I suggest that we discuss this at a time which will not risk your good name and reputation?'

'I think you might have much in common.'

'I am not a philosopher, nor French, nor dead for that matter.'

'Your personality is changed—'

'You based this on our one brief conversation during a ball?'

'Yes. As well, your sister reports your personality is changed and you have experienced a traumatic event,' Miss Barton persisted, in those strong, clinical tones.

Anger, fierce and sudden, pushed through his numbness and calm control. Despite the lingering pain, he was up from his bed. He cared nothing for his scars. He cared nothing that he wore only loose pantaloons and that his chest was bare. Every muscle had tautened. His shoulders hunched and his hands balled.

'You—do—not—know—me.' He ground out the words, almost barking each syllable.

She stood. For once, she seemed unsure. He heard her swallow. Her green eyes widened. Her breath quickened as her mouth dropped slightly open.

It pleased him to see her rattled, to see cracks appear within that calm façade.

The nightgown revealed the creamy skin of her chest and the occasional freckle. He stepped forward. She was a tall woman, but even so her head was only at the level of his chin. Her hair had been pulled back into a single, short plait, but loose tendrils curled at the neck and framed her face.

Even in the half-light, he saw colour rise into her cheeks. Her lips parted. The silvery gleam of the moonlight made fascinating shadows so that her long eyelashes formed shadowy fans against her cheeks.

Without conscious thought, he touched the smooth line of her jaw, tilting her chin up. He saw her eyes widen and heard that quick exhalation of breath as he leaned into her, touching her lips with his own.

Tony hadn't 'felt' anything for months.

But he *felt* now. The onslaught of emotion

was huge like water from a dam breaking during spring flooding. It was tumultuous, overwhelming. His kiss deepened, his tongue teasing at her soft lips.

He felt her startle. Her fingers rose to his shoulders, perhaps initially to push him away, but instead instinctively gripping his shoulders. Then, more wonderfully, her mouth opened under his own. Her body had stiffened, but then arched sinuously into him so that he could feel the warmth of her skin through the fine linen of her nightgown against his bare torso.

Thought and reason ceased, swamped in a wild, driving, growing need. The emotion that he had not felt poured into him, drummed through him, making his pulse throb and his heart pound. Nothing mattered, nothing existed, save for the touch of her lips, that instinctive bending of her body into him, the soft swell of her breasts against his chest and the eager press of her fingers on his shoulders and winding into his hair.

He pulled her even closer. His hands spanned her back, feeling the curve of her waist. He inhaled the slightly soapy scent of her. His fingers slid up her spine. He touched the soft skin at the nape of her neck and the silky strands of hair not captured in the plait. He loved the feel of her; the warmth of her and her humanness. The connection was sexual, but also about the physical connection of being human and alive.

He felt…alive.

For the first time in for ever, he felt alive.

His fingers moved, exploring her curves as he slid down the length of her spine and felt the curve of her buttocks. He heard her quick gasp, felt her startle and then yield at his touch. Instinctively, she pressed against him and he heard her soft, muted groan.

That moan, her eager unschooled fingers tracing his shoulders and arms and the needy arch of her body against his own fuelled him. He pulled on the silky ribbons at the neckline of her gown. He tugged roughly, the delay intolerable. The strings released. The gown fell loose. He pushed it past the soft smooth skin of her shoulder, exposing one breast.

He stepped forward, inching her backwards until the back of her legs touched the side of the bed.

He pressed kisses along her collarbone, conscious of the quick rapid beat of her pulse. His hand touched her breast. He felt the nipple's pucker and her gasp as she half-tumbled on to the bed. Her hair had loosened from the plait and now haloed about her head in a wash of brilliant red. The cloth of her nightgown had fallen to her waist, revealing soft, creamy alabaster skin.

Her arms reached for him.

He lay beside her and raised himself over her. He kissed her neck, her collarbone, her breasts—

It was his wound which brought him to his senses. It was his wound that jerked him back to reality with a stab of pain, twisting through his ribcage just where the bullet had lodged.

He froze.

The air chilled against his heated skin.

He heard her muted moan of protest, her hand instinctively reaching for him, her body pushing against his own. Dazedly, he realised he was sprawling on top of this beautiful, young, wide-eyed innocent—his sister's guest.

In the moonlight, he saw his hand, scarred and deformed.

He rolled off her and pulled himself upright. He heard his own ragged breaths and her own, mingled with the quickened beat of his heart.

'I apologise,' he managed to gasp.

For a long second she did not move.

'For God's sake, cover yourself,' he said.

His harsh words energised her. She stood, pulling her nightgown over her shoulders, clasping the cloth and silk ties at her neck. Her hair was wild and tousled. Her cheeks were flushed and her lips red and swollen from his kisses.

'I—I—didn't know. I didn't know I could feel like that,' she said, with eyes that made him want to forget about his honour or that he no longer had the physique that was pleasing to the female eye.

'Go. For God's sake, go,' he said.

She stepped towards the door. For a moment she paused, silhouetted against the curtains and the shimmering grey light of the new dawn.

'Try...try not to shout the house down again,' she said. 'And in the event that you cannot sleep, read Goethe. I believe he writes about his wartime experience.'

He glared. He had lived, was living with his wartime experience. He had no desire to read some philosophic treatise about it.

'I will keep that in mind,' he said, although obliteration through sleep or brandy seemed a more preferable solution.

Letty stood within the entrance of her bedchamber, staring at the simple furnishings as she might a foreign landscape. Her breath came quickly. Her cheeks felt hot as though on fire.

Feelings and sensations entirely foreign to her flooded her body and mind. She had wanted... she still wanted...

She crossed the bedchamber to the window and lay her forehead against the cool comfort of the pane. She took deep, gulping breaths as though starved of oxygen. She tried to focus on the immediate present: the feel of the sill under her hand, the cold wooden floor on her bare feet, the chill glass against her forehead and the rasping intake of her breath.

It didn't work. All she could feel was the memory of his kisses and the welcome invasion of his tongue. She remembered the hard, angular, muscled strength of his body and the sizzling heat which had darted like fire sparks within her. And she recalled her need, her compulsion to arch against him, to seemingly meld herself with him and to feel, without embarrassment but rather a great joy, the evidence of his need for her.

She shook her head as though to shake herself free of wayward thoughts and memories. She must be scientific. Logic had never failed her. She would collate the data from this new experience as she might organise any information.

Indeed, any human experience would serve to enhance her work.

Except her logical brain, for once, did not function. Her thoughts spun. Her feelings defied logic.

It was not logical to want and to need something which could well jeopardise her future and her delicate, carefully constructed present.

It was not logical to want to bed a man she did not know and who was autocratic and angry—and hurt.

It was not logical to want to become so physically close to an individual with whom she could never be emotionally close. She could never tell him about her odd double life. All dreams came with a price. She'd made a choice. She'd stepped away from the rigid confines of womanhood with all its conformity.

She had to live with this choice.

But never before had she thought that living with this choice might be hard. It seemed she had glimpsed a whole different side to herself, a part so foreign, so impulsive, so instinctual—nor could she tie this experience to any pre-existing knowledge.

Even in her training, these feelings were not mentioned. Rather it seemed that wives did their duty, hapless girls were pressured into poor choices, while only whores enjoyed physical intimacy or feigned this enjoyment.

But her feelings…there had been no pretence.

Letty stretched her fingers further along the sill, staring at the infinitesimal lightening of the sky as dawn approached.

She remembered the girls, their bellies big with children they didn't want. She remembered the frightened maids, begging for herbs or some magic potion, eyes huge with fear and worry.

Letty had never judged. She had always acted with kindness and with empathy. And yet she had not understood. She had not comprehended how any need, any emotion, any urge could make one ignore consequence.

One girl, she remembered, had been brittle with bravado. 'It was worth it,' she'd said. 'I'd do it again.'

Of course, Letty knew it wasn't. No moment could be worth a life in ruins.

Yet… Letty lifted her hand, tracing her fingertips across the cool glass. Today in this grey dawn she felt less certain. Today, she thought, it might just be possible that someone eminently sensible, sane and intelligent could indeed be overcome by emotion.

But this very thought set her adrift. It was illogical, and logic was her anchor. It was her way of being. Indeed, that was one thing on which her parents had agreed.

It does not do to wear your heart on your sleeve, her mother had said. *It gives others an advantage.*

And her father—she could hear his words now. *Emotions are fickle things. Logic and reason provide a stronger foundation.*

Letty again leaned against the window frame. Her father was right. Reason was a more reliable guide than emotion. And reason dictated that she should be so thankful, so grateful, so relieved that nothing more untoward had occurred and she need fear no consequence.

And she was grateful and relieved.

Except underneath the thankfulness, the gratitude and the relief, she felt stirrings of other emotions, complex, confusing and contradictory.

And a longing that seemed stronger than reason or logic which, indeed, defied both.

He had been attracted to her.

Tony stared at the ceiling above his bed until he felt the pale cream paint was burned into his eye. Sleep eluded him. The candle flickered.

Tony had not known he could still experience such emotion. Since his injuries, he'd felt this numbness that was both physical and emotional, precluding lust.

All his feelings had felt restrained, inhibited. Even his love for Elsie had seemed more driven by duty than that combination of affection and irritation he'd felt in earlier years.

In many ways, he liked that feeling of calm, of distance. Since arriving at Beauchamp, he'd drunk less and had settled into a routine, a carefully muted half-life. It was predictable and controllable.

He did not want feelings. Such emotion belonged to a younger man, a healthy man, a whole man. Certainly, he had no wish to be attracted to this odd, annoying, impulsive, eccentric, intriguing woman. The only thing he sought in his life right now was calm, peace, control and not this riot of emotion, this urgent need.

It felt… He frowned. He wasn't certain how it felt. It felt wonderful but wrong. It was wrong. It was wrong that he should feel so alive. It was wrong that he should enjoy sunsets, or horse rides, or music or art.

It was wrong that he should be able to feel her touch against his skin, the whisper of her breath or the way the candlelight made her hair glint like burnished gold.

Edgar and George would never enjoy anything again. George would not meet his child. He would not hear the infant's first words or feel a small hand placed within his own. Nor would Edgar serve and enjoy the estate he had loved. He would not advise his tenants nor survey the emerald-green multitude of his fields.

And all the other young men—all the other corpses abandoned in the muck—they could not feel warm sun or breeze or food or wine—never mind a woman's touch.

He ran his fingers across the scar on his cheek. Oddly, it reassured him to feel the puckered skin so that, finally, he slept.

This time he did not wake screaming. Indeed, he could not remember his dreams, but when he woke he was conscious of a deep aching sadness.

He touched his cheek again. It was wet as though he had been crying.

Pulling himself upright, he stared about the brightness of his bedchamber and at the morning sunshine flickered through the curtaining, the cloth moving lazily with the breeze.

Memories from the night flooded back—a

mix of joy and guilt, layers of emotion he could not discern.

He stood with sudden and unusual energy, ignoring the pain snaking through his side as he rang for Mason. He must shave and dress.

With the clarity of daylight, one thing was clear. A single concept stood out against all the confused mush of convoluted emotion.

Odd or not, Letty Barton was an innocent.

Therefore, broken or not, he must do the honourable thing.

Letty found her own dress neatly sponged clean and hanging on the hook behind the door. Thankfully, she got up, pulling off the linen nightgown with its disconcerting memories. Hastily, she put on the familiar dress, as though its unfashionable shape and colour would protect her from other further flights of aberrant behaviour.

Across the room, she caught sight of the fairy-tale dress from the night previous. Its gold threads glinted within the sunlight. She stepped to it, touching its soft silk and tentatively running her fingers along the cloth.

It was beautiful. And she had felt beautiful. For the first time ever, she had felt beautiful. It was a fantasy dress and had perhaps helped her step briefly into a fantasy life.

But fantasy was not reality.

And last night was some odd, wonderful, illusory experience.

Turning away from the dress, she sat at the writing desk, sandwiched into the far corner of the room. She'd write to Elsie. She would politely thank her for everything and then leave with all possible dispatch. And she would return to the routine of her own life, which did not include fairy-tale dresses or night-time encounters.

With this in mind, she rang for the maid and requested that the horse and carriage be brought around as soon as was possible.

'What about breakfast, miss? It is ready and laid out in the breakfast room.'

At the mention of food, her stomach gurgled and she realised that she was hungry. She hesitated. She did not want to see Lord Anthony. However, it was entirely unlikely that he would be up already. He did not seem an early riser. In fact, his sister had specifically stated that he slept late.

Besides, the thought of travelling for more than an hour on an empty stomach was not appealing and she supposed she should ensure that

Mr Cummings was still recovering. Infection was always possible.

'Very well,' she agreed. 'If you could direct me to the breakfast room that would be helpful. And how is Mr Cummings today?'

'He's left already, miss. Apparently, he has gone home and has sent a message to Dr Jeffers in London, demanding his prompt return.'

'Then that would suggest that rational thought has returned,' she said tartly.

The maid led her through a warren of convoluted hallways and into the breakfast room, a small chamber pleasantly lit by bright beams of yellow sunlight.

Her body felt his presence even before she had become fully cognitively aware that he sat at the table. It was like a jolt, a cold, prickling chill, oddly combining with a flush of heat and quickened breath.

'Good morning, Miss Barton,' he said, his tone as bland as tapioca. He glanced towards the footman standing at the buffet.

'We have tea or coffee and help yourself to kippers, if you would like.'

Kippers? She definitely would not like. Her stomach somersaulted at the thought, any feelings of hunger vanquished.

'No, thank you. I will just have tea and toast.' She sat with attempted composure. 'And if possible, could you also ring for the carriage so I might return home as promptly as is convenient?'

Tony nodded abstractedly, as though the kippers were of far greater consequence than her travel arrangements. Then he nodded towards the footman, who brought in her tea and left.

The door closed behind him.

They were alone.

That was worse. Her stomach knotted. Goosebumps prickled. Letty chewed nervously on her lower lip.

Had she imagined the night before? Lord Anthony seemed so entirely composed. Or were both nightmares and kisses entirely a matter of course to him and of no consequence? No, she had not imagined it. She was not of a personality prone to imagination.

Besides, what did she expect? They would hardly chat about kissing over kippers. Anyway, as a member of the aristocracy it was likely hardly worthy of comment.

'I will go to speak to your brother immediately,' he said.

Her butter knife dropped against her plate with a sharp clank. 'Ramsey? You will? Why?'

'To get his permission to marry you.'

'Marry?' Her voice squeaked unpleasantly. 'No. I mean, there is no need.'

He frowned. 'Miss Barton, I acted with dishonour last night. Asking your brother's permission to marry you might seem hypocritical now, but it is the right thing to do. Besides, he will have questions regarding my finances and my ability to look after you. I want to start things off well with your family. Even if this—if I—'

'No, please,' she interrupted. 'I mean, Ramsey would greatly enjoy the chat and would be much relieved, even if he pretended not to be. But—I will not marry you.'

Chapter Seven

⁓⁓⁓⁓⁓

Letty spoke quite calmly. The very calmness of her rejection angered him. His jaw tightened. He felt throbbing pain from the scar on his cheek and from his ribcage.

'But—Miss Barton—Letty—I must make things right.'

'As I said, there is no need. I certainly behaved with a lack of self-discipline myself, which is quite contrary to my natural disposition.' She paused, dropping her gaze and studying her plate as though contemplating something of great complexity. 'Indeed, I have always been somewhat judgemental of others. I felt that individuals who engaged in such intimate relations lacked judgement and self-discipline. Perhaps I didn't understand. I hadn't realised how powerful physical attraction could be. This has—enhanced my knowledge.'

She fell silent, continuing to stare intently at her plate and toast, and he found this studious, almost scientific analysis extremely disconcerting.

'Miss Barton,' he said at last. 'I have lost much, but I have not lost my sense of honour. Of course I will marry you and, while we have little in common, I am certain we will rub along as well as many couples. My estate, Oddsmore, is not too far from here and is a pleasant place. My income is more than adequate and I have a peerage. I am happy for you to go to London and buy trinkets and bonnets and...and things.'

She shook her head, glancing at him with that unique calmness. 'Lord Anthony, do I look as though I enjoy trinkets or give a rap about bonnets?'

She raised one eyebrow with quirky humour which he found appealing.

'No,' he admitted.

'And I know sufficient about procreation to recognise that there is no chance I am with child. Therefore, you need feel absolutely no reason or necessity to marry me. Anyway, you have done the honourable thing and offered, so think no more about it.'

His moment of humour was again overtaken by the anger which twisted through him and, underneath the anger, a painful hurt.

He had spoken of this as a matter of honour but, beneath this rationale, there was something more. This odd woman had given him something. He'd felt...

And this firm, definite, positive refusal hurt.

But then why would she want to tie herself to a broken man? He could not yet walk or run with any fluidity. His face was scarred. And she had witnessed his emotional weakness and the dreams which haunted his nights. He stood, pacing the small room.

'It is because of my scars? All right for a temporary dalliance, but nothing long term.'

'No.' She stood also. 'How can you say that?'

'Rejecting my offer of marriage might have something to do with my supposition.'

'You hadn't even thought of marrying anyone and certainly not me until last night. And aren't men always kissing women and not marrying them?'

'Not honourable men with honourable women. True enough, I hadn't considered marriage, but I must do my duty to the estate. So really it is not such a bad idea.'

'How reassuring,' she said. 'Well, for me, it is a bad idea. Marriage is of no interest to me. It has nothing to do with your injuries. Indeed, it is not personal. I just do not wish to be married.'

She spoke with absolute certainty. He glanced at her, taking in the strong line of her jaw and straight purposeful mouth. He saw no girlish coyness or maidenly blushes. Nor did he see any wavering or indecision.

He was conscious of a heavy, leaden feeling which should have been relief. Estate or no estate, obviously, he had no wish to hurry into a marriage with this eccentric female. She was the last type of woman he needed.

With a nod, he stood. 'Very well. I see you are determined. Obviously, neither of us would want the marriage, but I felt I should offer to ensure your good reputation and my own honour. Indeed, I am still willing to do my duty in the event that your reputation suffers as a consequence of my actions.'

She stood also, the toast untouched. 'I do not think you need to sacrifice yourself to the altar of duty, my lord. Lady Beauchamp was in residence so my reputation will survive.'

'Then we both have reason to be thankful. Good day.' Turning, with a slight bow, he walked from the room as swiftly as possible, the familiar pain twisting through his ribs again reminding him of his limitations.

A week followed, made eventful only by an unfortunate tumble out of a tree by one of the Maven boys and the delivery of Mrs Ebbs's fourth child. But despite the fine weather, Mrs Ebbs's good health and a bottle of homemade wine provided by the grateful Mrs Maven, Letty did not sleep well. Indeed, she found herself oddly restless.

Usually, she remembered everything she read with clarity. Now, she found herself staring outside when she should be reading or reviewing an entire page and remembering nothing. Such behaviour was highly out of character.

She, or rather, Dr Hatfield, even received a letter from Sir Humphry Davy regarding his experiment with nitrous oxide and his views on its use during surgery. Normally, she would have found his note exciting, or at least edifying. Under normal circumstances she would have likely replied immediately, but now she found her attention wandering.

Indeed, even her own research into childbirth fever did not grip her as it should.

Of even greater concern, her mind lingered not on issues of medicine as would be natural, but rather on Lord Anthony's various features: chin, shoulders, eyes...

She kept on seeing his grey-blue eyes framed by straight brows. She remembered the dark hair, falling forward in a way which made her want to brush it back. She remembered the touch of his fingers against her skin and that slight sand-paper dryness that sent tingles and sensations throughout her body.

Of course, she could not marry Lord Anthony.

The idea was ludicrous and unnecessary. Her entire life had been spent in ensuring that she need not marry anyone. She had engaged in subterfuge and masquerade. She had sat in the back rows of cold classrooms and listened to dry lectures. She had observed surgeries and had listened to self-important physicians. She had wrapped wounds and watched illegal autopsies. She had performed illegal autopsies. She had nursed incurable patients and walked through the slums of Southwark. She had lain awake at night both excited and fearful while the inevitable 'what ifs' had rotated through her mind like a child's spinning top.

At times, she had not known which she feared most—if her gender was discovered by the rough men walking the Thames's banks or by the aristocracy in their perfect salons.

But she had reaped rewards. She had a way to make her living. She had a purpose. She was a doctor.

She could not and would not throw it away.

And yet... The feelings overrode thought. She both wished that night, that kiss, had not happened and, conversely, found herself reliving the moment and holding on to each detail as one would something precious.

She was filled with new thoughts, new ideas and new feelings tangled together with horrid, niggling discontent and self-doubt, which was both new to her and decidedly out of character.

Her mother's note came twenty-four hours after the delivery of Mrs Ebbs's child. It informed Letty that Mrs Barton was established at the Dower House for two weeks and requested that her daughter visit that day.

Letty was drinking her breakfast tea when the missive arrived. She frowned, pushing her spectacles more firmly upon her nose, as she studied the didactic directive. She was in Miss Barton's breakfast room, a small space lacking in character. She stared about its confines, trying to think of some possible, plausible excuse. Perhaps she could say that Archimedes was taken lame? Except her mother would merely send her own carriage.

Or she could say that she had another social engagement, but then Mrs Barton would pepper her with questions...

Besides, she could hardly avoid the visit for two weeks and, if she tried, her mother would appear again on her own doorstep.

Therefore, with breakfast over, she went upstairs and summoned Sarah.

'It appears I must visit my mother,' she said.

'I thought that might have been a summons,' Sarah said, nodding with apparent approval at her ability to foretell the future.

'Can you ask Arnold to get Archimedes ready for noon?'

'Yes, miss, and shall I do your hair?'

'No—I—' She had been about to refuse, but then remembered the rather pleasant feeling of having her hair in loose waves. 'Perhaps we could try. And I will wear that new blue dress you insisted I purchase.'

'Yes, miss.'

'Lady Elsie dressed me up the other night and it was rather odd. I felt—I felt a little more confident knowing that I looked quite well.'

Sarah chuckled. 'Yes, miss, I believe the rest of the female population learned that while still in their nappies. Likely you would have, too, if you'd listened to me and if Mrs Barton had not been quite so enthusiastic about ruffles and colour.'

'Well, let's make me as presentable as possible and we'll see if it helps me feel more confident with my mother. I wonder if Flo will be there?'

It was always more pleasant to spend time with her mother in Flo's company. Perhaps she was relieved by the tangible proof that at least *one* of her children had made a suitable marriage.

'I believe Mrs Barton went up with Mr Ramsey to London,' Sarah said.

'Right,' Letty said.

'But do try to get on with your mother. You know she only wants what is best for you.'

Letty shook her head. 'I think she only wants

what is best for the image of me—the daughter she would want to have. It is just she has never got to know the real "me".'

'Perhaps because you never gave her the opportunity?'

'You mean if I were to explain how I masquerade as a man so that I can work as a doctor, she would embrace the notion?'

'Well, perhaps not when you put it that way,' Sarah said.

At the appointed hour, Arnold pulled to a stop in front of Dower House. It was much smaller than Oddsmore, a small brick structure with honeysuckle covering the walls and well-weeded rose gardens lining a small horseshoe-shaped drive.

Letty got out of the carriage, patted Archimedes's rump as she walked past him and entered the somewhat narrow entrance way.

'Don't worry, Staples,' she said to her mother's stately butler whose expression always suggested that he was privy to impending disaster. 'I can find my own way.'

She need not have bothered. As was his habit, Staples ignored this instruction, throwing open the doors on to the drawing room and announcing her arrival.

Her mother was alone, to Letty's considerable relief. She'd half-wondered whether, in her desperation, her mother might have decided to invite yet another potential suitor. Visions of Mr Chester or some other worthy had unpleasantly peopled her imagination.

Her mother presented her cheek for Letty's dutiful kiss.

'Do sit down,' she invited. 'And would you like tea?'

'Thank you,' Letty said, sitting in the chair opposite.

Her mother rang for tea and then proceeded to the matter in hand, fixing Letty with her astute gaze.

'I hear you acted very strangely at Beauchamp the other day.'

'I did?' The memory of those moments in Tony's bed made her cheeks burn and her fingers move nervously across the fabric of her dress, scrunching it into tight balls.

'I am glad you have the grace to blush. You are actually invited to a suitable establishment by a member of the local aristocracy and you choose to drag along an injured gentleman.'

'I did not exactly choose to do so. What would you have me do—leave him bleeding on the path?'

Her mother appeared to consider this comment before stating, 'Transportation was perhaps a necessity, but there was no requirement for you to become so involved once at Beauchamp. I heard you caused all manner of nuisance.'

'I stopped his bleeding, largely considered beneficial for all concerned, particularly Mr Cummings.'

'My cook heard from the cook at Beauchamp that…' Her mother paused, lowering her voice as though she feared an eavesdropper within her drawing room '…that you applied the stitches yourself.'

'Indeed, all that needlework came in handy after all.'

Irritation flickered across her mother's face, visible in the tightening of her lips. 'There are doctors and others paid to do such things.'

'None was available.'

Her mother frowned, but apparently decided the effort to pursue this line of questioning was not worth the questioning. 'And it is true, you have become friends with Lady Elsie Beauchamp?'

'We are acquainted.'

'Well, I am glad of that. It is appropriate...in fact, beneficial for you to be friends with Lady Beauchamp.'

At that moment, the door opened and Mrs Petch, the housekeeper, entered with the tea trolley.

They paused while this was set down and her mother busied herself in pouring the tea and handing around the pastries.

'And what of Lord Anthony? I hear he was also present and that you dined with him?'

'It was too late for me to return so Lady Beauchamp asked me to stay.'

'And you dined with Lord Anthony?' Her mother repeated the question.

Again she felt that irritating tell-tale flush. 'Yes.'

'It would be an excellent match. He is titled. How bad is his scarring and his infirmity?'

'What?' A flash of something close to fury flickered through her, stunning her with its intensity. 'Lord Anthony is a hero. He fought for this country and you dissect him and analyse his wounds.'

Her mother sipped her tea, raising one well-shaped brow. 'Such concern for someone you hardly know.'

'Yes, well, I think we should all have care and show compassion for an individual injured in the service to this country. Anyway, he has a slight cut on his cheek and is still healing from a wound to his ribs, I believe,' Letty said.

'He should be able to sire children?'

Her cheeks crimsoned. 'I would suppose so, but I cannot see what possible business it is of yours or mine.'

Her mother replaced her cup. 'Oh, do stop being so foolish. It is completely obvious that you care for him and about time, if I may say so.'

'I—I—' Letty was about to say that she did not care, but something stopped her. Instead, she concluded somewhat lamely. 'I have no intention of marrying Lord Anthony.'

'Well, I suggest that you change your intentions. And quickly. This is an apt time. He may feel more needy now because of his medical afflictions.'

'Grab him in a moment of weakness, you mean, when he might be more apt to settle for an inferior match?'

'I would not be quite so crass. I would suggest that it is suitable and advantageous for both you and him. There will be other young ladies, you know, if you tarry.'

'I hope so. I wish him well. However, I am everything he does not need in a wife. Indeed, I don't know how you can be so—so cold and calculating.'

Her mother replaced her teacup. 'I am calculating because I did not have the luxury to be otherwise. I was a housekeeper in a small establishment. I had to work for my living. I was still young and pretty so the women were jealous and the men—'

She stopped, as though suddenly remembering her audience.

'And Father?'

'Your father was kind and brilliant and a hopeless businessman. I told him that we should marry. I would escape a life of service and he would gain someone to run his house and ensure that some scurrilous businessman did not take advantage of his invention. It worked well enough. It was a union based on mutual respect and good sense.'

Letty watched the emotions flicker across her mother's face. Usually, she was so guarded, seldom showing her feelings as though fearing they might be perceived as a sign of weakness, even to her family. 'I never thought about how hard your life would have been as a housekeeper.'

'And I did not want you to. I brought you up as a lady, not having to care about those things. I tried to give you the skills so that you could secure a level of ease and belonging in your life. Ramsey has made a good match and if you were to marry a lord—'

'I would be hopeless. I watched you. I saw how you tried to be accepted. I saw how you tried to wear the right clothes and invite the right people and it never worked. I will never be accepted by society. At least you knew how to say the right things.'

'Our situations are entirely different. I used to be a housekeeper. The gentry do not forget. But your father was a gentleman and you'd be married to a peer and related to Lady Elsie and Florence. Besides, I am certain you could learn to say the right things if you tried. It is your wilfulness which impedes you. If you can learn Greek and Latin and all that nonsense your father permitted, you could certainly retain the rudiments of a dance and say something of interest now and again.'

'But I do say interesting things! It is just that they only interest me.' The words burst from her.

They were not loud, but their very impulsivity gave them weight and urgency.

Her mother made no response and the silence seemed heavy. A fly had had the temerity to enter the room and Letty could hear its drone. It was, she realised, one of the most honest conversations they'd had.

She leaned forward, almost wanting to touch her mother's hand, seeking some tangible connection. For a moment, she wished she could confide about her being Dr Hatfield. Perhaps her mother might understand? Was her own drive to study medicine and her mother's drive to escape servitude but different sides of the same coin?

But her mother spoke, breaking the silence. The fleeting moment evaporated. 'Florence could help. Her conversational arts are exceptional. And I understand that Lady Elsie is well known for her style.'

'I'm sure both Flo and Lady Elsie would try, but I cannot marry Lord Anthony or anyone because I do not have the skills or the motivation to be the type of wife a member of the aristocracy requires. It is different than with you and Father. You both benefitted. Lord Anthony and I would hurt each other. I have never been accepted by society. A marriage and lessons in fashion won't change that. I would hate that life and I would be a quite dreadful wife. He needs someone able to help him take his place in society and accept the role inherited from his brother. I think it will be hard for him and he needs a helpmeet, not an added burden.'

'You have thought a lot about this,' her mother said, as their gazes met.

'Yes.'

'Very well,' her mother said at length. 'I just always hoped you would change.'

Letty heard the quickness of hooves striking the cobbles. She was reading by the light of a candle, having sent Sarah to bed. Her maid did not approve of such late-night reading, advising that it would result in either blindness or a house fire.

Rising quickly, Letty crossed the room and pushed open the curtain. This was not the lumbering gait of a farm horse or the rattle of a wagon or cart. In the darkness, she could see the dark bulk of a coach, illuminated by its twin lamps. It had stopped outside the doctor's house and the footman had already dismounted. She could see the fast movement of his silhouette illuminated by the coach lamp. He raised his fist to the door, the knocking sharp and urgent within the night's quiet.

The Beauchamp insignia was visible emblazoned on the coach.

Letty's hand squeezed tight against the curtains. Elsie—it must be.

From the window, she saw Arnold open the doctor's door. He held a candle. His nightcap was askew and the light from a candle flickered across his face.

Letty let the curtain fall into place, turning quickly. 'Sarah!' she shouted. 'Wake up! Get me my doctor's gear.'

She dressed quickly, pulling on her doctor's trousers, coat, powdered wig and spectacles. Sarah brought in the bag and Letty glanced through its contents. Holding it tightly, she hastened out the back door of the house and through the doctor's house into the waiting coach.

Usually she drove herself, so this comfortable transportation was an unusual luxury and certainly more expeditious than Archimedes. And yet she almost wished she was outside. Driving would have occupied her mind and this birth would have felt more routine. Instead, she was aware of a pent-energy and anxiety, far greater than was usual.

She rubbed her fingers against the plush velvet. What if Elsie had the fits…what if she was unable to deliver the child safely…what if she needed forceps or took the fever?

What if Elsie died?

She is all I have.

The pain in those words had touched her. Since hearing them, she'd become aware both of his vulnerability and her own. He was a desperate, hurt and powerful man. The loss of his sister on top of all else he had endured would either break him or make him determined to seek vengeance.

Or both.

She knew she was good. She knew she was competent, but she was no miracle worker and the practice of medicine came with no guarantees.

He would never forgive her if Elsie died on her watch. And if he recognised her…

Bother. She closed her eyes. She should rest. The birth of a first child could be a lengthy process and it was wise to slumber whenever possible. But sleep eluded her and it was a relief when she felt the coach turn up the drive, stopping abruptly.

She peered outside. Beauchamp looked different at night. It was even bigger, less civilised and more Gothic, a dark hulk outlined against the starry sky.

Within seconds of the coach's arrival, the front door opened, yellow lamplight spilling into the evening. Tony stepped forward. Seeing him, his tall dark silhouette outlined within the light, caused a jolt of something: energy, apprehension, awareness, excitement.

She pushed the thoughts away, focusing on his speech. He was saying something. She saw his mouth moving even before she could hear the words.

The footman opened the carriage door and Letty clambered out.

'The baby's coming.' Even in the dim light, he looked haggard. Dark circles rimmed his eyes. He seemed unnaturally pale and his injured hand hung limp.

She felt an urgent wish to comfort him.

Pushing the thought away, she walked towards him, stiffening her spine and making her stride long and her voice gruff.

'This way.' Without further words or greeting, he turned sharply and disappeared into the house's interior.

He said nothing more, leading her through the

convoluted passages and stopping on the threshold of the confinement room. She entered. As was customary, it was stuffy. The windows and curtains were both tightly closed. The smell of sweat already laced the air and the fire burned bright, sparks crackling up the chimney. Elsie lay on the bed. Perspiration shone on her forehead. Her hair stuck damply to her skin in wet strands and her breath came in quick, uneven gasps, her eyes wide.

In that moment, the 'what ifs' that had been circling Letty's mind stopped. It did not matter that these sheets were fine-quality linen. It did not matter that the bedchamber was part of this huge mausoleum of a palace or that Elsie likely spent more on a single gown than most of Letty's patients spent in a lifetime.

All that mattered was this exhausted, spent woman with her wide, frightened eyes.

'You are doing wonderfully,' Letty said, approaching the bed and keeping her voice gruff, more for the maidservant than Elsie.

'It hurts—so much. And it—it is too early,' Elsie gasped.

'A little, yes. But you are very close to your eighth month. The child might be small, but likely perfectly fine,' she soothed.

'Truly?'

'Absolutely. How far are the pains apart?' she asked, turning to the maid.

'I don't know, sir.'

'You have not timed them?'

'No.' The maid shook her head to underscore the negative.

'Do so now. And heat some water on that fire. I will wash my hands and do the examination.'

The maid turned to do so and Letty took a towel. She made it wet and then carefully wiped the sweat from Elsie's forehead as her face again contorted in pain, her fingers twisting into the sheets.

When the contraction had passed, Letty plunged her hands into the hot water that the maid had prepared. She took the soap, cleaning carefully, even under the nails.

Very gently, she lifted Elsie's nightgown. With careful hands, she felt the baby's form through the woman's tightly stretched skin. Not breeched, thank goodness. Indeed, given Elsie's tendency to swelling, this early birth was likely the best thing to prevent the fits.

'The baby seems in an excellent position,' she said, her words interrupted by Elsie's cries as another contraction struck her.

Letty again dampened the towel, wiping away the sweat. Elsie relaxed, the hurried pants of her breath slowing as the pain lessened.

'That is good. Take advantage of the lull between the pains,' Letty said.

'They are too short... There is no rest...'

'I know. But it means you will soon hold your son or daughter in your arms.' Letty again touched Elsie's forehead with the damp cloth.

'Thank you,' she said. 'You're quite gentle for a man.'

Letty froze, her hand clenched around the cloth. Did Elsie guess? Suspect? Her glance darted to the maid, but she appeared not to have heard.

Before anything more could be said, Elsie again contorted with pain and, once the contraction had dissipated, was too spent to question Letty further.

'In the next pause between pains, I will complete an internal exam, but I am certain you are making most excellent progress,' Letty said.

Elsie nodded.

Just after she had completed this examination Letty heard a rap on the outer door of Elsie's sitting room, which was attached to the bedchamber. The maid answered, quickly returning.

'Dr Hatfield, sir. It is His Lordship, sir. He is that worried. He wondered if you could give him an update, sir?'

'I am somewhat busy,' Letty said. She did not particularly wish to see His Lordship. She not only feared he might recognise her, but also felt a complexity of emotion which interfered with the clarity of her thoughts. 'Tell him—'

'Go—go to him. Just for a moment,' Elsie said, her words punctuated with gasps. 'He pretends not—to fear losing me—but I know it—it haunts him. Please.'

'I…' Letty paused, but nodded as she felt the tight clutch of Elsie's hands against her own. 'Of course, if it will provide comfort.'

'He's waiting in the corridor, sir,' the maid explained.

Letty left the chamber and went through the outer sitting room and into the hallway, allowing the door to close.

Tony was pacing with his back to her. He swung around immediately as she exited the room, striding quickly forward. 'How is she?' His voice was raw, his face haggard and his hair rumpled as though he had been running his hands through it.

'Strong and healthy. Everything is proceeding well,' she said.

'I worry…' He paused. The candlelight enlarged and darkened the circles under his eyes. 'I can't lose her.'

'I will do everything possible. I promise.'

Perhaps his obvious pain made her gentle her voice and add those last words. Or maybe it was another trick of the candles, the golden light touching her face in such a way that it softened her features.

Confusion, followed by a quick flash of disbelief, flickered across his face. His straight dark brows pulled sharply together, his grey-blue eyes darkened.

'Dr Hatfield?'

'Indeed.' She deepened her voice so that even to her own ears she sounded like a child in a theatrical production. The effect was heightened by the nervous tremor in her tone.

Disbelief shifted to sudden understanding and fury.

'Miss Barton…?' He paused, his gaze scrutinising her face while his hand lifted as though to pull off the dreadful wig. 'Is it you?'

He did not remove the wig, instead letting his hand drop with a soft thwack against his leg.

But she knew it was too late. Wig or no wig, he knew the truth. The quick protective movement of her hand and trembling voice had said it all.

Heat flushed into her cheeks. Her mouth felt dry, her tongue cleaving to its roof. She swallowed. Months earlier she'd devised practised excuses. She'd say Dr Hatfield had a twin sister or some such tall tale, but none of that came to her now. Instead, she merely gaped, entrapped by the fury in his eyes.

From the room behind her, she heard Elsie's cry.

'I need to go—' Letty said, not bothering to deepen her voice.

Anger contorted his features. 'No.' He put his hand on her forearm. She felt the outline of his fingers. 'I do not want you within twenty miles of my sister. You are a fraud. You are a fraud and a trickster. I thought you were honest. I trusted you. You lied to me.'

'I didn't want to. Besides, right now this has nothing to do with you. It is Elsie—'

'I offered to marry you.'

'That has nothing to do with this.' Again, she heard Elsie's muffled cry. 'I must go. She needs—'

'Not you. She—does—not—need—you.

She—does—not—need—lies.' He stepped forward, blocking her progress back into the room. He had removed his hand from her arm and now gripped her shoulders. His face was inches from her own. She felt his heat, his breath, his anger. She backed from him. He stepped forward, following her retreat, so that they moved in an odd, menacing dance.

Elsie screamed again.

Briefly, her cry stilled both their movement.

With an effort that seemed huge, Letty squared her shoulders, pulling herself to her full height. She was tall, but even so the top of her head only grazed his chin. She shook off his grasp.

'Right now your sister needs help. I need to help her. You have to put your anger and outrage aside. I can help her and I will help her. She is my patient. Not you.'

Their gazes locked. Something snaked between them; anger and something else.

At last, his gaze dropped. He stepped away, letting her pass.

'Very well,' he said. 'Stay with Elsie. I will send for a proper doctor. Don't deliver the baby until he arrives.'

'I will inform both child and mother of your instructions,' she retorted, before stalking past him towards her patient.

Chapter Eight

Throughout the night and into the next day, Elsie's needs occupied Letty's mind. She'd always had an ability to focus, excluding all distractions, and it served her well now. She rubbed Elsie's back. She supported her as she paced the room, making low guttural groans which seemed to come from some primal source deep in her belly. She helped her to squat on the birthing stool, stroking her shoulders and back. She wiped her sweat and held her hand until her own fingers felt numb.

'You are doing so well,' she said.

Elsie stared at her, almost sightless with pain. Then, as the pain eased slightly, she moved again, pacing, as though by moving she could outdistance the pain.

Thankfully, Tony had said nothing to Elsie, likely intelligent enough to know that distrust in her physician would only place Elsie at greater risk, although she knew from the maid that Jeffers had been summoned.

Sometimes Letty heard the pace of Tony's footsteps in the hallway outside and felt the fear tighten, making her stomach leaden. He could tell everyone. Florence would be implicated. Her mother. Ramsey.

But there was time enough for that. Right now, she needed to focus on Elsie as they worked in tandem, helping her find her strength and courage for what was yet to come.

Night turned into day and the chamber brightened, sunlight pushing through the gaps within the drawn curtaining. Elsie's pains came more frequently now. 'That means your child will be born soon,' she assured the exhausted mother.

Hours passed. The sun set, glimmerings of the red sky just visible. And then, at last, with a final, low, excruciating primal sound, the child was born.

Letty held the child, as always filled with that mix of emotions: joy, relief and worry. For a moment, he did not cry. The worry grew. Carefully, she cut the cord. He was so tiny, red and wizened, with tufts of dark hair.

She lay him gently on the towel, carefully massaging his tiny, fragile chest.

'Is he—is he all right?' Elsie gasped.

Letty held her breath as she continued to pump the tiny fragile ribcage.

At last his red wizened, newborn face contorted. He took his first breath, crying lustily.

Letty exhaled. Then they both laughed and cried and Letty saw the joy, relief and pain mirrored in the other woman's eyes.

'He's perfect,' Letty said.

'Can I see him and hold him?' Elsie asked, reaching forward, her face glistening wet with a mix of sweat and tears.

'Of course, you can. Elsie—Lady Beauchamp— he is so beautiful. So perfect.'

Gently, she swaddled the infant, handing him to Elsie. She watched as the young woman took him, gazing down with a look that touched something deep in Letty's heart, making her eyes sting as a lump formed in her throat.

'Thank you,' Elsie whispered. Gently, with shaking tentative fingers, she touched his small head.

Letty swallowed. 'You did all the work.'

'You helped.' Tears trickled down Elsie's cheeks so that they hung pendulous at her chin. Her blonde hair lay in lank curls about her.

She looked beautiful.

'He isn't too small?' she asked.

'Do you hear that lusty cry? He is small, but strong.' Letty paused, savouring the moment. This was the best part of her life—a mother's joy and the scream of new life dwarfed all else.

'And Tony? You'll tell him?' Elsie asked. 'Please, as soon as possible. I know he has been worried.'

Reality thudded back. Letty's stomach tightened. She tasted bile.

'Yes.' Very slowly, barely conscious of her movement, she tidied the soiled clothes, sheets and blankets. She went to the bowl and washed her hands. The blood swirled from her fingers, mixing into the clear water. She stared at it, watching the water's movement and the flicker of the candlelight against its surface. In that moment she saw her hopes, her dreams, her carefully constructed life, swirl away.

She'd always dreaded this.

'Dr Hatfield,' Elsie said from bed. 'Can you tell him now? Tell him he is a proud uncle to a beautiful, beautiful boy. Tell him to come.'

'Yes, I will tell him,' Letty said.

She had always known the risk. Intellectu-

ally, she'd known that at some point she could—
would—be caught.

But she'd hoped…she'd hoped to have a few
more years.

A brisk knock startled her. She jerked up,
swinging towards the sitting room. Water
dripped from her hands and on to her trousers.
The door opened.

A maid entered. 'Dr Jeffers has arrived.' she
said.

The man entered. Letty knew him by sight.
He was short, portly and walked with a swagger, visible even in his first few steps. His clothes
appeared to be of good material, but grubby,
his complexion was pallid except for his nose
which was overly red. His hair was thinning and
slightly oily, combed sideways as though to hide
his balding head.

'Dr Hatfield, Lord Anthony summoned me. I
am sorry it took me so long. I was attending another medical matter. However, I am here now
and ready to provide you with my considerable
expertise,' the little man announced, striding
with that swagger towards the bed.

'The child has been delivered already,' Letty
said.

'Oh.' There was a momentary pause. 'And
the afterbirth?'

'No.'

'Then I will examine the patient immediately.'

'Lady Beauchamp. Her name is Lady Beau-champ,' Letty said dully.

'Quite so. Well, I am here. Lady Beauchamp, we'll just have a look see, shall we?' He rolled up his sleeves.

'You have not washed,' Letty said.

He glanced back as though confused by her presence or statement. 'You are my maid now?'

'No, but Lady Beauchamp is still my patient.'

Letty stepped back so that she was between the doctor and the lying-in bed on which Elsie reclined, almost oblivious to them both as she still held the child, staring down with doting adoration.

'Maria, clean out the water and refill the bowl with fresh, hot water and soap so the doctor can wash,' Letty directed.

'What? What nonsense are you spouting now, man?' Jeffers asked.

Man—so Tony had not told him either. A wave of relief, gratitude even, washed over her.

'I am suggesting that you clean your hands before examining Lady Beauchamp,' she said, energy piercing the dullness.

'That introduces unnecessary delay.'

'Lady Beauchamp is in no distress. The child is born. We are just waiting for the afterbirth. Therefore, there is no need for a delay to worry you.'

The man stared. His mouth opened. His chest expanded as his cheeks flushed, puffing slightly with the intake of air. 'I have been practising for twenty years. Twenty years! You are a—a young pup. A boy. You dare to lecture me?'

'Yes, when your practice accounts for more childbirth fatalities than any other doctor or midwife in the area.'

'I—what?' The man's eyes appeared to bulge, his face now purpling. 'Are you suggesting a lack of competence on my part?'

'It wasn't a suggestion.'

There was a brief moment of silence. His eyes opened, his jaw slackening, as though he could hardly believe the words and did not know how to react. 'You—you—you upstart!' he exploded. 'My God, I should take you out by the shirt tails and trounce you thoroughly. Get out of my way.'

'Wash your hands and I will do so.'

Just then the door from the outer hallway swung open. It banged against the wall and a draught of cooler air whistled inwards. Tony stood on the threshold, a huge, dark angry figure.

'I am summoned to see my sister and nephew and all I can hear are you two brawling as though in a tavern.'

He did not shout, but Elsie must have heard her brother's voice. 'Tony! Tony! Come in, I am quite decent and want so much to introduce you to your nephew. And please encourage Dr Hatfield to stay. He has been so wonderful. I really do not think I need any other physician.'

If possible, Tony glowered even more, fixing Letty with his angry stare. '*He* has, hasn't *he*,' he muttered, adding more loudly for Elsie's benefit, 'Dr Hatfield is lacking credentials. Dr Jeffers will provide your medical care. He has more experience. Dr Hatfield will step aside.'

He fixed Letty with his angry glare. She met his gaze but did not move.

'Of course,' she agreed equitably. 'Provided Dr Jeffers washes his hands.'

The woman stood in her ridiculous man's garb with her chin outthrust, green eyes huge behind smeared glasses, wig askew with several damp, red curls protruding from under the yellowed hair piece.

He could not imagine a less impressive sight.

And the ludicrous woman still wanted to set the rules and prevent Jeffers from doing his job.

And he had trusted this fraud. This imposter.

And as for Miss Barton—he'd thought her odd, eccentric but honest. Oh, yes, he'd even admired her forthright bluntness. In a society known for *double-entendre* and façade, he had thought her the exception.

And all the while, she'd been keeping this secret and he had allowed himself to feel…something.

'Tony.' Elsie's voice, faint but also laced with joy, jolted him from his reverie.

He swung around from the puppet of a doctor. He was an uncle. His sister had survived the birth and the child was also healthy.

He would not let this person take that from him. Striding forward, he went to Elsie. She looked tired but, despite her pallid countenance and the dark circles under her eyes, a smile lit up her face.

A happiness, almost frightening in its intensity flared through him, dwarfing all else to insignificance.

He knelt beside the bed.

'Meet Theodore George Edgar. Isn't he beautiful?' Elsie whispered.

He looked down at the tiny bundle held so carefully to her chest. He was not quite certain if beautiful was the right word to describe the squashed, red face with the surprising mop of dark hair, but he felt something: a warmth, a softening, a joy, a hope…

'A rather long name for such a small mite,' he said, gazing down at both mother and child. 'But I like it. And he is a miracle.'

He pressed a kiss to Elsie's forehead. The skin felt damp but cool. He watched as the infant's tiny hand, pink and fragile as a bird's wing, escaped from the swaddling blanket. The infant stretched each tiny finger, the movement strangely slow, purposeful and delicate. Tony placed his finger between the tiny digits and felt their instinctive clutch.

'His grip is strong,' he said, aware of a mix of laughter and tears threading his voice. His happiness felt fragile as though it might disappear like a soap bubble, gone within the moment.

'Strong and beautiful and wonderful,' Elsie said. 'I wish George could know he had a son.'

He watched as the other hand escaped from the swaddling blanket. The tiny fingers seemed almost impossibly small with nails which looked as thin and delicate as a butterfly's wing.

'We will make certain that Theodore George Edgar knows he had the most wonderful, brave, kind and loving father.'

Elsie smiled, but he saw her lids growing heavy. He removed his hand from the tiny fingers, stepping back. 'Elsie, you should get some rest. We can get the nanny and the nurse to help.'

'Not yet, I just want to hold him and look at him,' she said.

Tony knew a similar feeling. He had been immutably altered by this tiny newcomer and was aware of a peculiar prickling fear which made him want to both hold the child and mother and alternatively flee from the room.

At that moment, Dr Jeffers cleared his throat and Tony turned sharply, momentarily surprised by the man's presence.

'I was just about to do an examination, my lord,' Jeffers said.

Tony straightened. 'Yes, yes, of course. I will wait outside.'

'Dr Hatfield,' he said pointedly, angling his head towards the door. But the ridiculous woman still stood rooted to the spot between Jeffers and the bed, like an unnecessary, trumped-up bodyguard.

'Lord Anthony.' She made no move, nor softened her pugilistic posture.

'Dr Hatfield, I wished to talk to you and I believe Dr Jeffers has this in hand. Perhaps we might adjourn to the library.'

'Dr Jeffers is not examining anyone until he washes first.' Letty pressed her lips together in a firm, stubborn line. 'Maria has the water ready.'

'As I said before, I do not like your tone, young man,' Jeffers started.

'You do not need to like my tone or anything about me. I just want to ensure that you wash prior to examining my patient.'

'*My* patient,' Jeffers corrected, snapping his lips together and emphasising the pronoun. 'And I'll have you know that I was practising long before you became qualified. Likely you were still in nappies or mewling in your mother's arms.'

'Quite possibly. I am not certain of your age. However, I do know that the mortality rate among new mothers whose labour you attend is high.'

'Again! Again, you impugn my reputation? You are an upstart!'

'Stop,' Tony said. 'Enough of this. I will not have either of you frighten my sister with talk of mortality. Nor disturb her with this bickering. Jeffers, wash your hands if only to quieten this—this person. It can hardly do any harm and perhaps then he will leave the room.'

'The soap and water is over there,' Letty said pleasantly, stepping aside.

With a final angry glance, Jeffers went towards the water as Letty walked to the door.

'As for you...' Tony followed her, lowering his voice '...for goodness sake find a maid and change. And wait for me in the library.'

The corridor felt pleasantly cool after the warmth in the bedroom. Sweat prickled on her forehead and her cheeks felt flushed as though on fire. For a moment Letty stood quite still. No one was in the hall. For the first time in hours— indeed, since Tony had recognised her—she was alone.

Letty leaned against the wall, glad of its sturdy coolness at her spine. The exhaustion felt so heavy, it was a physical thing. Her limbs seemed almost to vibrate as though unable to bear her weight.

Tears prickled, clogging her throat and goosebumps prickled, oddly mixed with the dampness of sweat.

What should she do? She stared at the white

wall opposite as though it might provide direction. From somewhere down the passage, she heard a clock, its ticking rhythmic. Behind her, she could hear the muffled tones of voices.

Tony would be out soon. He would not remain during the medical exam.

She straightened. She needed to escape. She did not want to see Lord Anthony. Not now. Not until she'd had time to think, to sleep, to push away the tears which already blurred her vision.

Nor did she want to find some confused maid and explain why the male doctor required a dress. Besides, then she would be truly rumbled and some unacknowledged part of her still hoped.

With desperate energy, she inhaled, squared her shoulders and started down the corridor. Why hadn't she insisted on bringing her own buggy? She wanted only to leave, to escape into the darkness, curl into the comfort of her own bed, slow the rotating thoughts that circled within her mind.

But she was Dr Hatfield. As long as Tony had not disclosed her secret, she still had that identity and its authority.

By some miracle, she found her way to the front hall. Dobson still stood at the door. Had

he been there all night, impervious to fatigue?
Did he know…?

As she neared him, he allowed his proper features to relax.

'It is a happy day for this house, sir,' he said.
He did not know.

Her body felt limp with relief, but she kept
her figure straight and her tone masculine and
imperious. 'Indeed—however, I require a carriage immediately.'

'You are leaving, sir? Mrs Greene, the housekeeper, has made up a bedchamber in case you
wanted to rest and we thought you and Dr Jeffers and Lord Anthony might want to drink to
the new lad.'

'Thank you. It is already after dawn and I
have patients to see. I am certain Dr Jeffers will
be able to do any drinking necessary.'

'Yes, sir. You did not want a small repast?'

'No, I wish only to leave and I am not used to
these questions,' she snapped.

Later she might regret her sharpness. Such
impatience was not in her nature, but right now
she was a desperate wounded animal, wanting
only to return to its lair.

'Yes, sir. I will order the carriage directly.'

She stood within the hallway, like a fugitive.

Every noise, the creak of a board under a servant's foot or the muffled sound of a door closing, made her startle. She could not see Tony again. Not now. Not today. Not yet. She needed to get away. She needed to make sense of the situation and determine how best to cope.

She needed to keep Dr Hatfield, his strength and autonomy, for at least another day.

Finally, she heard the clatter of horse's hooves outside. Dobson opened the door, as always imbuing the simple motion with ceremony. She slipped out, hurrying down the stone steps into the chill grey light of early morning. Phillips swung open the carriage door.

She entered, leaning back against the padded cushioning with a relief that was close to elation. The door shut and the vehicle jolted forward, its wheels rattling over the drive. Through the window, she watched as the house became smaller and more distant, at last disappearing as they swung into the wooded copse.

She squeezed her eyes shut, feeling the sting of tears. Her lids felt so heavy it was though leaden weights were tied to them. The full gamut of emotion rocked her: joy at the birth, desolation at discovery, frustration and whatever it was that she felt for Lord Anthony with his hard, intelligent, sad eyes.

She heard the distaste lacing his words—*You are a fraud. You are a fraud and a trickster... A fraud...a trickster.* The words became a part of the wheels' rhythm, repeating over and over.

Of course, she'd known she would be found out. Logically, she'd known it was always only a matter of time. But she hadn't expected this level of pain. She hadn't expected to see his hard, steely grey-blue gaze piercing her whenever her lids fell shut. She hadn't expected to hear the reverberation of his cold tone throughout her head, or the ache at the hurt disappointment lacing his words.

She'd anticipated anger, worry, scandal, consequences...

But not this personal pain. She had not expected to feel this awful hopelessness as though something infinitely precious had been lost.

Nor had she expected this flickering of guilt—as though she had somehow let him down or robbed him of something.

At last she dozed, a fitful sleep filled with confused images which left her feeling more exhausted when she startled awake.

The vehicle had stopped. The village appeared as it always did, a tranquil place. Phillips opened the door and she stumbled down, shivering. She felt as cold as though it were winter and not summer's end. Indeed, goosebumps prickled her arms, despite the warm sun, and she shuddered as she stepped towards the door.

It opened. Arnold's wonderfully solid and familiar figure stood within the portal. She blinked. It would not do for Phillips to see her cry, she thought, as she half-stumbled through the doorway.

'I'll just go and make sure the horse gets food and water,' Arnold said.

For a moment, she stood quite still. She heard his footsteps, voices and at last the horse's hooves click-clacking down the cobbled village street.

She went to the study and sat. Her mind felt blank, empty or numb.

'You're still here. You should be over to the other house,' Arnold said, when he re-entered. 'I'm guessing you had breakfast. Or are you wanting something to eat? A little luncheon? Sarah went out to get some milk, but she should be back soon enough.'

'No, that is fine. I am more tired than hungry.'

'You should go to bed.'

'Yes, I should go,' she agreed, making no move to do so.

He nodded. 'You do look a mite worn, if I may say so. You'll feel better after a rest.'

'Yes,' she said, thankful for his calm, familiar, reassuring kindness, even though she knew it wasn't true. She wouldn't feel better.

She was glad Sarah was away. Sarah cared, but would likely demonstrate this by worry, nagging and perhaps even an 'I told you so'.

Just then she did not think she could cope with Sarah's kindness—or her worry.

'You go over to the other house now,' Arnold prompted. 'I can help you up if you need. Sarah will get you later for lunch or supper.'

'No, I'm fine.' She rose. The energy required for the simple movements felt huge and her limbs weighted. She exited through the back door and crossed to the other house, her movements still pedestrian, her movements awkward and leaden.

As always, Sarah had turned down the bed and Letty knew there would be a warm brick at her feet. Moving slowly, Letty pulled off the powdered wig, the jacket, the soiled shirt and trousers.

She stared at them, studying the outline of

the trousers and shirts against the blue rug. Useless. Obsolete.

Pulling on her nightgown, she threw herself into her bed and under the covers. She lay there quite still, feeling her body relax as finally she allowed the tears to fall, wetting her cheeks and her pillow.

She had never wanted to be a fraud. She had never wanted to put on the ludicrous wig, trousers and spectacles. Was it her fault that society thought her genitalia affected her ability to learn? Or that she would swoon or faint at the sight of blood? How could they judge? How could Lord Anthony judge? Had he seen her in the morgues or with the stolen bodies in the anatomy lab? Had he inhaled the air reeking with the smell of decomposition and alcohol? Or walked beside her as she hurried home past brothels and beggars?

Had he seen the wounds she had stitched or the child that had survived at Guy's even though everyone had anticipated his death?

Now he would likely expose her secret. Her family would be ridiculed.

And, even if he did not, she had lost his good regard. Those moments playing cards had felt as close to friendship as she had ever experienced with a male. And then later—

She pressed her hands to her eyes as though that might stop the thoughts which circled, crazy like a child's spinning top, so that it seemed she'd never sleep but would twist and turn, mired in her own linen, dampened with sweat.

How was it fair that she had lost the regard of a man who likely owed his life to the medical profession because she had wanted to join its ranks? She had wanted to learn…to heal…

Exhaustion won. She fell into a heavy sleep marked by dreams where Tony was shouting at her only to peculiarly morph into a clergyman, vaguely remembered from her childhood parish. She hadn't liked him. He'd stood at the pulpit, wagging his finger and staring at her as though able to read her soul.

'A fraud' and *'a trickster'*…except now it was not the clergyman but Tony. *'A fraud'* and *'a trickster'*…

'Miss—miss—wake up.'

Sarah's voice pulled her out of sleep.

'Huh? What—what is it?' she asked. 'What time is it?'

'Morning. You're slept more than fifteen

hours straight. I couldn't even wake you for supper last night.'

'Really,' Letty rubbed her head, staring around the bedchamber as though something in her surroundings might help her track down the missing hours.

'His Lordship, Lord Anthony, he's here and he wants to see you.'

Letty started at her maid's words, sitting up, instantly alert. 'Is it Elsie? The baby?'

'No, no. I mean it can't be. He didn't ask for Dr Hatfield, but you, miss. Most specific he was.'

'Unfortunately, that doesn't preclude that possibility,' Letty said.

'What?' Sarah froze, her hand tight about the cup of chocolate she was about to place on the night table.

Letty saw the maid's fingers, swollen from arthritis, turn a mottled, yellowed white from the pressure on the cup.

'Does—does he know, miss?' Sarah asked.
'Yes.'

Her maid's face blanched. Her hand shook so that a drop of chocolate spilled. She did not seem to notice as she sat on the bed, a heavy movement which made the mattress wheeze.
'Oh, miss.'

'It's not the end of the world,' Letty said robustly, although the slight tremor in her voice made her tone sound fake even to her own ears.

'It's the end of your world, miss.'

'Yes,' Letty said, unable to pretend.

'But I don't think there's anything wrong with the baby or Lady Beauchamp, miss. He did not seem unduly worried.'

'And, let us be honest, he would ask for Jeffers, in that event. I presume he has come to inform me of—of what he intends to do with this information.'

'Oh, miss, but I am sure he is a gentleman. Likely he will suggest that you stop and that he won't say nothing.'

'Perhaps,' she said. 'But that is hardly consoling.'

'It is better than a scandal, miss.'

'Yes,' she agreed. After all, she did not want Flo or Ramsey dragged through the mud. But for herself... For herself, stopping would be the worst of it.

It hurt that Sarah, who knew her better than anyone, did not really understand.

'I knew this would happen sometime,' Sarah said.

'It does not take a clairvoyant to see that, I suppose.' Letty spoke tartly, swinging her legs over the edge of the bed. 'Well, I guess I'd best get this over with.'

'Yes, miss. I'm sorry, miss.'

'I know.'

Chapter Nine

Miss Barton's cottage was small and scrupulously neat. The furnishings were simple. The shelves appeared clean and had very few ornaments or novels and certainly none of the scientific books he had anticipated.

Just then the door swung open and Letty entered. She walked quickly, her back ramrod-straight and her hair again pulled severely into a small tight bun.

'Your sister and the baby? They are well? There is no sign of fever?' she asked instantly, before even greeting him, her dark brows fiercely furrowed.

'They are well,' he said, her concern for his family briefly derailing his anger.

She looked very pale. Dark shadows ringed her eyes. The grey dress did her no favours, if anything serving to emphasise her slim frame and ashen complexion.

'You did not need to leave last night,' he said. 'You must have been very tired.'

He hadn't liked the thought of her sitting alone in the carriage as it wound through the countryside. Indeed, she must have been frightened at what he would do and say.

Of course, she deserved to be damned scared and yet, conversely, he didn't like to think of her either alone or scared.

'I felt it would distress your maid unduly if Dr Hatfield suddenly asked for a dress,' she said, eschewing any prevarication, with just the hint of amusement lacing her tones.

He felt reluctant admiration at her ability to see humour in the face of adversity. They could have been friends, he thought suddenly. In a different life, they could have been friends.

And, he reminded himself, if she hadn't decided to participate in this ludicrous sham—this ruse. Amusement morphed into anger. He valued honesty and integrity. Why had she done it? If she were desperate for funds, surely his offer of marriage would have been a better solution.

'You wished to see me?' she prompted.

'Yes,' he said irritably. 'It would seem we have something to discuss given the recent revelation.'

'Indeed,' she said, quite calmly.

'Like why?' His anger spilled out. 'Why this huge deception? Why do this?'

'It seemed like the best option at the time.' She sat, waving a hand to suggest he do the same.

'Working under false pretences. Pretending to have credentials you do not have? Tricking your patients? That seemed like the best option!' he snapped, refusing to sit, but pacing.

'Yes,' she said, but dully as though forcibly muting her emotions, her tone colourless as her complexion.

'Was it for money?'

'No, potatoes.'

'Pardon?'

'My patients tend to pay me more often in potatoes and other vegetables. Fruit when in season, eggs and butter,' she said. 'Honey and wine on occasion.'

'Miss Barton, this is no joking matter. You have put me in an untenable situation.'

'Rest assured, I did not choose this double life merely to place you in an inconvenient position.'

His anger grew, fuelled by this fake calm façade. She must *feel* something. She should feel something. My God, he was feeling something. He was feeling more emotion than he had felt in months. Indeed, more than he ever wanted to feel. But Miss Barton appeared calm and composed. *He* could not stay still while she sat with a singular lack of motion as though a bloody statue.

'Can you at least explain *why* you did this? Don't I deserve that much?'

'I can't see why you would,' she said.

'I offered you my hand in marriage. I trusted you. I trusted you with my sister's care. You put her at risk—' He stepped closer with the words.

'No!' That single word blasted from her, shattering any calm façade. She bolted upright. Colour flushed into her pale face, the hue intense. Her green eyes sparkled with sudden fire. 'No!'

The transformation took his breath away. Perhaps it was the change from calm to fury or the wash of colour, the sparkle in her green luminous eyes or even the strong straight brows, dark and at odds with the ruddy hair.

They stood quite close. She was taller than most women. Indeed, there was only half a head between them.

Even though they were not touching, he was aware of her every breath and curve and angle.

'Lord Anthony, let me make one thing quite clear. I have never put anyone at risk. In fact, I know more about birth than any doctor because I have spoken to midwives and have the humility to learn from them. I have lost very few patients. I have done everything I can—everything I am allowed to do—to be qualified. I did not put your sister at risk. I have never knowingly put anyone at risk.'

She had said most of this in a single breath and now stopped. Her eyes still flashed in a way which was magnificent. The anger vibrated through her. Her fists had tightened, her chin jutted out and her breath had quickened. He could smell the fresh clean scent of her soap and noticed the tiny freckles sprinkled across her nose and the sheen of moisture on her full lips.

Damn.

He turned from her. He strode to the window, needing distance and separation. He was insane. He should not be thinking about her lips. She was a fraud. He should not be thinking about kissing her. Or considering kissing anyone. He should not be feeling this ludicrous riot of emotion.

He pushed his injured hand through his hair as his other hand rested on the sill as though needing the physical support of bricks and mortar in a world gone mad.

'You should not be practising medicine if you have no licence to do so,' he ground out, clinging to this truth.

'Really? That is your answer. Tell me where I can get that licence in my own name and I will do so.'

'You're a—a lady. You shouldn't be doing it—or wanting to do it.'

Why would anyone want to immerse themselves in death and injury? For a moment, he saw the field, pitted by cannon fire and dotted with the bodies, their guts spilling through soiled uniforms and their open eyes staring sightless to the heavens. He forced the image away. He made himself look at the overgrown garden outside, a tangled green wilderness of moss, ferns and long grasses.

He made himself concentrate on its vibrancy, the splashes of sunshine and even the bee as it circled lazily over pollen laden flowers.

Life.

He lifted his good hand and spread his fingers on the pane, feeling the cool glass under his fingertips as he breathed, inhaling the dusty scent of cosy fires long extinguished.

'Miss Barton, you don't need to do this. I offered you marriage, a viable alternative despite my injuries,' he said, breaking the quiet.

'Lord Anthony, I am not a street worker, I am a doctor. And I do not need to be rescued and I do *need* to do this. Indeed, I could have multiple offers of marriage and I would still need to do so.'

She spoke with such certainty. He could not remember when he had felt such surety about anything. Even before Waterloo, he had tended to drift amiably.

He did not know why her words hurt and made him feel a heavy, hopeless feeling. Perhaps *he* should not have come here today. Perhaps he should have stayed at Beauchamp with its ordered routine.

Miss Barton was not his concern. He could put his sister and nephew in the hands of Dr Jeffers and place the eccentric Miss Barton in the hands of her mother, brother, a solicitor, the Bow Street Runners, a mad house or any number of options which would not have involved him coming here.

Definitely, he should not be standing here in this tiny, close room with this woman who preferred to immerse herself in death and sickness rather than marriage or anything that a typical woman would do.

He gazed again at Miss Barton's overgrown garden. Edgar would not have approved of its green chaos. Oddsmore had always been immaculate. He'd pored over articles about crops and innovations. He'd pestered Mr Sykes to try new procedures.

Although if Oddsmore had been so damned important to him, maybe he should never have gone off to war.

'Why? Why would one want to?' he muttered.

'I still can't answer that,' Miss Barton said.

He felt a quick confused start of surprise at her voice.

'Any more than I can answer why a child is motivated to walk or talk,' she continued. 'It is a need, as strong in me as movement or communication.'

'But walking and talking is not illegal or unethical.'

'Would it matter if it were?' she asked.

He turned from the garden, meeting her direct, green gaze. He felt a peculiar intensity which seemed to mark their interaction, as though everything else and everyone else had dwarfed to insignificance and she was brightly luminous in a grey world.

'What?' he questioned, realising that he had forgotten her words in his study of her eyes, her lashes and kissable lips. *Damn.*

'Would you stay dumb if a government said that men should not speak, but the edict made no sense to you?' she asked.

'You are talking nonsense now.'

'People tend to say that when they have no answer.'

He drew his gaze away from her, because somehow when he looked at her he found it hard to think, to construct sensible, logical arguments.

He stared again through the window at the grey paving stones half-hidden under moss and dandelions. 'I have an answer. You can't decide to do something despite the law. There are laws for a reason.'

'Really? And what is the reason in this case?

'I—' He felt tongue-tied, confused and in the wrong when he knew he was in the right. 'It is against the law to impersonate someone and to pretend to be something you are not.'

'I do not pretend. I heal. That is the truth.'

'You are not Dr Hatfield. That is also the

truth. Just because you do not agree with the law does not mean that you can flout it. We would have anarchy. My brother and Elsie's husband died for this country and its laws. Edgar believed in this country so much that he volunteered. I still see—'

He paused, closing his eyes, willing the images away. He swallowed. The room grew still, the moment unnaturally long. He wished he could pull back the words, reeling them in as one might a fishing line.

'You still see them in your dreams and nightmares.' She spoke quietly, but in matter-of-fact tones.

'Yes,' he said.

There was a pause. He had not spoken of his nightmares to anyone. He had not spoken of the weird mix of guilt and fear and hopelessness that haunted his nights. And days.

He did not want to talk about them.

He did not want to talk about the sightless, bloodied, corpse that had been George. He did not want to talk about the severed foot with the laces so perfectly tied. Or how the cannons made the earth shake, the vibrations striking deep into its core and peppering the earth so that it liquefied to mud.

Even now, with the cannons long silenced, his body shuddered. He still heard the haunting echoes: the shouts, screams and the piercing whistle of a cannon just prior to its strike. He still saw things he wanted only to forget.

But he had no wish to talk or even acknowledge his peculiar vulnerability—indeed, that a sound, a movement or smell could seemingly transport him back into the nightmare.

'Tony.'

It was the first time she had used his name and her soft voice cut through the noise and chaos that was his mind. She had edged closer to him. He could feel her body as they stood, side by side, staring through the glass at the overgrown garden. Again, he smelled the clean, soapy scent of her hair. A loose tendril tickled his chin. The top button of the drab dress had fallen open, revealing a triangle of pale skin, scattered with freckles like brown sugar. She bit her lower lip. It was well shaped, full, sensuous and intriguingly at odds with the prim hair and dress.

'Tell me about Edgar and George,' she said.

Even the names hurt. He closed his eyes as though that would obscure the images littering his mind.

Edgar had looked after him. He had looked after everyone.

He'd dragged a ladder from the stable when Tony got stuck up a tree and bailed him out when he lost to a card shark on his first night in London. He'd even kept both events secret so that Tony never had to confess his foolishness to his father.

And then there was that time that Edgar had appeared in the nick of time just when he was about to challenge Lord Winsborough to a duel. Winsborough was known largely for his pockmarked face, a predilection for very young women, a skill with pistols and a disregard for the lives of his opponents.

Somehow, Edgar had extricated him with his honour and all body parts intact.

Sometimes, Tony wondered if Edgar had only come to Waterloo in some ludicrous attempt to keep him safe.

Tony pushed the thought away. He stepped away from the window, moving as fast as his injury would allow in his need to distance himself from her, from his thoughts.

'I certainly didn't come here to talk about personal issues,' he said.

'No?' She turned also. 'But you want to discuss my role as Dr Hatfield. That is very personal to me.'

'I wanted...' He paused. He tightened his injured hand on the mantel, almost welcoming the pain. 'The two issues are in no way comparable.'

She said nothing.

He inhaled, keeping his voice under tight control. 'Actually, I did not wish to discuss anything. There is no need for discussion. I came here to inform you of my decision regarding this Dr Hatfield masquerade. I don't want to cause you or your family scandal. I demand only that you stop this pretence. You must stop being Dr Hatfield. It is fraud. I cannot be a party to that.'

Briefly, their gazes locked. Just before she looked away, he saw the shimmer of tears and the movement of her throat as she swallowed. He wondered if there would be weeping. Women tended to be emotional. He felt lousy to have hurt her, but could see no other choice.

But Miss Barton did not weep. Instead, she merely stepped across the floor towards the door.

'Now that we have clarified that issue, I must ask you to excuse me. I need to garden before it becomes too hot outside. Sarah will see you out.'

Without waiting for his response, she opened the door. A draught of cooler air whistled inwards. Pausing, she glanced back before exiting the room. 'When Dr Jeffers visits Lady Beauchamp, please ensure that he washes his hands before any form of examination.'

Tony did not return to Beauchamp immediately. He felt too angry and unsettled. Instead, he allowed Jester to canter down the road and towards the open field. It was the fastest he'd ridden since his injury. For a moment, he felt that familiar thrill of speed and freedom before the jolting pain twisting throughout his torso became unbearable. He cursed at the bullet that had shattered his rib and seared his flesh.

For a few paces, he refused to slow, pushing his animal forward and grinding his teeth against the pain as his hands tightened into fists against the reins. He had loved riding. He had loved the freedom of it, the rhythmic movement, the way it encompassed one's whole attention and dwarfed all petty worries into insignificance.

And he'd loved jumping even more.

There was the excitement, the happy camaraderie as he and George had vied with each other. George had known more about horseflesh, but Tony had been the better rider. But a good jump was more than that—there was a beauty in that perfect moment when man and beast became one, beating gravity and soaring over fence or hedge.

With a second muttered curse, he slowed Jester to a plodding walk. Even that slow laborious pace hurt, but now there was no exhilaration, no blurring of fields or wind whistling past his ears in that wonderful combination of sight and sound and movement.

In contrast, the horse moved slowly. On either side, the fields spread in a patchwork quilt of greens, a criss-crossing of hedgerows punctuated with the darker greens of woodland copses. If he were to keep riding south-west, he'd come to Oddsmore. He'd need only cross the sparkling brook that threaded through the valley's base, crest the hill and then down the other side. He knew the route well. His parents and Lord and Lady Beauchamp had often visited. He and Edgar would spend long days with George, often with Elsie as the unwanted tag-along.

George would fish with a single-minded determination while Tony sat with him, dabbling his feet in the chill brook, before searching for a more interesting pastime like digging out worms or other insects. He'd captured a frog once and put it in a drawer in the nursery. It had been a disappointing enterprise. George's nanny had not batted an eye and he'd had an early bedtime for a week in addition to one of his father's lectures about responsibility.

His father had been fond of lectures. Tony had always run too much, galloped too fast, shouted too loud, gambled too often.

Turning Jester around, he headed back. Despite his earlier desire for Beauchamp, he still found himself reluctant to return. He glanced towards the village. It was but a short distance on his left, a pleasant place, with a twisting main road, and a small collection of buildings and cottages, centred about the church and inn.

During school holidays, they'd come here often. Of course, they'd fished less and, with age, the taproom had become their favourite haunt. They'd sup ale within the dim, shadowy room and feel like men.

Leaning forward, he touched Jester's sweaty flank. Given the day's heat, he should stop and get him water before heading back to Beauchamp. It must be close to mid-afternoon and the sun beat down with an unusual heat. Hesitating, he spurred Jester towards the tavern. It would be pleasant to get away from the day's warmth. The stone walls and green ivy made the taproom a cool, dim, pleasant place.

He even remembered one of the barmaids, the owner's daughter, a pleasant girl with long blonde hair. He'd visited the pub with George and then sat dumbstruck, unable even to place their order.

Smiling, he shifted the stallion forward. Why not go in for a drink and some food? He had eaten little for breakfast and there was reason to celebrate. Perhaps he could buy the punters an ale and they could drink to the health of young Theodore George Edgar.

Swinging off the horse, he handed the reins to a groom before taking the back door and entering the corridor. It was narrow, of stone construction, and, upon entering, he had the peculiar feeling that he had been transported in time.

The pub was so exactly as it had been in his adolescence. It smelled the same, a mix of ale, pipe smoke, sweat and food. The taproom looked the same with tables constructed of a dark wood and small, narrow windows dotting the walls at irregular intervals. The ceiling was low and made of thick beams, blackened by age and smoke while the window panes were still largely obscured by ivy so that the sunlight cast a flickering green light.

Tony stared, struck at the very timelessness of the scene. The toothless farmer still sat in a dark corner, nursing his one ale and chewing on a grass straw, its stalk pressed between his lips and toothless gums. And Mr Gunther, the owner, seemed equally unchanged, his cheery face framed by white whiskers and his shirt sleeves rolled high over arms made strong by lifting kegs of beer and changing the barrels. Beside him, his daughter sat with her long blonde hair and smile. Likely the comely serving wench now featured in the dreams of a new generation of young adolescents.

There should be a comfort in the very familiarity of the place and yet there was not. Instead, its very timelessness enraged. And hurt. How could this place remain the same when everything in his own life had shattered?

He was no longer a healthy lad ogling a pretty girl, but was instead a maimed man with a bullet hole in his ribs, a scar snaking down his cheek and his left hand burned. He could not gallop on his horse without pain. He could not approach a young woman without shame. He could not dream without nightmares.

Fury thundered through him. It twisted into his shoulders until every muscle felt as rigid and hard as steel. He balled his hands. The movement hurt as the skin on his hand tautened, fuelling his anger. His heart beat fast. His jaws were clenched tight so that they hurt.

He didn't even know who he was angry at— the war, Edgar with his damned honour, George who'd married Elsie weeks before leaving for battle? Napoleon? Or those bloody awful notes congratulating him on his good fortune that he was alive.

'My lord?' Mr Gunther spoke and Tony realised he was standing stock still with his hands balled.

'Are you quite well, my lord?'

'Quite,' he snapped.

'Would you care for a drink, my lord?'

'No.'

Tony turned, striding down the corridor, wanting only to escape its familiar smells and memories.

He entered the courtyard, letting the door slam behind him. Grabbing Jester's reins from the groom, he threw coins at the lad and swung on to the animal. Careless of his injury, he spurred the horse forward.

As he exited the courtyard, he glanced towards Miss Barton's house. He realised now that he would have little reason to see her. In fact, he would have every reason to avoid her.

Skirting the house, he took the back route, wanting only to get home to Beauchamp where he could find oblivion at the bottom of a brandy bottle.

Letty had pulled out every weed, tossing them away with such energy that clumps of earth scattered in a shower of dirt. Then she'd taken clippers, hacking at overgrown bushes and errant branches before digging furiously at alder trees rooted in the wrong place.

Every muscle ached. Her head thumped. Her face was hot and sore from the sun and her body damp with sweat. She could not rest. She could not even sit.

She had been Dr Hatfield or working towards being Dr Hatfield for so long that she now felt adrift without identity, as though free floating in space. If she was not Dr Hatfield, then who was she? Who could she be?

There was no 'Miss Barton'. There was the child, Lettuce, and the adult, Dr Hatfield, but no 'Miss Barton'. Of course, she'd pretended. She'd

attended the theatre, balls, dances and other out-
ings to appease her mother while in London.

She'd conversed politely about nothing or,
more frequently, allowed her brain to wander
while keeping a smile plastered to her face. But
all that had been an act, no more real that Gar-
rick's theatrical performances.

Casting her gardening tools aside, she went
inside. Briefly, she stood in Miss Barton's immaculate drawing room, staring at its empty
shelves and nondescript furnishings. It struck
her that this house, this drawing room, was but
a stage set. It felt uncomfortable, an alien landscape.

'I can't stay here.' Turning on her heel, she ran
up the stairs, her dress half-undone before she'd
even reached her room. Tearing it off, she threw
it on to the bed. Then she pulled on her trousers,
shirt and jacket, pushed her spectacles higher on
to her nose and grabbed her wig.

She needed her books. Even if she could no
longer practise, she needed to immerse herself
in their pages. She needed to feel that pulse of
interest, to connect research with experience,
present with past.

For a moment, she stopped, staring at herself
in the looking glass. Why had she even bothered

with her costume, her disguise? The play was over. Done. The curtain had fallen.

But people are creatures of habit. She'd never entered the doctor's house as a female and even now adhered to that self-imposed edict.

Shrugging, she turned from the glass, hurrying down the stairway and across the small gunnel separating the two homes. She pushed open the back door, stepping down the narrow corridor and into the drawing room, now modified as a study.

Pausing on the threshold, she inhaled the dusty air, perfumed with old leather, ink and paper. She looked at the tall shelves. They lined all four walls, reaching floor to ceiling. As a child, she'd dreamed of a house with its every wall lined with books.

She went to them now. She touched each spine, running her fingers across the dry leather and embossed title as though greeting a friend.

How could years of effort be wiped out by one single person in a single night? Tears stung. She rubbed them away. For some reason, it hurt even more because it was Tony—Lord Anthony. She had experienced feelings for him that no other man had inspired. She'd allowed him liberties— Moreover, an odd, foolish, ludicrous part of her

had believed even last night that he would understand—that she could make him understand—

Damn. Pulling at the powdered wig, she threw
it to the floor, kicking it so that it flew across
the wood like a moth-eaten rat. Her hopes, her
dreams, lay tumbled about her like a jumble of
children's blocks.

If only she could break something, throw
something, kick or stomp like a child might.

Or if he would listen? If she could explain and
prove to him her knowledge. Did he think she
came up with this plan on an impulse to trick the
British public or earn a few shillings or potatoes?
This was the result of long hours of planning and
dreaming. It was the result of sacrifice, determination and days of reading, writing, studying
and dissecting bodies, the flesh already rotting
from the bones.

This life was her own personal miracle.

A furious pounding on the outside door interrupted her thoughts. She heard Sarah's brisk
footsteps. She heard the whine of hinges and a
murmur of voices. Usually, she would have been
at the door, doctor's bag in hand. But she stilled
her movement. This was no longer her life—
could not be her life. Even if she were prepared

to risk her own disgrace, she could not expose her mother, her brother or Flo to scandal.

Sarah entered, closing the door behind her.

'Yes?' Letty asked dully.

'It's Mr Jamison. His youngest boy has fallen and is lying on the ground. He is screaming and can't feel his arm.'

'Cedric?' She remembered the lad swinging on the fence, with his wide smile and freckled face.

'Will you go?' Sarah asked.

Letty felt the urge, the energy, the momentum pulse through her limbs. She bent towards her bag, then stopped.

'I can't,' she said.

'But you can't leave the lad.'

'Lord Anthony says he will expose me. I cannot allow that. My brother and Flo would be implicated. There would be scandal. It would kill my mother. You know it.'

'Oh, miss—'

'Tell Arnold to fetch Jeffers.'

Just then they heard a knock on the study door. By habit, Letty bent to the floor, grabbing the wig and pulling it quickly over her red hair.

'Doctor?' Mr Jamison entered. Sweat beaded on his forehead, his cheeks were red and his breath laboured. He held his cap between large hands, twisting the cloth.

'Yes?' Letty said, stepping forward and deepening her voice. 'I understand Cedric is hurt?'

'Please, sir. I don't have much money, but we're got a great apple crop and I'll give you all I can. But the lad is screaming that much, it's a wonder you can't hear him from here. He fell out of the apple tree, just close to your stable.'

'It is his arm?'

'Yes.'

'But he is still conscious?'

'Aye, he is that and screaming to beat the band,' Mr Jamison said.

'Believe it or not, that is a good sign. I can't go myself, but I can send for Jeffers,' she said.

'No! Please, sir. Come yourself. You know Dr Jeffers don't come out for simple folk.'

Letty hesitated. She glanced down, unable to look the man in the eye, as she rubbed her damp hands against the cloth of her trousers. The material rustled. 'Really, I can't.'

'Is it the money? I can borrow summat from my brother. I hate to see the lad in that much pain. And his mother will be that upset it will turn her milk. I'm sure of it. We were coming into town when the axel broke. While I was fixing it, he went and shimmied up a tree, as lads will.'

Mr Jamison paused as though out of breath. In the room's sudden quiet, she thought she heard the child's scream. 'I can pay for Dr Jeffers,' she said.

'But it will take Jeffers an hour at least to get here and his shoulder looks that odd.'

'You said he can't feel his fingers?'

'That what he said. And he's screaming that much. I ain't heard nothing like it.'

'He is close, you say?' Letty said, glancing about the small study as though expecting to be watched, even in this private place.

'Just down the lane.'

She paced to the window. If the boy's fingers were numb, his circulation might be impacted and the limb would die. And if the limb died, so would the boy.

'Very well,' she said, turning sharply and peering through her lenses at the man's worried face. Since when had she been paralysed by fear?

'I will come.'

She would not have her last act as a doctor to be one of cowardice.

Chapter Ten

Grabbing the doctor's bag, she followed Mr Jamison through the front door and past the fresh fragrant growth of the herb garden.

'I don't hear him.' Mr Jamison looked at her, his red face suddenly pale. 'I think the silence is worse than the screams.'

Together, they hurried down the uneven paving stones, through the gate and past the stable, almost running down the rutted road.

They came upon the horse first, a large, angular, stalwart beast. Beside the animal, she saw the cart, newly repaired and freshly filled with hay.

'There he be,' Jamison said.

The boy lay under the apple tree, a small, crumpled, silent form, one arm out flung and oddly angled.

'Cedric!' Letty ran to him.

Kneeling beside him, she checked for his pulse. It was strong, thank God.

Her touch revived him and his eyes flickered open, brightly blue in his frighteningly white face. His tears had made long white lines through the grime and still clung, pendulous, to his lashes.

'Hurts,' he managed to say.

'You had a fall, but we are going to look after you. I am just going to feel your arms and legs for breaks. Let me know if anything really hurts.'

'My shoulder.'

'I know. I want to see if any limbs are broken.'

Carefully, she ran her fingers down his legs and arms, feeling for abnormal swelling or angles through the roughness of the cloth. But his legs and arms felt sturdy. She could not find any areas of swelling or, thankfully, any bones which had broken through the skin.

She met the boy's worried gaze, talking, as she always did, in calm steadying tones. 'No broken bones. But I think your shoulder is dislocated.'

'Is that bad, sir?' Mr Jamison asked.

Cedric said nothing, his eyes wide with fear and pain.

'Painful but fixable. Much better than a break. I will adjust it. Mr Jamison, you will need to help and, Cedric, you will have to be brave.'

'Yes, sir,' the boy muttered, nodding his head and then wincing with the motion.

Inhaling, Letty gave herself a moment to think, to run through the procedure in her mind. She had done it several times at Guy's, but that was some time ago and she had never manipulated a child's bones. They were smaller and would require less force.

'Right,' she said. 'Ready?'

Mr Jamison nodded and, taking the boy's arm, she raised it. The boy groaned. 'Hold his arm upwards,' she directed.

The man did so, his large ham hands shaking.

'Good,' Letty said. 'You are doing fine.'

With care, she took a tie from her bag, winding it about the lad's torso so that she could better exert pressure on the blade. Then with a swift firm movement, she twisted.

The boy screamed. It was an awful sound more like a wounded animal than human. For a moment, she feared the movement had not worked. Then the blade fit into place. Cedric's body relaxed and the awful high-pitched scream lessened into muffled sobs while tears still ran from his eyes.

'You were so brave. That was the worst of it, I promise,' she said, nodding to Mr Jamison to lower the arm.

'Dr Hatfield!'

The two words blasted at her. The voice so startled her that Letty lost her balance, sitting inelegantly on her bottom.

'Lord Anthony,' she gasped.

He sat mounted on a black beast of a horse directly behind her, more like a rider of the apocalypse than human form.

'What do you think you are doing?' He did not shout, but the fury lacing his tone made it worse than a thousand bellows.

'I—I am helping—'

'Torturing, more like. I heard his scream.'

She could feel his anger. It emanated from him with a physical force. Standing awkwardly, Letty tried to collect her scattered wits. She pulled herself to her full height, squaring her shoulders and jutting out her jaw. 'And he is not screaming now, if you noticed.'

'He is helping my lad, sir—' Mr Jamison started. 'I mean, my lord.'

'I did not ask you.' Lord Anthony swung down from his mount, his movements awkward.

'There is no cause to be rude to Mr Jamison,' Letty said. 'Besides, we should go—go elsewhere for this discussion.'

'You are lecturing me on manners?'

'No, but—'

'I think you might have concerns of greater import than whether I am sufficiently respectful, given your situation.'

'That's just it. Can we go inside to talk?'

'So now you ask for my discretion?' he mocked. 'If you are so proud of yourself, why wouldn't you want all and sundry to know? And why the hell did you not follow my direction? I told you to stop this nonsense. Did you not hear me earlier? Did I not make myself clear?'

'You were quite clear.'

'Then why are you disobeying my orders?'

'Because I am not your servant. I do not answer to you,' she snapped.

'You will answer to me. I will not have you flout the law of this land or make a mockery of its rules.'

'I took an oath.'

'A person that does not exist took an oath—'

'Tony—' She looked again towards the farmer.

'I told you I could not go along with this masquerade. I warned you. Not if you continued to practise and put others at risk. You should never have started this nonsense in the first place.'

'And I would not have done if I did not live in a backward society that fails to recognise my abilities because I am female. And, by the way, I have never put anyone at risk and I exist. A name or the lack of a name does not equate to non-existence.'

'I am not interested in a philosophic discussion.'

'Then are you interested in fact? I helped this boy. I relieved his pain. It does not matter who I am. What matters is my skill and my knowledge.'

'You are a fraud.'

The words hung in the silence. Anger and fury fired through her.

'I—am—no—fraud!' She ground the words out, pushing each syllable through clenched teeth. 'Come! Come here if you are so certain I am a fraud!'

The fury energised her. She could feel it in the wild thump of her heart, her quickened breath and the heat in her cheeks. She pushed past him, brushing against the black magnificence of his horse, beyond the bewildered Mr Jamison, the waiting cart and grazing cart horse.

She went through her gate where Arnold stood, his kindly face lined with worry.

'Look after His Lordship's horse,' she directed.

Then she strode up the uneven path and through the long grasses which brushed against her trousers, filling the air with fragrance. She opened the doctor's back door with such force that it banged against the wall.

Still without pause, she went into the dark coolness of the corridor and through to the front room. She did not stop until she was again surrounded by her books and papers and filled with that swift surge of familiarity and home coming.

'Here!' she said. 'Look here! And tell me if I am a fraud.'

Tony stared. Huge wooden bookshelves covered every wall from floor boards to ceiling. Books lined the shelves, huge tomes and smaller volumes, old and new. Their embossed titles glinted. A desk stood in the centre of the room, also piled high with books, journals and papers. Beside the desk, more volumes were stacked in huge toppling towers.

He stepped forward. He touched the shelves, running his fingers across the dry leather of the spines. The books were meticulously arranged in alphabetical order. There were volumes from Greek and Roman times, obscure treaties and familiar texts from Rogerius Salernitanus, and Andreas Vesalius. There were newer works, Treling and Pott, as well as huge bound copies of medical journals.

Admiration flickered, but he tamped it down. 'So, you have an extensive library. That doesn't mean you can set yourself up as a doctor. Reading about—about an operation does not mean you can perform it.'

'I recognise that,' she said, going to the desk and yanking open the drawer with such angry energy he feared it would spill its contents on to the floor.

'This display of emotion serves no purpose. You could have retired "Dr Hatfield" with dignity if you had followed my direction. Now it is entirely likely that Jamison will tell everyone.'

She paused, standing straight and placing her hands at her waist. 'Do you practise being pompous or does it come naturally? Anyway, if Mr Jamison does speak, whose fault is that?'

'Yours because you chose to ignore me. Yours

because you chose to start this enterprise and thought books, interest and the desire to help could take the place of training and knowledge.'

But he recognised his own culpability, at least in speaking so openly in front of Jamison. He'd allowed fury and emotion to overwhelm good sense and restraint.

The boy's scream had done it—those cries had catapulted him down a rabbit hole of memory.

It hadn't given him that awful disengaged feeling—that peculiar numbness—he'd experienced previously. He hadn't seen mud or bodies. Instead, he'd remembered—or thought he remembered— although, truthfully, he still was unsure if it was a real memory or nightmare.

As he'd exited the inn's courtyard, he heard Cedric's scream. He remembered the boy's cry. He remembered spurring his horse forward. He remembered a flash of fear, frustration and a driving, overwhelming need to do something.

Then he'd seen Letty bending over the boy. He'd seen the movement of her arm or elbow pulling upwards.

And in that moment, images had flashed before his mind's eye, snippets and snatches, disconnected and disjointed. There'd been a lad on the battlefield. He remembered him. He was sure he remembered him. He could picture his face. The lad had looked too young to be a soldier with his blond hair and stubbly chin. He could not yet grow a full beard.

He'd lain on the ground with wide blue eyes and a bayonet sticking out from his gut.

Tony remembered crawling over to the boy. George was dead. The mud from the heavy rains on the day previous made movement slow as his knees and hands sank foot deep into the wet dirt. He could feel the sun, but could not see it. Everything was shrouded with swirls of mist and the air tasted of gunpowder.

At first, he could not see the boy, but could only hear his screams. Then he saw the lad's crumpled form with the bayonet projecting from his intestines.

The boy had stopped screaming at his approach and almost smiled. 'Help. Please, sir, please. Take it out! Take it out!'

So Tony had.

'Cedric was in pain. What would you have me do?' Letty asked, her firm strong tones interrupted his reverie.

'What?'

'Cedric was in pain. What would you have me do?' Letty repeated.

'Send a servant for a doctor who is qualified,' he said. 'Helping when you don't know what you're doing merely does more harm. Good intentions count for nothing—'

'Do it!' the boy had said. 'Get it out of me!'

The blood had gone everywhere, a red fountain.

Within a second, the boy had died.

One moment he had been conscious, talking, and in the next his eyes had glazed with the blank look of death.

'Except I do know what I am doing.' Letty said, her clear tones again pulling his thoughts back. 'That is what you don't understand.'

'I understand that you want to help. I know that you have read articles and likely talked to midwives, perhaps you even observed their work. But that does not mean that you know more than someone who has trained. It is not the same—'

'I know more because of this.' She bent down again, pulling out the contents of the opened drawer and piling the bundle of papers on to the desk. 'And this!'

She yanked open the bottom drawer with such

force that it hit the floor, disgorging its contents. Bundles of papers, neatly tied with black ribbon, scattered. She grabbed one, picking it up and banging it on the desk. A flurry of dust sparkles danced upwards, visible within the sunbeam.

'And this!' She opened another drawer. Again it hit the ground, its contents spreading across the floor in a riot of paper.

'And, these also!'

'Stop! Stop! What is all this?' Tony said.

She thrust a bundle at him. 'Take it.'

He folded his fingers around the thick package. He looked down. Tightly written lines and diagrams filled every page. Sandwiched between the text, he saw illustrations. There was a hand and an ankle, meticulous in its every detail.

'My notes,' she said.

'You drew these? And wrote these?'

'Yes.'

'From the books?'

'No, from my anatomy lab actually,' she said.

The words hung in the room.

'You attended an anatomy lab?'

'Several. It was at Guy's and led by Mr Harting. The notes are here.' She tapped one of the bundles on the desk. 'And these were taken during a chemistry class with Professor Lindenburgh. And here are some additional notes on anatomy. Please forgive the messiness. They were written during an autopsy and might be marked with blood.'

He stared at the pages. The words swam before him. 'How long were you there?'

'Eighteen months.'

'You went to Guy's for eighteen months.'

'Yes.'

'But how? Where did you live?'

'I lived with Flo. I attended boring soirées to make my mother happy as Miss Barton. As few as possible, naturally. Then I studied as Dr Hatfield. I had to miss a few lectures, but generally I managed quite well.'

He stared as she stood there in her ludicrous outfit. At least, she'd discarded the wig, although her hair was so rumpled that it now framed her face like a rat's nest. Her jaw was thrust out. Anger had made her cheeks flush and her green eyes sparkled behind the thick lenses.

'What do you think this proves? What am I to do with these notes? Why would you subject yourself to such hardship, to illness and death when you could have a good life?'

She said nothing and he felt a confused mix of anger, admiration and hurt. He felt tricked.

The level of subterfuge astounded. No wonder she had wanted no part of his proposal.

He turned away with a final angry look at the notes and papers strewn across the desk. 'This proves nothing. It proves nothing except that you are not just eccentric, but bloody crazy.'

Tony strode from the house. The door slammed behind him. His ribs hurt and his head thumped.

'Arnold!' he shouted.

The man appeared. Tony took his horse from the servant, swinging himself awkwardly on to the animal and wincing at the pain. He needed to leave. He needed to think. Spurring his horse forward, he rode through the gate and back on to the lane.

The farmer, cart, horse and injured boy were still there. He stared in surprise. It seemed a strangely long time since he'd entered the house and he'd thought they would be long gone.

'Jamison!' Tony pulled to a halt in front of the farmer.

The man stood at the back of the cart, apparently checking that the gate was secure. The boy lay in it, reclining on a hay bale. Mr Jamison looked up, touching his cap. 'Yes, sir. My lord.'

'I don't know what you heard before, but you will not speak of this to anyone.'

'I am not one to gossip, my lord,' Mr Jamison said, with surprising dignity. He rubbed his hand over his forehead to wipe clean the beads of sweat. 'But I'll say this much, my lord, Dr Hatfield helped my son. And the wife, too, when she had our last child.'

'I am sure Dr Hatfield will keep you in mind if requiring a character reference,' Tony said, then immediately felt remorse that he had spoken unkindly.

'He's a good doctor,' Jamison said with a certain mulishness.

'Good or not, he will not be practising in the future. How is the boy?' Tony asked, nodding his head towards the lad. His colour had returned.

'Much better, my lord.'

'Send a message to Beauchamp, if he needs anything.'

Without waiting for an answer, Tony turned his horse around, moving as swiftly as he could, given the rutted ground and his own injuries.

That evening Tony drank most of an expensive bottle of brandy. Elsie was still in bed so he had his dinner served in the library and glared with animosity at the empty hearth.

The memory of the injured soldier on the battlefield seemed particularly clear, more vivid than hearth or books as though to compensate for the months he had forgotten. Truthfully, the recollection seemed both old and new, as though the image had always been there…waiting… lurking just beyond the fringes of consciousness.

He wished he could tell Letty.

The thought came without warning. He had never wanted to speak of his experiences with anyone. And why Miss Barton? He hardly knew the woman and what he knew was hardly conducive to trust. But it seemed as he sat within the still dim room that he would like to talk to her. She would not be shocked. She would not look away as though by even mentioning such things he was breaching some rule of etiquette. And that social norms and manners were more important than the boy with a bayonet in his gut.

Of course, Miss Barton would hardly want to talk to him. He glared with further enmity at the hearth, studying the uneven pattern of the blackened bricks. As he remembered his last words to her, he felt discomfort and then irritation at his own discomfort.

You are not just eccentric, but bloody crazy.

He had not meant to be cruel. Indeed, Miss Barton's masquerade had not been sensible.

It was not sane or safe for a woman to work for eighteen months through the rough district around Guy's. Her disguise was hardly foolproof and, male or not, she hardly looked capable of winning a fist fight.

And what if she continued in this charade? What if she moved to a different county or back to the city? And what of disease? By the very nature of her occupation, she was putting herself in harm's way.

His hand tightened against the arm of the chair. The thought of something happening to Letty hurt with a deep pain, stealing his breath. She had such vitality, strength and single-minded determination. What would it be like to feel such drive and purpose?

He stood. The room rocked unpleasantly. He put down his brandy snifter, reaching for the bottle. He picked it up, holding it up to the flickering sconce to study its contents.

'Almost empty,' he said to no one.

Grabbing the empty brandy snifter, he lurched unsteadily towards the door while still gripping the bottle. He went to the bedroom, placing the bottle on the side table while sitting in the chair and stretching out his long legs. The candles had been lit. Mason was waiting.

'Go away,' he muttered, with a wave of the snifter.

'I was going to get you ready for the night.'

'Can do that myself,' he said. 'Go find me another bottle.'

'There is some in this bottle here. Will that suffice?' Mason poured out a small measure into the snifter.

Tony peered at it suspiciously. 'Suppose so.'

'Did you wish me to shave you, my lord, or light a fire?'

'No. You can go. Will ring you when I need you.' He waved the snifter towards Mason and the door.

'Yes, my lord,' his man said.

The door closed. Tony stared about the bed-chamber. Sometimes he delayed going to bed. At times he wondered if he was afraid to sleep, afraid of the nightmares. But his dreams had decreased recently. In fact, he had not had a bad one since that night when Letty had come in.

Her image flickered before his eyes, the voluminous nightgown which was so short that he could see her feet and ankles and draped in such a way that he was aware of the comely shape of her long legs. He remembered the feel of the silk ties as he pulled them, pushing the cloth past her shoulders and then tumbling her on to the bed. He could picture her with the nightgown draped about her waist, the white skin gleaming in the candlelight and the red hair spread about her in a fiery halo.

As he had kissed her, all the numbness had dissipated. There was lust, of course. And desire... but integral to the physical attraction there had been something else: hope, joy, rebirth and new beginnings.

And even though she had refused his offer of marriage, the hope that she would form some part of his life had persisted. A portion of his mind had recognised that the feelings she engendered were special and could not be ignored. There had been a connection, both physical and emotional. He had liked her wit, her bluntness and her intelligence. He'd liked the way that, despite his scars and his nightmares, she had not looked at him as though he was an oddity.

He had felt a man again.

And when he'd learned about her double life, it seemed as though fate laughed at him. He'd actually felt something for another human being, only to find he'd loved a mirage.

Loved?

No, it was not love. He could not love someone he didn't know. Besides, he didn't even think he was capable of the emotion. He should push Miss Barton—or Dr Hatfield—from his mind. There was no reason for him or his family to have anything more to do with the woman.

But he couldn't. The image of green eyes fringed with long dark lashes lingered as his mind swung like a pendulum. On one hand she must be mad to take such risks to work with death and illness and the worst of human life.

On the other she demonstrated more determination and purpose than he'd ever witnessed before.

What would it be like to feel such purpose?

He would like to see her again. Despite the masquerade, he'd like to see her. There was something about her; she angered him, frustrated him, confused him, but she had accepted him.

He took another sip of the harsh liquid so that it burned his throat. She had accepted him.

A thought came with sudden clarity, darting

through his brain, almost visual like print upon the page.

She had accepted him—but he could not say the same.

The brandy made him sleep late and it was past noon when he woke, stumbling out of bed and staring blearily at the painful brightness outside. He rang for Mason.

'Make me as decent as you can,' he muttered, touching the twisting line of his scar. 'Don't want to scare her ladyship or give the child nightmares.'

'Yes, sir. Would you be wanting something to eat, sir?'

'Later in the library.'

'Yes, sir.'

'And don't look so damned disapproving. If you are not careful your face might set that way. One needs to eat.'

'Indeed, my lord, and we highly encourage eating. However, eating later in the library usually involves drinking. And might I say, sir, that you are not yet without the effects of the last bottle.'

'You forget yourself.'

'Yes, sir.'

'And who is this "we"? You are not the bloody King of England.'

'No, sir.'

'I have no need for a wife or a nursemaid. And I already have a mother. Though not a father, dropped dead, you know. Dropped dead when he heard about Edgar.'

Elsie was sleeping when Tony tiptoed in. She looked pale and he noted the dark shadows circling her eyes. However, the maid and Nanny reported that there had been no sign of fits or fever.

Theodore George Edgar lay in his cradle beside her. His face looked less red, but still wizened and oddly wise for one so newly arrived. Tony smiled, reaching forward to touch the tiny hand.

'Hello, Theodore George Edgar,' he murmured, as the fragile perfect fingers clutched his own.

'I am going to call him Teddy for short,' Elsie murmured sleepily.

'Sorry to wake you.'

'I was just dozing. But, Tony?' She raised herself on one elbow, a frown puckering her forehead.

'What is it?' He knew his sister well enough

and could see the anxiety lurking in her eyes and furrowed forehead. 'You are well?'

'Yes.'

'And Teddy seems well.'

'Yes.'

'Then why do you appear so apprehensive?' He sat in the chair between the bed and cradle, placing his hand against his sister's forehead. It felt quite cool, particularly given the room's stuffy heat.

'Teddy was a little fussy last night, but I suppose babies are like that.'

'I wouldn't know.' Tony eyed the infant as it lay in the cradle, one hand reaching upwards as though conducting some silent unknown orchestra.

'Does he feel warm to you? Elsie asked.

He reached into the cradle, touching the boy's forehead. 'Not particularly.'

'Good, I thought he did.'

'Likely because it is hot as Hades in here and stuffy.'

'That is Nanny. She insists that the windows and curtains are closed so that we keep out bad spirits.'

'Likely it will keep out anyone who needs to breathe. George's Nanny is as old as Methuselah. Indeed, she already seemed ancient when I put the frog on her desk,' Tony said.

'You did? I don't remember.'

'Likely you were too young. She didn't bat an eye, but I got a dreadful lecture.'

'Father was always rather good with lectures.' Elsie smiled. 'He wanted us all to be like Edgar.'

'Edgar was a rather hard act to follow.'

'I suppose. Easier for me because I was youngest and a girl. Must have been hard for you. Father always thought Edgar was so perfect. Mother always wanted me to be clever and to be a good singer. I am neither.'

'I'd say you're clever enough and you can thump out a decent tune on the piano.'

'Only due to diligent practice. It used to bother me, but then I fell in love with George. And George loved me,' she said somewhat drowsily. 'He loved me just for being me. I'll always have that. You should fall in love.'

'The latter seems very unlikely,' he said.

'And I do know how to dress people. I am good at that. Really, I must invite Miss Barton over again.'

'Miss Barton? You must?' He heard his voice lift. He felt a ludicrous pulse of happiness.

'Indeed, I thought I could lend her more dresses. Didn't she look lovely in that gold one?'

'I suppose,' he said, shifting. The memory of that golden, glittering dress flickered before him.

Just then Teddy coughed or hiccoughed. Elsie sat up, any drowsiness forgotten. She leaned over the child, touching his head.

Again, he saw her apprehension, her gaze worried and the shadows under her eyes deepening.

'Tony, I really think he feels warm. There is whooping cough going about the village. Indeed, one of our servants has come down with it, you know.'

'I didn't. But if you are worried, fetch Jeffers. Let him take a look. I don't want you worrying.'

'What about Dr Hatfield?'

'No,' he said.

He saw a confused frown flicker across her face, but she did not push the point, again touching Teddy's forehead.

'Perhaps I am fussing or imagining a fever. I mean babies do cough and hiccough. It is just that he is such a miracle. Sometimes, I love him so much, I feel scared. I sit and look at him even when I should be sleeping.'

Just then Nanny entered. She always wore her

grey hair pulled into a bun and a frown of disapproval. She had looked after George and his father and while she looked old, there was also a timelessness about her. Indeed, she had aged little from when he was a young fellow. Rather it was as though she was born old and had failed to age during the intervening years.

'Now don't you be disturbing her ladyship. She needs her rest,' she said, making a *tsk*ing sound.

This was accompanied by a shooing gesture with her hands so that Tony rather felt like an obstreperous fowl being chased into the hen house. He left and started towards the library as was his habit.

But some impulse made him stop. Slowly, he turned, walking instead to the study. He halted. He placed his hand on the door handle and then slowly twisted. The hinges creaked as he pushed open the door, stepping inside.

He had not been here since George's death.

He'd walked past the room often enough. His hand had even rested on the knob, but he had always turned away.

Tony stood on the threshold. The room was exactly as it had been during his childhood and more recently when he had visited George after his marriage to Elsie. Tony stepped further into the room, allowing the door to close behind him, as he sat on the familiar armchair. The cushioning wheezed under his weight. They'd often played cards, chess or discussed politics. Like George, the study had a quiet, strong, unpretentious comfort. The furnishings were shabby but cosy and pleasantly moulded to one's frame. The view looked on to the green vista of the park and a collection of paintings covered the walls. Generally, they were of stiff animals planted in the centre of a pastoral landscape. George had had a better eye for animals than art.

Tony remembered bringing over new horses. George would run his hands over the animal's mane and down the smooth glossy coat as though able to feel its health and temperament through his fingertips. Later, they would go out to the field and watch the horse's movement and gait.

George refused to be hurried. He'd ask the groom to lead the animal around the paddock, watching with narrowed eyes until Tony felt bored and stiff. Then, just when Tony had feared he must fall asleep, George would straighten, nod and say with sudden decisiveness, 'That one's a keeper.'

Tony always wondered what differentiated

that final walk from all the rest. Then they'd have a ride or, if it was late, walk up to the house to see Elsie. On occasion, if the weather was suitable, they'd grab a fishing rod.

Time with George had always felt pleasant and somehow lessened that restless spirit which had been a part of him since childhood.

Tentatively, Tony leaned back within the comfortable chair, as he had done so many times with George. His eyes closed. It was, he thought, one of the first times he'd allowed himself to remember not only the man's death but his life. It seemed that his memory had bounced between the boy and the corpse.

But never the man.

The door opened, banging and crashing against the wall. Elsie tumbled inwards.

'Tony!' Her face was white, her hair wild and she wore only her nightgown.

'My God—what is it?' He stood up from the chair, hurrying to his sister as she seemed likely to collapse.

'Theodore—I was right. He is sick. Within a half-hour, his fever has worsened. It has gone up so quickly. Indeed, he's burning up.' She ran to Tony. Tears tracked down her cheeks. She reached forward, holding his arm with tight, desperate fingers. 'I can't lose him. I can't lose him. I've lost George. I can't lose him, too.'

He saw the desperation in her wide blue eyes. 'Have you sent for the doctor?'

'Yes, I just sent for Jeffers, but he has not come yet. Maybe if you go, you can explain. And make him come, except the servants think he might be out of town. And I don't know what to do.'

For a moment, it seemed time froze. He could feel his mind work as he interpreted this rush of words. Through the open door, he heard a child's cry, peppered with coughs. It was getting quite late in the day. He had become immersed both in memories and in estate business which should have been done weeks ago.

Beside him, his sister stood with her white face and hands so desperately clenched against his arm.

He thought of George. He thought of Jeffers's amiable countenance, reddened with drink. He thought of Miss Barton.

It is a need, as strong in me as movement or communication... I took an oath... I helped a child...

It was crazy. She was crazy. And she was brilliant.

'I'll get help,' he said. 'I'll get Dr Hatfield.'

Jester sprang through the dark night. Tony hunkered down, ignoring the pain that still shuddered through his side. It was a clear night and he knew the woods well. He pushed Jester fast so that they thundered down the narrow pathway as fast as was safe. Branches snapped his face and he ducked to avoid low-hanging boughs.

The silence was profound, broken only by the thud of hooves, the crack of breaking twigs and the hurried beat of his own heart.

His nephew was a week old. Not even—six days. And he'd spent so little time with him. Of course, men don't spend time with babies. And yet, was this his reasoning? Was he ruled by society's custom or was he ruled by fear.

He'd worried that he would love again and lose.

Except loss might happen anyway.

And if Teddy died—he stumbled against the word—if he died he'd curse himself. He'd curse himself that he had not held the tiny hand more often. He'd curse himself that he had not sat in the dark and listened to the soft rhythm of his baby breath or watched the wave of that minute hand conducting an invisible orchestra.

There was no escape from pain. No guarantees.

It was not a long ride—an hour at most. But it seemed endless. Every second felt like a minute and every minute interminable.

At last he broke out of the copse and Jester gathered speed, cantering smoothly down the dirt road sandwiched between fields and farms. He felt raw, cut open, bleeding and hopeless. He saw images of George and the other men who haunted his dreams. Sometimes, dead faces appeared within the moonlight's spectral shadows. That same frustrated impotence that he'd felt on the battlefield filled him. 'What ifs' rotated through his mind. What if Letty could not help Theodore? What if he died before she came? What if she wouldn't come? What if she couldn't help the little boy any more than he could help the brave men?

The questions swirled. And all the while he was haunted by the infant's bright eyes turning dark…sightless…

Leaning forward, he angled his body as though, by doing so, he was measurably closer to his destination. Every movement hurt. Perspiration prickled his head and neck.

At last, the village neared. On either side, he could make out the grey shapes of the farm houses and barns, now clustered more closely. Under Jester's hooves, the dirt road turned to cobbles and the noise of the animal's footsteps made a clipped sound, no longer muted by the dirt road.

The small house stood on the right. One light glimmered from a lower window.

Jerking Jester to a halt, he swung off, pushing through the gate and hurrying up the path. Raising his fist, he hammered on the door. The noise was loud, reverberating through the quiet street.

He held his breath. It felt as though his heart had stopped and, in that moment, he had an awful, absolute certainty that Letty was away.

The door opened. Letty stood within the portal, backlit by the lamp within the hallway.

A huge speechless relief washed over him.

Chapter Eleven

'Lord Anthony,' Letty gasped.

He was staring at her wildly. A confused anger mixed with fear flashed through her. She felt an almost physical weakness as though the sudden impact of his presence made her own knees wobble.

She gripped the door frame more tightly. She refused to go weak at the knees over a judgemental, inebriated aristocrat who had likely come merely to hurl accusations at her head.

'You forgot a pertinent insult? Indeed, now it is you who look mad. Are you in your cups?' she asked tartly.

'Letty—' There was a desperation in his tone which made her study him with new focus and narrowed gaze.

Sweat beaded on his forehead and upper lip. His face was grey, his exhalations quick.

'Tony? Come in. What is it? What's wrong?'

'The baby,' he said, his voice ragged. 'He has a high fever and is coughing. Please, she can't lose him. I can't lose him.'

'I'm so sorry—'

'You'll come. You'll come despite what I said?' he asked.

'Of course I will come,' she said. 'I will just get my bag.'

'Thank you,' he said.

'Rest while I get everything I might need. I will ask Sarah to bring you food and water.'

He nodded. He sank into the straight-backed chair within the hall, his exhaustion visible within every line of his slumped body.

'Will you change?'

She paused, uncertain.

'No,' she said. 'Let us not introduce any delay. I'll just get my bag and any draughts I might require.'

'Thank you.' His pain and hopelessness seemed almost palpable and her heart hurt for him. Standing on the first rung of the stairs, she glanced back at him.

'And, Tony, I will do everything possible.'

They rode in silence. Jester was spent and they'd left him with Arnold. They'd debated about getting a horse from the inn, but had decided that it would be as quick to take Archimedes. This animal, spurred by Tony's use of the stirrups, moved at a faster pace than his usual rolling gait, his tail flicking behind him in irritation.

Letty rode in front of Tony. It was quicker to take the horse than the trap.

She was conscious of his solid strength. She felt his muscled chest behind her, the firmness of his arm and the hardness of his thighs tight about her. She catalogued the sensations.

At some time, she thought, when she was not so worried, she would want to feel this. She would want to remember the soft thud of hooves, the night air softly perfumed with the woodsy scent of bark and moss and branches darkly outlined against the starry sky.

And she would remember that he had needed her. He valued her, not only as a woman, but as a doctor.

Finally, they broke out of the forest shadows and into Beauchamp's park. The lanterns were lit, strung along the curved driveway and casting bright pools of light. At its end, she saw the dark shape of the house, its walls punctuated with yellow lamplight.

Now that they had arrived, the urgency returned also, growing huge. Anxiety dampened her palms, tightening the muscles in her shoulders and neck and keeping her worried gaze fixed on the house.

The second Archimedes stopped, she swung off, landing lightly on the drive and almost running up the steps to the dark lacquered door.

It opened instantly. Dobson stood in the portal, his silhouette darkly outlined against the lamplight.

'Any news?' Tony asked.

The man shook his head.

Without pause, they ran inside and up the steps which hugged the wall, leading to the second storey.

'This way,' Tony said, pushing open the nursery door.

The room was hot. The fire had been stoked so that the flames were high, flickering and crackling up into the chimney. The window was tightly closed. The crib stood in the centre of the room and Elsie, her maid and an old woman, likely the nanny, clustered about it.

'Letty? What? Why are you here?' Elsie asked, her worried puzzled gaze resting on Tony.

There was a pause, a brief moment of silence.

'Because she is the best,' he said.

'He's having fits! He's having fits!' the maid suddenly screamed.

Letty pushed through only to be blocked by the nanny's stout form. 'Miss Barton? Where's Dr Jeffers?'

'Let her through!' Tony said.

'But, sir—'

'Now.'

Letty bent over Theodore. He was, indeed, having fits. The infant was tightly swaddled. His face was red and his breathing laboured. She noted also an unnatural twitching and stiffening racking his small body.

Reaching down, she loosened the tightly wrapped blankets, feeling his hot, tiny body as she did so.

'How long has he been twitching?'

''E just started, miss,' the maid said.

'The seizure is caused by his temperature. He is very hot so our first job is to decrease his temperature. I want the window opened and the fire doused. Then we will give him a sponge bath. I want a basin of lukewarm water. Not hot.'

'Really, I do not think that any of this will help—' the nanny started to say.

'Then your presence isn't needed here. I do

not have the time or energy to convince you so you would be better off leaving,' Letty retorted.

Letty, the maid Maria, and Elsie worked together with single-minded concentration. Letty made herself focus only on the child, refusing to look at Elsie's pale face and haunted eyes. Together they sponged off Teddy's hot body while giving him a tincture of elder and yarrow, delivered via a tiny silver teaspoon. The fire was doused and downstairs the cook stoked the fire and heated huge kettles of water. This was poured into huge steaming bowls which were brought up by the maids and distributed about the room so that the windows and looking glass became foggy with steam.

Thankfully, the seizures had stopped, but Teddy was still too hot. Despite the steam, he coughed with that awful dry hack, typical of whooping cough. Too often he seemed to lose his breath, his tiny body convulsing as he fought for air. At these times, his face turned a bright-red colour, close to purple, while his lips looked almost blue and his body shook with the violence of the cough.

And then he would gulp in the air. His colour would return and Letty would breathe again.

* * *

The hours merged. Night turned into day and day back into night. Letty worked without respite. With endless patience, she put water on to a spoon, gently easing it between the child's lips. Elsie tried to nurse him, but the coughs too often racked his tiny body so that he vomited the fluid, the smell of sour milk scenting the room already filled with sweat.

'I wish he could keep something down,' Elsie said, looking at Letty with eyes which looked much too big for her face. 'He will starve.'

'He still has tears and is not without fluid. And he is getting more respite from the coughing. He will not starve.'

Occasionally, Elsie would lie down in the small chamber attached to the nursery, but she never ventured to her own room. Nor did she really sleep, always jerking awake at any sound from the child. Indeed, she only agreed to rest because Letty said that Theodore would need his mother's strength and energy throughout his recovery.

As for Tony, he would look in, his face a pitiful mix of hope and fear. Sometimes, he'd coax them out to eat, but they'd take little more than soup or tea before returning to the nursery.

Of course, a bedchamber had been provided for Letty, but she went there infrequently, lying down for little more than an hour. More often she fell asleep in the nursery, propped up against the chair.

It was sometime on the third or fourth night that the fever broke. Letty must have fallen sleep because she jumped, disoriented at Elsie's scream.

'What?' She leapt up from the chair, leaning over the cot while still half-asleep.

'I cannot hear him breathe. And he feels so cool,' Elsie said. 'Is he…? Is he…?'

She couldn't say the word, instead fixing Letty with huge, fearful eyes. The room was lit only by candle and its flickering light emphasised the hollows and shadows marking her face.

With a pounding heart, Letty reached forward. The child was cool, but not cold. She felt his breath against her hand and saw the restful look of healthy sleep.

She smiled, joy pulsing through her. 'He is breathing. He is breathing normally. The fever—it has broken.'

'You mean…?' Elsie stared at her.

'I think he should recover.'

* * *

They sat together until dawn broke and the room became lit with the early sunlight. By then, Letty was quite certain Teddy was well on the way to recovery. He was breathing well and coughing much less frequently and never with that awful breathlessness, as though his breath had been taken and could not be regained.

Hungry once more, Elsie was able to nurse him and though he coughed a bit, he was able to ingest some fluid and then fall asleep, snuggled at her breast.

'Thank you,' she whispered, looking over Teddy's tiny, damp, blond curls. 'Thank you.'

'Get some rest,' Letty said. 'You both need it. I will tell the servants to keep steaming the room.'

Exhausted, Letty stepped into the corridor. Tony was waiting for her. 'He's better?'

'Yes.'

'May I see them?'

'Of course.'

'I have asked that the maid bring some food to your bedchamber and then you must rest,' he said.

'That is considerate.' Almost too exhausted to

remain vertical, to place one foot after the other as she navigated the hallway.

'And thank you,' he said.

Letty stood on the terrace, propping her elbows on the stone balustrade and gazing into the garden. She was conscious of the evening air. She had slept close to ten hours straight and day had turned to night.

September was approaching. The air had that cool, crisp autumnal feel, different from summer's heat. A few leaves had fallen and moved across the grey flagstones in tiny, rustling, spiralling swirls.

There was a full moon. Its light shimmered on an ornamental pond, illuminating the bushes and trees with silvery radiance. She wondered how many days had passed since Teddy had first been taken ill. The moon had not been full when she'd arrived. At least, she didn't think it had. It should be easy enough to remember, she thought. But her mind still felt dull, muddled as though still hazy with sleep.

She felt his presence, even before she heard his footsteps. It was in the quickening of her breath. It was in the exquisite sensitivity of her every nerve and in the goosebumps prickling her arms and neck, which had nothing to do with September's chill.

He stood beside her, also leaning against the stone balustrade, tall in his lanky, big-boned way. He was close, but not so near that they physically touched. Yet her awareness of him could not have been greater. It made her breathing quicken and her pulse race.

Glancing sideways, she saw that he had no jacket and had rolled up his shirtsleeves. He'd placed his hands on the balustrade and she could see the muscles in his forearm. For once, the glove had been removed and his injured hand was visible. Distorted by flame, the skin was stretched painfully across the bones.

'Thank you,' he said once more.

'I didn't do that much. Doctors still know so little.'

'You fought for him. You never gave up.'

'And you believed in me. It is the first time that anyone has believed in me—I mean, as opposed to Dr Hatfield.'

'Were you able to rest?'

'Yes, for hours. I got up only a short while go. I checked on Teddy and Elsie. They are both sleeping.'

'I sent most of the servants to bed early, too.

I don't think they'd slept either while Teddy was ill.'

They fell silent again, staring across the velvet darkness of the garden. The leaves still danced, rustling over flagstones as light, wispy clouds fluttered across the sky.

'You can work as Dr Hatfield for as long as you want. I'll say nothing. I don't think Jamison will either.'

'Thank you. What about the servants here? They must guess?'

'They will say nothing.'

She glanced at him. In profile, his scar was not noticeable and she could see only the strong lines of his chin. He reached somewhat cumbersomely across his body, resting his uninjured hand upon her own. His palm was warm and dry and her entire awareness seemed focused on his touch.

She turned slightly towards him and, very gently, touched his wounded hand, feeling the taut, tight skin where the wound had so recently healed.

He made to move it away.

'Don't,' she whispered.

Tenderly, she ran her finger light across his palm. 'I am glad you have taken off the glove.'

'Why?'

They stood so close that she could feel the whisper of his breath.

'Because it shows that you survived. It is not a sign of weakness, but strength.'

'Is it? Is it strength to survive?' he asked. 'Or merely a twist of fate?'

He spoke so quietly that Letty had to shift closer to hear him.

'It takes strength to keep going.'

Tony closed his eyes, squeezing them tight. He thought of George and Edgar and the nameless boy with the bayonet stuck in his gut.

'I see them, too,' she said.

'What?'

She looked towards the garden. 'I see them. The people I could not help. Patients. And my father. He died quite suddenly. It was his heart. I felt like I should have been able to help. Even as a child I'd read about medicine. I thought I should have been able to do something. With all those hours of reading, I should have been able to help my own father.'

'But you couldn't?'

'No. He died in front of my eyes. I know it is not the same, but I wanted you to know—'

'I see George,' he cut in. 'I see George.' Not really, George, of course. Rather the remnants of what had been George. 'And this boy. He had a bayonet in his stomach. I pulled it out. He died.'

'You blame yourself?'

He glanced at her, expecting to see condemnation in her clear gaze. 'Yes. Wouldn't you?'

'No. You did your best. That is all any of us can do. Likely the bayonet was preventing blood loss by placing pressure on a severed vessel. But he couldn't have been saved. At least he died knowing someone cared and wanted to help.'

'He shouldn't have died.'

'None of those young men should have died. Young men should not be sent to battle as cannon fodder at the whim of politicians. But it is not your fault. Your survival did not make them die. There is no correlation. No causal effect.'

His lips twisted into a wry smile. Always the bloody scientist. Yet, despite their oddness, her words comforted more than the polite platitudes that had been sent in all those pretty, gushing notes with their black-trimmed edges and copperplate penmanship.

'Oddly, that helps,' he said.

They were silent for a moment and it struck him that the silence was comfortable. Even as a healthy young man, he'd felt a restlessness, a need to move, to climb, to run, to talk and to fill in the quiet moments. Since his accident, he'd hated the company of others yet, conversely, dreaded solitude. He supposed that was why he'd sought the oblivion of brandy which provided a facsimile of peace.

But here, with this woman, he felt an ease.

'Why did you tell me to read Goethe?' he asked.

She showed no surprise at his sudden change in topic. 'He described the sound of the incoming shells at the Battle of Valmy. He said he felt different afterwards, less of a person. No, maybe it was not that he was less of a person, but that he was isolated, remote from others in a way he had not been before.'

'Perhaps I *should* read Goethe.'

'If you read enough literature and with sufficient variety, there will always be something to comfort or inform. I find books more reliable than people.'

He smiled, but it was true. Knowing that Goethe had also experienced this odd, peculiar, awful disconnected sensation helped. He was not alone. Or mad. Or, if he were mad, it was a madness shared by others—Goethe and that French fellow who fell into the canal.

He felt a flicker of humour and was conscious of that unusual mix of emotion, which Letty always engendered.

Muddled in with the humour, there was a stirring, an awareness of their solitude and that the moonshine highlighted her cheeks, making her long lashes cast lacy shadows. Perhaps it was the mention of Goethe which made him remember that other night with sudden clarity. In that moment, he saw her in the voluminous nightdress, her hair wildly dishevelled, her lips parted.

Or maybe, more seductive than all the rest, was the notion that tonight, on this terrace and in this moment, he was not a solitary creature.

The comfort of her presence morphed into something else. He found his gaze drawn to her profile, to the turn of her cheek, the pert outline of her nose and the fullness of her lips. The moonlight gleamed on the gold wire of her spectacles through which her eyes looked huge and green and luminous. The breeze made a stray strand brush against her cheek.

Gently, he reached forward and, with one finger, touched her soft skin, gently tucking her hair behind her ear. He felt her start at his touch. He heard her gasp and saw her eyes widen.

'I am going to remove your spectacles.'

'Why?' Her word was more exhalation than speech.

'Because your eyes are beautiful.' Gently, he removed her eyewear. 'Besides, your spectacles will get in the way when I kiss you.'

With equal deliberation, he touched her chin, tipping it slightly upwards and bending forward to kiss her pert, upturned nose, her forehead, her cheek and, at last, her lips. He heard her muted gasp. He heard the rustle of her clothes as she shifted forward towards him.

A sense of life, of promise, of need, pulsed through him, filling him and making him forget about his marked face and scarred shoulder.

Her lips parted with a sound which seemed half-pleasure and half-surprise. Her hand reached up, touching his chin and the nape of his neck.

This time he felt no impulsivity, but a certainty. The kiss deepened. His grip tightened, his fingers splayed against the fabric of her gown, pulling her tighter to him.

A need, a desire, like a primal life force, engulfed him.

He cupped her face with his hands, despite his injury. He stared down at her, as though memorising the curve of her cheek and the strong lines of brow and chin.

For long seconds, they stood bound together and then, by mutual accord, turned from the garden view towards the house as though a question had been asked and answered.

Chapter Twelve

The balcony door clicked shut behind them as they moved down the long hallway towards her bedchamber. Infrequent wall sconces lit their way, providing puddles of warm yellow light.

They stopped at the door. She placed her hand upon the brass doorknob and he was aware of this moment as a single entity—as though disconnected from past or future.

She glanced at him. She opened the door and then turned, reaching for his hand. He folded her fingers within his own. He felt the slight roughness of her skin which should be odd in a woman's hand, but wasn't.

'Letty—' The word was dragged from him.

He should leave. He must leave.

'I don't want you to leave,' she said.

'Letty, Letty, I…we…' He tried to hold on to sense…restraint.

'I've never felt like this before.' She spoke with an appealing wonder, curiosity threading the soft huskiness of her tone.

With exploratory fingers, she reached up to his face. She touched his chin. She ran her fingers along his jawline and touched the tip of the scar as it snaked down his cheek. On tiptoe, she pressed a kiss to his lips. The touch was sweet and chaste.

Its very chastity undid all restraint.

Gently, he tipped her chin upwards. Her lips parted with a muted gasp. He claimed her mouth, tasting her sweetness. She leaned into him, her movement unschooled and spontaneous.

The door was already ajar and, as his kiss deepened, they pushed it open, half-stumbling as they stepped over the threshold. The chamber was dark save for the fire's amber glimmer and the curtains had not yet been drawn. The moon and a myriad of stars twinkled in the dark velvet sky visible through the leaded panes and casting diamonds of silvery moonshine on to the wooden floor.

He caught her lips, no longer tentative.

Bending further, he kissed the smooth line

of her jaw, her neck and the sweet spot on her collarbone where he could feel the beat of her pulse. He kissed the small triangle of skin visible at the neckline of her dress. Her skin had a dewy softness. She smelled of— He chortled. She smelled of soap.

His hands dropped to her waist. He could feel her curves through the cloth. His fingers ran up her back, until he found the buttons.

He undid them one by one so that her bodice loosened and he was able to push it down from her shoulders. She wore only a chemise and the pale skin of her shoulders and neck gleamed in the lamplight. Through the thin cotton, he could see the darker outline of her nipples straining through the cloth. Her hair had come undone and fell in loose tangles about her face.

'You are so beautiful,' he said. He touched the thin cloth of her shift and felt the nipple pucker, pressing against his hand. He heard her quickened exhalation.

Letty knew that scientifically she was not beautiful. She did not fit the criteria for classical beauty and yet, as Tony's hand cupped her breast and she felt the warm, strength of his other hand, sliding down her spine, it did not matter.

She *felt*…beautiful.

Instinctively, she pressed herself closer so that she could feel the strong, hard lines of his body. She lifted her arms, caressing the hard muscles of his shoulders and running her fingers into his hair. She heard the wild drumming of her own pulse. It seemed that her body became molten, no longer stiff bone, but sensuous and fluid.

Thought ceased, swamped in sensation. Letty knew a wild freedom. She moved without thought, instinctively responding to the driving heat which started at her core, pulsing and expanding throughout her body.

She felt an exaltation, an awareness of her body and a cessation of thought and reason with a singularity of focus on this one moment. She felt his urgency as he pulled at the ties of her chemise. He tugged at them, pushing the cloth aside so that it hung about her waist. Her skin was bare.

They stood so close that she could feel the cotton of his shirt brush against her. Her hands slipped from his shoulders, moving under the cloth of his shirt. She wanted to feel his skin. She wanted to feel the tiny hairs on his chest, the flat male nipples and the sinewy movement of his muscles.

She felt him respond to her touch and thrilled to his soft needful groan.

They shifted backwards in an intimate dance until she felt the mattress at the back of her legs. Half-stumbling, they fell to the bed. The mattress sank under their weight. He kissed her, long drugging kisses. For a brief moment he moved away. She heard him remove his shirt. Through half-closed eyes, she watched the way his muscles moved, highlighted within the low amber glow of the fire and by the moon's light.

He bent forward, kissing her stomach, her breasts, her neck.

Cupping her face, he caressed her slowly, gently, tenderly.

'You're sure?' he whispered.

'Yes.'

She could not turn from this. It was bigger than thought or logic. She couldn't turn from this, from him or from this wild, new, wonderful part of herself.

Life was not just about saving life. It was also about living, she thought with a drugged part of herself until thinking stopped.

He pulled off his trousers and lay beside her. He felt warm and strong. He kissed her slowly, gently, so that she arched against him, wanting him faster, harder, deeper.

Darts of feeling, that mix of pain and pleasure, pulsed through her. She clung to him, her body demanding something which was foreign to her, but in a heady, wonderful way.

Tony groaned as he pulled at her skirts and underclothes, peeling them off her body, until she lay nude. She felt the whisper of air against her nakedness, but knew no hesitation or embarrassment.

Instead, she felt only a needful joy as he lowered himself so that his body covered her own.

When Tony awoke, Letty was sitting at the desk in the corner of her room. It appeared to be still early. The sun was not yet high in the sky.

Letty had put on her serviceable gown and tied her hair back into a neat bun as was her custom. With head bowed, she was writing. He could hear the scratch of the nib and the concentration apparent in the lines of her body.

For a moment he was content to watch. Early morning sun bathed her, making her red hair gleam. Every so often, she would pause and chew her lip or conversely drum her fingers against the desktop. Then, after a moment of apparent contemplation, she would bend her head again and the chamber would become quiet, the silence punctuated only by the scratch of her nib.

Finally, when she showed no sign of pausing, he sat up. The cloth rustled and she turned to him, flushing quite delightfully. 'Hello.'

'Hello.'

They both paused as though ludicrously uncertain how next to respond. 'I am glad you are awake,' she said in those clear, firm tones that were typical for her—except for that wonderful, husky breathiness yesterday.

'Indeed. Although I would prefer to have you awake and beside me and wearing considerably fewer clothes.'

'I would like that, too,' she said. 'But, well, I thought we should talk.'

'Definitely not what a man wants to hear after a night of lovemaking. Do you regret last night?' he said, sitting up straighter.

'No, no. Absolutely not.'

'Good.' He smiled with some satisfaction.

'But I have done some calculations.'

'Calculations?'

He reached forward to take a sip from the water glass on the bedside table. Prior to Waterloo he'd had one or two dalliances and he could not recall ever waking to find his amour doing mathematical calculations.

'You will be glad to know that there is very little chance I am with child.'

'What—?' He put the tumbler down so heavily that the liquid splashed.

'I looked at the dates on the calendar and determined it is unlikely I would have conceived last night. I wish I could say that I was sufficiently logical that I completed the calculations prior to making love, but that would not be entirely accurate.'

Again he felt that wash of emotions, each so intense, so intertwined that he could not discern each feeling: embarrassment, confusion, irritation, desire and, under it all, sadness.

A dream he hadn't even known he'd built tumbled into sudden disarray.

'So even after last night, you do not wish to get married.' He spoke flatly, a statement, not a question.

He had thought…he had hoped…he had assumed…

'What? No, I mean, unless my calculations are wrong which I hope they are not. Please do not mistake my meaning, I— I—' She had the grace to blush more furiously, glancing down and rubbing the grey fabric between her fingers. It made a scratching noise. 'I am glad and thankful and joyful about last night. I learned so much—'

Learned? *Learned?*

He pulled on his trousers, standing. 'So glad to know that making love with me has had a similar impact to that of a dusty tome or dictionary.'

'You are angry?'

'Not at all. I've always aspired to be likened to a scientific tome.'

'No—no. This is coming out all wrong. I should revise. It is just that I know that I am not the type of wife you need—'

'I do not—'

She waved a hand at his instinctive protest. 'You will. You will eventually want and need a wife who can help you assume your role as lord.'

'It is a role I never wanted and for which I have no training.'

'Which is why it is even more important that you have a wife to support you now. Someone who knows how to socialise and run a house and host parties. Even if I am no longer practising as Dr Hatfield, that part of my life might be disclosed. Mr Jamison knows. Your servants here must suspect. It would cause scandal. You are a peer. You have a place in the House of Lords.'

'I don't care if—'

'You will. You will care. Your father and brother left you a legacy and you will want to honour that by being the best in that role. I can't be the person you need. Yesterday is something I will treasure but... I am not the type of woman you need for a wife.'

Except I love you.

The thought slammed through him. He jolted with its impact. It struck not only in his mind, but also like a blow to his gut and searing pain beneath his breast bone.

He hadn't realised this. He hadn't thought he could still love, not like this. He had perhaps imagined a duty-bound sentiment, more about his estate and England than any deep feeling. Or perhaps a light flirtation, if he healed sufficiently.

But not this. Not this big, confusing and all-encompassing emotion.

The idea of a life without her stretched bleakly. 'Letty, I don't need a certain type of wife. I want you.'

'Eventually you will,' she said. 'Your life will have purpose again.'

'It has now—'

She shook her head. 'Maybe as Teddy's uncle. But you have an estate. Oddsmore was greatly loved by your father and brother. You will assume that role and you will need a helpmeet.'

He went to her, the movement swift, despite the pain in his side. There must be words. He could not lose this woman. He could not lose this feeling of hope...of rebirth. He sat at the table, leaning forward to hold her hand, small but capable.

'Letty, I don't care about being a peer. I don't want some simpering debutante.'

Lifting his arm, he leaned further to touch the tendrils framing her face. The movement dislodged the papers. They fell from the table in a scattering of rectangles across the floor. Each sheet was covered with neat script, tables and diagrams. He frowned, puzzled.

Loosening his hand, she bent to get them, the movement oddly urgent.

'What is all this?' he asked.

Colour washed into her face. She took them from him. 'I was just recording Teddy's treatment.'

'All this is about Teddy?' He glanced over what appeared to be hundreds of pages.

'Some,' she said.

'And the rest?'

'It is a project I've been working on. I—um—tend to take the notes with me.' She spoke with uncharacteristic hesitation.

'What is the project about?'

She bit her lip and then gave a wide smile which was always the more striking by its very rarity. 'I've always wanted to understand why some women die after the delivery of a healthy child due to fever. The birth goes smoothly. Everything looks positive and then, often around the third day, she sickens and dies.'

'Puerperal fever. I have heard of it. You are looking for a cure or a way to prevent it?'

'Yes. Both. I am sure there is a way.' Her eyes sparkled behind the thick lenses, her enthusiasm contagious and overcoming her previous hesitation. 'That is what medicine is about—learning and discovering. I don't know if I will find the reason or if it will be found in my lifetime or even Teddy's. But I believe every illness has a physiological cause and therefore a physiological cure.'

He sat, the movement heavy as though suddenly too tired or overwhelmed to keep himself upright.

'So you are trying to find a cure for child-bed fever?'

'And maybe the antecedent, how to prevent it. Why do some individuals contract it and others do not?'

'Explain it to me,' he said. 'Help me to understand.'

She stilled. 'Do you really want to know?'

He was reminded of that first question so long ago in Lord Entwhistle's library. 'Yes,' he said.

Very carefully, she collected the pages. She placed them on the table, arranging them as though they were infinitely precious. He watched her gentle fingers and the precision of each movement.

'You see these are all the live births from the villages close to here,' she explained, pointing to a column in a neatly drawn table.

'And you have identified the attending physician or midwife.'

'Yes—Jeffers, Hedley, Marcham, Belrose, Simons.' She tapped each name as she spoke.

'And these—' She pulled forward a second sheet, again neatly organised with the names of women, villages and physicians. 'These indicate births where the mother or the child died.'

He nodded, gazing at the list, which was too

long, his hand tightening reflexively against the chair arm. 'It makes me so thankful for Elsie and Teddy.'

'But these are the cases I am most interested in.' She pulled forward a third chart.

'Why?'

'Because the child and mother were both healthy after the birth. These women should not have died. There were no complications, no great blood loss. The child was not in a breech position.' Again, she smoothed out the page, her fingers almost reverent. 'They are the cases of puerperal fever.'

'So you are trying to see if there is a particular doctor or midwife who attended those births?' He pointed to the column with the heading 'physician attending'.

'Jeffers, Hedley and Simons. They are all doctors, not midwives.'

He leaned back, in his chair. 'So you think that a mother is more likely to contract a fever if a doctor attends the birth, as opposed to a midwife? That doesn't make sense.'

'I know. But science does not lie. I must believe that. I mean there are instances when a mother contracts fever when attended by a midwife, but they are consistently less frequent and that is across several communities and involving a number of different doctors and midwives.'

'Do you have any ideas why this might be?'

'It doesn't seem to matter if the doctor is young or old, experienced or inexperienced. I even controlled for the mother's age and social standing. In fact, the wealthier the individual, the more likely she is to take ill because these families can afford a doctor.'

'Perhaps a doctor may have further to travel and is unable to provide the help as expeditiously as the local midwife,' he suggested.

She shook her head. 'The deaths occurred several days after the birth. The births were successful and uncomplicated.'

'Are doctors less efficient? Do they drink too much?'

'Dr Hedley is quite puritanical and Mrs Belrose drinks like a fish. The biggest difference is that doctors often come from another sickbed or the morgue whereas midwives deal only with birth.'

He straightened. He pictured Letty in her Hatfield disguise, standing belligerently in front of Jeffers at Teddy's birth. 'My God, hand washing. That is why you are so insistent on the hand washing!'

'It is a hypothesis.'

'You think that the doctors are transmitting the illness?'

'Unwittingly. Maybe. Midwives do not go to the morgue as often and usually not immediately before a delivery. As women, they tend to wash more frequently, even if it is only due to the activities of cooking, washing or childcare. I still don't know the exact reason, but these records are consistent over years.'

'Years? How long have you been working on this?'

'Ten years.'

'Ten? But you wouldn't have even trained then? You would have been a child.'

'As an adolescent,' she said, 'I'd slip out and attend births with the midwives. One time there was a young mother with her first child. The birth was uncomplicated and she was so happy and everything seemed well. Then the next day she got a fever. Within a week she was dead. Her husband—he was a tall man—not much more than a lad. I remember him holding the baby in his huge hands like he didn't know what to do with it—as though it was a bizarre and foreign object. I asked the midwife what had happened and she said she didn't know. She said sometimes a mother just takes ill. It just happens, she said. She spoke as though it was expected. I couldn't accept that.'

'There are things one can't accept,' he said. He remembered the field, the mud and the dead faces.

He remembered the boy with the bayonet in his gut.

'I had to do something. At that time, I didn't think I would ever be able to train or get medical knowledge, but I knew I could record births and deaths. I could make charts and graphs. I could look for patterns. I could see if there were similarities or commonalities between those who lived and died. Sometimes, you just have to start somewhere.'

Her face had flushed pink. Her eyes sparkled and he saw her excitement, the quickness of her breath, the pulse beating along her collarbone and that smile which always transformed her usually serious demeanour.

'Most girls look like that when describing diamonds,' he muttered.

'Diamonds? What have they to do with anything?'

'Apparently nothing.'

He stared at the papers. He felt oddly as though

he had gained a peek into a strange, unknown world. He could not imagine being so interested, so passionate, so determined and so persistent.

About anything.

He'd spent his youth in lively and pleasurable pursuits and his present staring down the neck of a bottle.

He was in awe of her dedication.

Oddly, he felt both hopeful and despairing. For humanity, he felt a lightness. She had worked her whole life towards knowledge and discovery, against the odds. It was not only a part of her, it was her. These neat notes, the tables, the headings, the illustrations and her scrupulous attention to detail—they were her life's work.

And while people like her existed, with this drive, this intelligence and this compassion, hope existed.

But he felt also heaviness and loss.

Letty had brought him back from the mud of battle. Without fully knowing it, he'd constructed vague but wonderful plans in a mind formerly blank with despair. And she was central to his every plan and happy daydream. He'd cast her as wife and mother, a role she did not want.

And by fulfilling this dream, he would take away her own.

He lifted his gaze from the papers and stared out of the window at the green expanse of Beauchamp's well-tended park. He had not worked his whole life towards anything. Edgar cared about the estate. George, too. But Tony had passed through life with interest, always seeking pleasure and entertainment but never with any great purpose. He'd gone to dances, house parties, fox hunts and horse races. He'd laughed over cards and flirted with pretty girls.

Yesterday, as they'd made love and later curled together within the warmth of her bed, he'd thought he'd found that purpose; to love her and to be with her.

But he would not ask her to live at Oddsmore. He could not take her from her practice. He could not tie her to children.

That would not be love.

And he loved Lettuce Barton. He loved every eccentric hair on her eccentric head.

He got up. He must go. The maid might come in any time. Slowly, he bent, picking up his shirt and pulling it over his head.

'Thank you,' he said. 'Thank you for telling me about your research. It is amazing. You are amazing. It helps me to understand why you can't marry. I see that this—is bigger than me or you.'

He walked to the door, placing his hand on the knob.

What did one say? Thank you for last night? I love you? I love you with every fibre of my being? I love you enough to set you free?

'I will go to Oddsmore as soon as Elsie and Teddy are fully recovered. I need to live up to my responsibilities—but if you ever need anything, you can find me there.'

He opened the door and stepped into the corridor. The door closed behind him. For a moment, he stood quite still. He exhaled, aware of the lingering pain in his torso and the smart of tears. Letty had woken him from a nightmare and, for a moment, a split second, an infinitesimal fraction of time, he'd believed in the daydream of a happy ending.

It was the first time Letty had shared her research with anyone. She'd explained it to Ramsey, but never shown him. She'd mentioned it at Guy's, but had largely met with dismissal.

But Tony had listened. He'd given her his full attention. He studied her ideas with intelligence. He hadn't scoffed or disparaged.

She'd always feared scorn. Everyone was so busy debating the issues of purification, bloodletting and inflammation that her own theory would seem simplistic in the extreme. But she'd seen Tony's expression. He understood. He was impressed even.

Yet, as Letty heard the door close, and his footsteps retreat down the hallway, something hurt, deep under her breast bone.

There was an intensity to the pain which she had not known was possible. She stood, walking to the window and squeezing her eyes tight.

As always, in times of uncertainty or stress, she reminded herself of her patients. She pictured children not yet born; the injuries she could set and the fevers she might heal. In general, such contemplation proved a pleasant diversion. Indeed, she'd often comforted herself when walking through London's streets or listening to yet another of her mother's lectures on bonnets or tea or etiquette.

But now Letty could not stay still. She paced the bedchamber. She went from one side of the room, turning swiftly, like a soldier on patrol.

She had never realised what it meant to be a woman. It sounded foolish. She was four and twenty. She knew more about female physiology, conception, childbirth than any other woman.

And she knew nothing. She'd thought that science and logic were more important than feeling or emotion. Sentiment was for those who were weaker or less disciplined.

But last night…

Tony made her feel whole, alive, vibrant, joyful, loved in a way she had not anticipated, as though she'd been existing in a shadowy half-life.

Return to the calmness, the routine and order of her life within her twin houses should appeal and it didn't. The hope that she might be able to continue as Dr Hatfield should engender joy, as opposed to this slight relief that was largely overshadowed by numbness.

Even her scientific tomes did not lure her.

Or her correspondence with Sir Humphry Davy. Quite recently he had replied to her enquiry about nitrous oxide and yet she felt no immediate urge to reply.

It felt as though she were going mad or that the landscape she knew, or had always known, had changed, morphing into something entirely unfamiliar. She'd never wanted a husband, love, or marriage. Moreover, it would be entirely self-ish to even consider Tony's proposal.

She could not be a suitable chatelaine to his estate. She could not plan meals or invite the right people and ensure that the numbers of dinner guests were suitably balanced.

With sudden frustration, she turned from the window. She pulled out the valise. Grabbing her few belongings, she stuffed them into the case. With quick, angry energy, she pulled it closed, snapping it shut.

She needed to get away from this house. No wonder she could think of nothing except Lord Anthony. Memories surrounded her. The bed was still rumpled from their lovemaking, the musky scent of him still lingered, even his cravat lay dishevelled, mixed within the linen.

Pausing, she looked at the silk fabric as it lay, dark blue against the white. Slowing for a moment, she picked it up. She ran the fabric between her fingers, feeling it slide softly against her skin.

Then she tossed it into the valise. It would not do for the maid to find it.

Home did not bring comfort. Letty still could not concentrate. Nor could she rest. Indeed, she continued to pace with such speed and heaviness of foot that Sarah came up to her bedchamber.

'Good heavens, you'll end up coming through the ceiling at this rate,' her maid said, folding her arms across her ample chest and narrowing her gaze.

'I'm thinking,' Letty said.

'Indeed. And would these thoughts be medical or personal in nature?'

'What? Both—I mean—I never thought there would be a difference. I mean being a doctor is at the heart of everything I do and everything I am. And I never thought I would want anything else than to be a doctor.'

'And now there is something else you would want?' Sarah asked, advancing into the room.

'What? No. Absolutely not.'

'I might say "I think she dost protest too much".'

'Please don't, I never liked Shakespeare. All his characters say everything in such a convoluted fashion. I am quite certain if they spoke plain English, there would be fewer misunderstandings. And I do not think that there is any potion which would feign death as was described in *Romeo and Juliet*.'

'I always knew it would happen,' Sarah said with a comfortable certainty.

'What?' Letty grumbled. 'Romeo would die?'

'You'd fall in love.'

Letty drew to an abrupt halt, putting her hands at her waist and glowering at her servant. 'Good heavens, Sarah, what a load of—of nonsense. I think you have been nipping at the cooking wine. I am surprised at you. Indeed, you are letting your imagination entirely get the better of you. If anything, I am still overtired because I was up for days fighting for Teddy. I am certainly not in the least bit in love. Indeed, I don't even like the expression. It sounds like a cheap romance and so very unscientific.'

'You may not like the expression and you may find it unscientific, but that doesn't mean it is not true.'

'It is total nonsense,' Letty repeated. 'And let me make myself crystal clear—it is completely and totally false and I will not tolerate any more suggestions which are so ludicrous in nature.'

'Now I know it's true. You always get on your high horse and sound like your mother when you're trying to pull the wool over my eyes.' Sarah bent over the valise, starting to unpack it. 'As I recall, you used to do that as a child. You never were so haughty as when you were in the middle of some odd experiment you hoped to hide.'

'I don't hope to hide anything and I am not sounding like my mother and I am not pulling the wool over anyone's eyes and I am certainly not harbouring any affection for Lord Anthony. Besides, even if I were, I am not the sort of wife Lord Anthony needs. I mean, he is a peer. He needs a proper wife. Someone who can host parties and dance and say witty things and go to London. Besides, I can't give up medicine. I could never live a life where all I did was sit around and sip tea or discuss bonnets. I don't know anything about bonnets and I only tolerate tea. And certainly not in those foolish delicate cups which are meant for people with miniature fingers. Besides, he doesn't love me and would only marry me for honour and—'

'And?' Sarah prompted as the speech finished in a sob.

Letty pulled out her handkerchief. She seldom cried. She had never found it a useful emotion and refused to become a leaky tap at this late date. 'If—if I were ever to marry, I would want to be loved.'

Sarah paused in her unpacking. She stepped

forward, taking Letty's hands and holding them between her palms. Her fingers were twisted from arthritis and her skin roughened from work.

'There, there. I have been a long time widowed, but I know a thing or two about love. And I know this. Lord Anthony was a broken man when he came back from the war. And he's started to heal. I don't think that healing and the way he feels about you is all about honour. I've seen him look at you. Besides, I don't think he's the sort of man who would take a maid to bed, if there weren't some serious feelings going on.'

'I—we—how did you know?' Letty gasped.

Sarah produced the cravat, handing it over. 'Now, miss, you can stay here and wear out the floor boards or you can talk to the man. Seems to me that if the two of you love each other, there's got to be a way to work things out. Except I doubt you'll be finding it pacing this here bedchamber.'

Tony went back to his study. He felt a heavy, achy lethargy.

He loved Lettuce Barton. He loved her eccentricities, her dedication, her serious, scientific intent, her moments of humour.

When had he fallen in love? Had it been when she'd come to his bed during his nightmare? Or when she'd touched his scar with gentle caring? Or years ago, when she'd sat in Lord Entwhistle's library in her vibrant green gown and lectured him on cowpox.

But he could not limit her.

He could not take her purpose, but must find his own. He had survived hell. For some reason, he'd lived. He had not asked for life and at times during his recovery he'd wished for death and still felt the heaviness of guilt that he could see and feel and breathe while others could not.

He had lived.

And he must ensure that he was worthy of this life. There was the estate. That had been his brother's purpose and now must be his own. He must do right by the tenants. He could no longer hide from Oddsmore or its memories. He must live up to his father's expectations of his brother. And he would be a good uncle and brother— the best.

That would be enough.

He leaned back in the chair. As he sat within the study's quiet, he felt the memories again: the mud, the stench, the low mist mixed with the smoke of musket and cannon. Usually, he tried to hide from those memories, today he didn't. Today, he watched them almost as he would watch the theatre. He saw them become clearer, superimposed on the study's books, hearth and comfy furniture.

He remembered the men, their frightened eyes as even the bravest among them cried for his mother. He remembered the severed limbs and the cold damp of the mud sodden by the heavy rains.

It had been cold. And then hot. The shudders had racked through him. He'd lain beside George's body and heard the tramp of the scavengers, their footsteps louder and nearer as the men died, an empire's discards.

It wasn't right. He remembered George and Elsie at their wedding. He remembered the way they laughed and smiled.

George had not deserved to die, but even more he had not deserved to be left to die alone. None of them had.

None of them…

Not George or Edgar or the boy with the bayonet in his gut.

Chapter Thirteen

Letty sat at the base of the oak tree on top of the hill which overlooked the village.

She had given up pacing the room.

It had been three days of pacing and sleeping fitfully. The only respite had been when Phillip Rant had required six stitches after falling off a barrel while in his cups.

Moreover, Sarah seemed intent on driving her mad, producing food when she was not hungry, suggesting exercise when her very bones felt lethargic and indulging in bouts of questioning and long-winded anecdotes.

Indeed, Sarah's sole purpose was to drive her into Lord Anthony's arms, but it appeared that admission into an insane asylum was the more likely result.

So today, she had found her energy and exited the house and now sat in solitude within the quiet of the outdoors.

Despite Sarah's soliloquies, one fact remained. Letty could not become the wife of a peer.

She could not be the type of woman her mother had always so desperately wanted her to be. Firstly, she doubted she even had the capacity to do so and, secondly, she would lose herself.

She could not give up on her research.

Moreover, the pain of loving Tony and knowing that he could not reciprocate the feeling would hurt too much.

Leaning back, she felt the solid bulk of the tree against her back. The leaves above were starting to change colour and a few had fallen and were scattered around her. A slight breeze moved the branches making the dappled sunlight flicker over her face.

In front of her, she could see the fields—some had turned to yellowed hay and waited for cutting while others were bright, emerald greens. Small copses of darker green, dotting the scene with foliage splashed with a smattering of yellows, reds and orange. The stream, low in its banks after the hot summer, formed a thin, sparkling stream.

She saw him. He rode his horse along the road

which threaded the valley. For a moment, she wondered if she had imagined him. Perhaps she had been thinking about him so much that she had conjured up his image.

Her breath caught.

She hadn't seen Tony for four days. She'd told herself that she did not 'love' him. Rather, she'd experienced this wild seesawing of emotion because she was naive, unschooled in the physical act of love, exhausted and elated after winning a battle with death.

Except when she saw his tall, thin, lanky figure at the base of the valley, she knew that was nonsense. It was the pap she was feeding herself.

She loved him. Absolutely she loved him.

Man and horse approached, darkly silhouetted against the green. Letty rose. A part of her wanted to retreat.

While another part wanted to run to him, throw herself into his arms, caution be damned.

Except she couldn't move. Instead, she watched him with a hungry avidity, unable to look away. She studied his movements, his broad shoulders, narrow hips and dark hair. Looking at him gave her both a mix of physical joy and pain.

As though drawn by the very intensity of her gaze, he glanced up. Their gazes locked.

Without conscious thought, she started to walk towards him, hardly aware that she was doing so.

He dismounted, dropping the reins.

They looked at each other with an eager, needful way. They did not speak. Hungrily, she took in the strength of his face, the dark intensity of his eyes, the sweep of his hair. Neither touched the other, but only stood, as though afraid to shatter the moment.

'Letty, I love you,' he said. 'I love you. I understand why you don't want to marry me, but you need to know that I love you.'

She looked up. She felt a joy which seemed too huge to be contained within her body. Tears smarted her eyes. 'You do?' she whispered, needing to hear it again.

'Yes.'

She felt a deep content. Just for now it was enough to be with him, to feel his breath on her cheek and to know she need only reach up to touch his dark hair, and strong jawline. 'I am inexperienced with love, but I love you, too.'

'Then we can't walk away from each other.'

'I can't be the type of wife you need—'

'I need *you*,' he said. 'I don't need a "type" of wife. I need your love. I need your wit. I need your brilliance. I need you. Letty, I've found my purpose.'

'You did?'

'The very worst thing about Waterloo was not the death and dying, but the way England sent men into battle and didn't properly save them or care for them. They were cast aside like they didn't matter. That is what I dream about.

'I can't be Edgar. But I can be myself. I can take my seat in the House of Lords and I can use it. I can advocate for future soldiers. I don't want us to leave people to die on a battlefield, to be plundered for their teeth.'

'So you will use your position to stop it.'

'To try. Or at least make people aware. As you said, you have to start somewhere.'

She reached for his hands, holding them within his own. 'It is a good purpose. A wonderful, worthwhile purpose. But, if you are going to take an active role in government, it is even more important that you are not connected to me, not if I am Dr Hatfield. And even if I am no longer actively practising, I still do not have the necessary social abilities.'

Tony took both his hands, cupping her chin. 'Letty, whether you are Hatfield or not, I will not be popular with those ideas. Or scandal free.

You know it. And I want you by my side. I need you by my side. I will not stop you from being Dr Hatfield, I promise. But there are other ways to contribute to medicine, as yourself.'

'What do you mean?'

'Work with me together to help to change society. Or start the change. Do your research. Help me learn about fevers and battle wounds. Research about childbed fever. Help me to advocate. Let us be two voices instead of one. Give me the knowledge that I need. Teach me. We will get your research published. I will talk about your work in the House of Lords. It will be a step towards changing people's minds—not pretending behind a powdered wig.'

'Yes!' Letty said. The single word blasted from her. 'Yes.'

It felt as though the world opened. Everything had felt narrow. Everything had felt divided between medicine and love, emotion and logic.

And with his simple words, the divide had gone.

But maybe there was no divide. Or the divide was only in her mind and in society. Minds and society could be changed.

She reached up, pressing a kiss to his lips. 'And if I am working less as Dr Hatfield, there are so many things I could research. How to have a better outcome for injured soldiers, how to stop disease, how to inoculate against other diseases and—'

He kissed her, stopping her words.

She arched into him, reaching into his hair and pulling him closer. Love. Hope. Joy.

Life would not be easy. There were no magic solutions. Together they might build a world where women had choices, doctors had tools and soldiers were not discarded on the battlefield. Or maybe they would just start that process.

You have to start somewhere.

Ideas flooded her mind. Perhaps she could research the effectiveness of her herbs—she had always wanted to design a more scientific study to properly analyse their success. There was yarrow and lavender and oregano and mint and—

'What are you thinking about?' he muttered, his lips moving against her own.

'Feverfew and oregano and—'

'I shouldn't have asked.'

And then his kiss became more passionate and she didn't think any more.

Epilogue

Letty exited the library and walked across Odd-smore's flagged terrace to where Elsie and Flo sat in the Spring sunshine. Well, Flo was sitting. Elsie had Teddy on her lap, but the child kept squirming off and attempting to walk.

'I don't know why I ever wanted him to walk early,' Elsie said, as she stood again, holding on to her young son as he took a few wobbly, tentative steps. 'Now I am forever chasing after him, and Maria is becoming positively athletic.'

Teddy lifted up his arms to be carried, but instantly tried to wriggle down again once Elsie had scooped him up.

'Goodness, you cannot decide what you want,' Elsie whispered fondly, pressing a kiss into his blond curls. 'I think it was the enforced immobility of the carriage ride and he is now determined to make up for lost time.'

Letty smiled. 'You are looking wonderfully healthy. You both are. Would you like tea?'

'Absolutely. I'll find Maria and have her look after this gentleman.' Elsie went into the house, while holding the still-squirming Teddy.

Letty turned to Flo, who was sitting, her hands resting on her increasing belly and her feet propped up on the chair opposite. She and Ramsey had arrived the day earlier.

'Tea sounds wonderful. Do tell me you ordered cream puffs,' she said.

'I did.'

'For the first three months I couldn't eat a thing and since then I have continually wanted cream puffs. Do you think that is normal?'

'I am certain it is.' Letty sat next to her sister-in-law. 'Indeed, I remember a farmer's wife who had never liked cheese and then craved that dreadfully strong stuff. You know, the type that smells like old socks.'

Flo smiled. 'Well, I cannot say that my liking for cream puffs is new, only more constant.'

The door swung open as Elsie returned without Teddy, but accompanied by Letty's mother.

Letty stood to kiss her mother's cheek. 'I was just about to order tea. Would you like some? Tony and Ramsey are in the study, but should be out soon.'

Letty watched as her mother sat, leaning over to enquire about Flo's health. Her concern for Flo was lovely to see. Indeed, she had taken up knitting and had several pretty garments put aside, ready for the birth.

Her mother had mellowed. She'd been thrilled when Tony and Letty married, but Letty had worried that their nuptials would not long satisfy her need for social advancement. However, while still suggesting that Letty pursue a more active and conventional social life, her mother was less persistent and more contented.

They might never properly understand each other, but had achieved a tentative acceptance.

Just then, Ramsey and Tony strode from the library, their footsteps brisk raps against the tiles.

Tony waved several pieces of paper. 'I have written the draft,' he said, sitting beside Letty and pressing a kiss against her cheek.

'For the House of Lords?'

'Yes. I read it to Ramsey. He doesn't think I'll be thrown out on my ear.'

'I wish I could see it all. They are very backward that they do not allow women to watch, although I understand some have managed to do so.'

'Not without more bother than it is worth,' Ramsey said, sitting beside Flo.

Just then Sarah came out with the tea tray. Letty leaned forward, starting to pour while Elsie took one of the cream puffs, handing it to Flo.

'And how is the final version of your article coming?' Ramsey asked.

'I need to make more revisions, but I believe it has clarity.' Letty spoke with caution.

'Which likely means it is absolutely brilliant,' Elsie said fondly.

'She is planning a follow up,' Tony added. 'Looking at statistics between midwives and doctors in London.'

'Do they keep such records?' Ramsey took a tea cup.

'That is what I hope to find out. I am going to Queen Charlotte's Hospital next week when we go up to London,' Letty explained.

'You do realise that those doctors may not want to talk to you?' her mother warned.

'Absolutely.' Letty smiled, reaching for Tony's hand and holding it tight within her own. 'But you have to start somewhere.'

His gaze caught her own, with a flicker of shared understanding and amusement. She leaned back after helping herself to a cream puff and licking the cream off her fingers with a contented sigh.

Here, within the rustic confines of the small estate, she felt that wonderful sense of belonging that had eluded her for so long. She might be an oddity within the larger community, still all arms, legs, elbows and a habit of over-analysis, but here she belonged.

She tightened her grip. Tony no longer hid the scar on his hand, and, while he had the occasional nightmare, he had achieved a peace and a determination to ensure that the past shaped a better future.

'My lady?' Sarah came out again. 'The gardener is at the back door. He thinks his son might have broken his ankle and is wondering whether you might be able to take a look?'

'I really don't know if that is quite the thing—' her mother started to say.

They all laughed. Letty could hear Ramsey's deep guffaw and Elsie's chuckle like silver bells.

'I don't think that matters to Letty,' Tony said.

She glanced back, taking in the merry group and love and understanding in her husband's steady gaze.

* * * * *

COMING SOON!

We really hope you enjoyed reading this book. If you're looking for more romance, be sure to head to the shops when new books are available on

Thursday 27th June

To see which titles are coming soon, please visit
millsandboon.co.uk/nextmonth

MILLS & BOON

Coming next month

THE DETERMINED LORD HADLEIGH
Virginia Heath

'Thank you for your kind assistance this evening, my lord.' Continued avoidance of basic good manners was petulant. Penny's eyes finally lifted to meet his and she immediately regretted it. It was as if he could see right through her, past the determined and proud façade, to the uncertain and lost woman beneath. 'It is much appreciated.'

'No, it isn't.' Hadleigh grinned, his intuitive eyes dancing, and the sight did funny things to her insides. Why couldn't he be wearing his bland and inscrutable expression tonight? She knew where she stood with that. 'You would have rather walked over hot coals than have me help you and I cannot say I blame you. I behaved poorly on both our last encounters. Boorish, high-handed and arrogant with a healthy dose of sanctimonious mixed in. I had no right to attempt to force my will upon you or to assume I knew what was best. I've mulled it over long and hard since and chastised myself repeatedly for my crassness.'

Another pretty apology. Why did he have to be so good at apologies when she wanted to remain annoyed at him? Being righteously annoyed justified overt formality.

'You have flour on your face.'

'I do?' Her free hand swiped at her chin.

'Here…allow me.' His fingers brushed her cheek and Penny swore she felt it all the way down to her toes. She found her breath hitching as he dusted it from her skin, not daring to breathe out in case it came out sounding scandalously erratic. Which it suddenly was. As if sensing the new, potent atmosphere between them, his unusual, insightful amber eyes locked with hers and held. They both blinked at each other before he severed the contact and took several steps back.

Did he realise that the dormant female part of her body had suddenly just sprung to life? That her pulse had quickened or her lips tingled?

Continue reading
THE DETERMINED LORD HADLEIGH
Virginia Heath

Available next month
www.millsandboon.co.uk

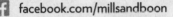